Beyond Morningstar Lane

Miriam C. Crouch

Black Rose Writing | Texas

First printing

This is a work of fiction. Names, characters, businesses, places, events, and incidents are either the products of the author's imagination or used in a fictitious manner. Any resemblance to actual persons, living or dead, or actual events is purely coincidental.

ISBN: 978-1-68433-600-5
PUBLISHED BY BLACK ROSE WRITING
www.blackrosewriting.com

Printed in the United States of America
Suggested Retail Price (SRP) $19.95

Beyond Morningstar Lane is printed in Book Antiqua

*As a planet-friendly publisher, Black Rose Writing does its best to eliminate unnecessary waste to reduce paper usage and energy costs, while never compromising the reading experience. As a result, the final word count vs. page count may not meet common expectations.

In memory and tribute to those who never give up believing in us. Their loving legacy of caring inspires us to make this world a better place.

Beyond
Morningstar Lane

VALENTINE

We are miracles. From first to final breath, we are awed and fascinated beginning with the miracle of birth to the mystery of death by our mystique continuing its intricate and complex journey. Simple concept but one I preferred to ignore, to my detriment.

We arrive pure and innocent to experience the beauty and joy of our existence until reality sets in. Childhood may account for a small percentage of our lifespan, but proportionately wields a mighty force. Whether a single grotesque event or a way of life lasting for months or years, dark moments steal our hope and joy. Unless rescued, the child's broken soul is abandoned to decay. As is true for most of us, I created my survival guide as I stumbled along. The core of who I am demanded the opposite of a sugary sweet concoction sprouting tiny hearts and flowers. I underwent a perpetual overhaul to blast free of the suffocating darkness or spend the rest of my days anchored to it.

Destiny stepped in and dealt me a second chance. The elusive intangibles needed to jumpstart me landed smack dab in my lap, but I had to make the choice. Pathetic and hopeless accompanied by anger and smoldering hate wasn't on my radar long term. Determined to contribute more to the world than as another emotionally distraught social misfit, I rejected living in denial. A part of me wanted to be like everyone else. Begin life with a clean slate. If derogatory marks were given, I should earn them and not because of some random act of so-called grown-ups. My beginnings with its notable humps, bumps, and bruises reflect the truth and wonder of who I am. I'm neither trivializing nor magnifying my ordeal, but in the process I discovered a girl worth saving, worth healing, and worth loving. I had setbacks, wrong turns, U-turns, detours, and barriers on my journey along life's pathway; it's no Autobahn. My *golden key* revealed from within to decode the way-- tap into my personal arsenal of adversity as stimulation for change. The tenacity of the human spirit serves as our powerhouse.

Poor, pitiful me story? No way and far from it. It's an uplifting tribute to those stalwarts who encouraged, inspired and challenged me and is a testament to the impact we have on each other. *Aunt Nona* encouraged and nurtured me with her strong spirit to assert my rightful birthright to happiness. I did not have to earn the right to be joyful. *Leland* guided me to overcome fear and to become my vision. *Jessica* encouraged and stood by me with her patient understanding and humor bound by unconditional friendship. With their love and support, I rebelled against the gravitational pull of lapses into the comfortable status quo and unapologetically proclaimed my place on wobbly emotional legs. Just as I began to see my way, my discovery of a family secret sent me reeling. I was forced to face yet another one of my debilitating character flaws. Life's constant demands to cope become our strength--from crutch to tool to dig deep and out of the ditch rather than sink and wallow. My goals may seem insignificant and my progress meager, but I hope we're inspired. The beginning dark stage isn't our fate until the final fade. Events and people leave their marks, discarding us broken, scared and scarred. But an event powerful enough to make or break does not have to control until our dying breath and is a compelling motivator for us to make a difference in the world. In our quest to live a fulfilling and rewarding life, we may discover the beauty and joy of our existence is in the challenge of finding our way.

Chapter 1
Storybook Haven

Mother said we would make a new life and a good life and leave our troubles behind. Mother's aunt was her only relative, and her doorstep was our target. With a five-year-old and no immediate family, Mother had few options. Aunt Nona Emmaline Monroe could have said no and no one in their right mind would have blamed her, but she never flinched much less hesitate. Whatever opinion you had of her, she was unflappable. Her kind and soft demeanor disguised her indisputable toughness developed over a lifetime of fighting her battles. Mother planned the exact moment of our arrival precisely heralded by a Sunday afternoon cloudless sky of brilliant blue. A cool whisper breeze promised relief from the months of continuous summer heat. Mother knew Aunt Nona would be in her place Sunday morning in pew at the First Baptist Church. She arranged our visit to 4112 Morningstar Lane conveniently after the services and the extended activities of a Sunday including lunch, visitation, and home visits to members ailing or in the hospital. We stood gazing at the dark red brick Tudor at exactly four o'clock. Mother took my hand as we made our way along the sidewalk leading up to the dark archway. An asparagus fern fanned from a colorful pot beside two tall cane back rocking chairs. Mother showed her brave side but had to be nervous. She reached for the doorbell, glowing amber in the dim porch. I wondered if Aunt Nona would answer and if she did whether she would regret it.

"Look Valentine. Isn't the little storybook house beautiful? It's just as I remembered." I had no inkling what she meant, but I agreed the house looked dark and imposing with its pointy roof and dark front entrance. Maybe Mother meant to say Grimm's fairy tale house.

Aunt Nona answered the doorbell after a minute or so, although it seemed we stood on the dark porch for eternity--wondering and waiting. She flung open the big oval wooden door, smiling and beaming. Then her face fell, her jaw dropped and her mouth opened wide. Surprise didn't begin to describe her reaction, more like shock. I hoped she didn't slam the door in our faces. I remembered thinking Mother should have phoned Aunt Nona before we dropped in. Whatever her reasoning for not phoning first, the strategy worked.

"Oh, Lila Jo. And this must be little Valentine! You two are the last two people I ever expected to see in my doorway. You might have given old auntie a little warning, though. I hope my old heart can stand the shock. You two are the sweetest dreams ever to come true on my doorstep, so get in this house."

She welcomed us verging on disbelief but with absolutely no sign of apprehension and took us in with open arms. She appeared undaunted, as if we were just another Sunday afternoon surprise. Whether Aunt Nona acted out of the kindness of her heart or whether she chose to avoid coping with an overwhelming burden of guilt for the rest of her days, who can say. We moved into the cozy house that Sunday as effortlessly as we slipped into the fresh cotton sheets of my aunt's beds. The process seemed preordained and uncomplicated. There were no interrogations or moments of causing us guilt or awkwardness or stabbing stares of what are you doing here, which obliged us to give a full accounting of our predicament. My aunt welcomed us instantaneously and wholeheartedly and opened her heart and her home to us. We were a family, and this was our home. Aunt Nona quieted my foreboding and made sure I understood she was my aunt, too.

"Oh, Valentine, this is an answered prayer! I can't tell you how often I've prayed for you and your mother and hoped to be a part of your lives."

After a short visit and time to recover from us, she became a whirlwind of changing sheets, grabbing blankets, pillows, and towels. A beaming energized human spinning top, rather than distressed or confused, she seemed overjoyed to have us fill up her house and to complicate her life. There were two extra bedrooms, so Mother had a room and so did I. The rooms were small but comfortable with a bed, night table, chest, and chair. The one bathroom for three women made it thorny at best, but we made it work. Natural light and the sweet smell of jasmine poured in through two cross pane windows overlooking the garden.

That night in my new bed, I strained to listen to the hushed conversation. Aunt Nona had her arms around my mother to comfort her. "Lila Jo, what you're going through is natural. But coming here is what you and Valentine and I need. *We all need family.* There's no reason for you to be embarrassed or ashamed. We all have occasions when we question our decisions and shake our beliefs and our confidence. Trust me because I've been there. The bad memories seem overwhelming but will be overshadowed by tomorrows. You and Valentine have a home now with me and whatever you experienced in the past can be overcome. Your and Valentine's future is here, and I'll do everything possible to make your lives as bright and hopeful as I can."

I fell asleep listening to their voices into the night. I wondered if Mother would tell Aunt Nona about him and what he did to us. I tried to stay awake but the blanket of relief proved too much. For the first time in my young life, I felt safe and secure. I belonged here. I didn't know my aunt, my surroundings, or my future, but my mother and I had found our refuge with little strangeness and no underlying mystery.

Mother got a waitress job at a local diner working six days a week. Willingly but occasionally begrudgingly, Aunt Nona did her best to take care of me with the help of a neighbor lady from the church. I was a handful. I was not intentionally a problem child, but I *was a child.*

Life eased into an uneventful, peaceful existence once I started school. My aunt and I shared a common goal. Get me out of the house and into a classroom. School was my escape and for my aunt a relief. She tried bravely to corral a pint-sized tyrant. As a teacher for forty years, she took to heart the schooling and discipline of her great niece. I read the bedtime stories for myself and printed easy one-syllable words. Aunt Nonie demonstrated self-sufficiency and independence as the highest goal for a young woman. She had never married nor depended on someone to take care of her. Under her supervision, I yielded to gentle but firm prodding. You can be a helpless little girl for simply so long and the time had ended for me. With the finer points of personal grooming instilled by Aunt Nona, I insisted to do it all without assistance. I liked to take care of myself, thank you, and enjoyed the freedom of independence. I picked out my clothes (simple since I had few outfits from which to choose), and I liked being self-reliant and took on more and more everyday responsibility. I made my bed and kept my room spotless, cleaned the bathroom, and helped with the dishes and general cleaning. I watched my aunt closely. I liked her instantly because she didn't need anyone, or so it appeared. Stubborn and intent to follow her lead, I took things into my hands. I liked to challenge my aunt even about the most mundane activities such as how to fold clothes, how to make a bed, how to get ready for school the next day. I developed a bad habit of arguing with her just to see who would win. My game of butting heads with Aunt Nona came to an abrupt end. Mother eventually had enough and intervened. She put an end to my challenging Aunt Nonie. I had driven her to the brink of insanity as she impatiently explained the obvious to her pig-headed daughter. How easily I had forgotten our predicament of being homeless except for the kindness of Aunt Nona. I had become entitled.

"Valentine, this is Aunt Nona's house. She is kind enough to let us live here. The least you can do is treat her with respect and be a help to her and not cause problems. You can be a good girl. Aunt Nona has feelings, too. Straighten up or you'll find yourself and your mother living on the streets. You don't want that, do you?" The mere fact Mother turned stern (seldom if ever) said it all. *I was in deep trouble.*

Anything Mother said became gospel; the way for me to stay out of trouble with my mother and my aunt was to mind Aunt Nonie and not cause her problems. From this first experience, I developed my mantra---blend in. My behavior got rewarded, and my life became easier. As though I needed a reminder, Mother and I were desperate and Aunt Nonie was in control, like it or not. No one of conscience would describe Aunt Nona as mean or unreasonable or even demanding. She had run her house and her life a certain way for six decades and would not change to accommodate an unruly six-year-old. I gradually became accustomed to her ways and began to appreciate her and her somewhat bizarre sense of humor. I liked to take advantage, but she didn't allow such nonsense, and didn't hesitate to tighten the reins. Children just happened to be her expertise and most times were easily maneuvered to do things her way. She regarded my strong will as an asset to be channeled. She was so shrewd and the process so subtle I hardly felt a thing. I began to admire and emulate her.

Mother spent her days working long hours at the diner. The 4:30 alarm blared through the still quiet as she dressed in her crisply starched white and blue waitress blouse and skirt with *the* flower on her left shoulder. Mother adored lilies, specifically those called Stargazers. Artificial but pretty in its brilliant white and stunning fuchsia pink, I wondered its purpose. "Mommy, why do you wear that flower every day?"

"Makes me happy, sweetheart, and maybe it will bring just a smidgen of good luck. I love everything about this flower--its name and the way it smells. Don't you think the petals are beautiful, so big and showy? Stargazer for sure."

Her vitality yet easygoing personality and ready smile encouraged the customers to be relaxed. The owner of the diner knew he had a gem in my mother and rewarded her with regular raises. Along with her tips, she made a living at a seemingly boring, mundane, and thankless dead-end job thanks to her smart creativity. She made her working hours enjoyable for both her and her customers and took to heart the names of her regulars and whatever other information they wished to share. She made the BluePlate a place where people wanted to go to be connected and became the catalyst making the BluePlate the café of choice. It takes more than a good menu and a good cook to stand out from the countless eating spots. It had the atmosphere of your neighborhood bar—regulars who wanted to hang out in a comfortable, safe place with people they felt they knew. Diners could enjoy the BluePlate with no pressure, no expectations, no trying to impress--a place with a spirit people liked to share. She particularly impressed one regular customer. He appeared on the red vinyl and chrome stool at the far right end of the counter for breakfast five days a week 6:30 a.m. sharp. He and Mother struck up easy conversation in the early hours, starting their day together every morning for three months before he got up the nerve to ask her for a date. My mother thrived on social interaction. She sought out the company of others easily and effortlessly. She enjoyed dinner at a white cloth restaurant and then dancing—a night on the town. She offered no pretense. The welcome atmosphere of music and dancing and some drinks offered relief from the cares and routine of the day-to-day. She felt comfortable with a regular customer of the diner. In contrast, I was not the least bit accepting, much less happy, about sharing her with a strange man. I hoped we would not need a man. Everything was perfect, and now the grown-ups insisted on messing it up.

"Mommy, I don't like you to be alone with a strange man. He might hurt you."

"No, honey, you don't have to worry. He's a good man."

"How do you know?"

"Well, he's been coming into the diner long before I started to work there, and Ray says he's a good guy."

I understood her wanting to dress up and go out. How could anyone be more beautiful? But my controlling nature took over, and I stubbornly insisted she was gone too much. She should find ways to satisfy her need to go out that included me.

Mother looked amazing in her dressy dress. The flowing navy and white polka dot circular skirt topped by a stiffly starched white pointed lace collar and short white cap sleeves had a self-tie belt to accentuate her tiny waist. Her smooth creamy skin glowed, topped off with red lipstick and white beads and earrings. Her passion for shoes shone in her new red patent sling-back pumps. She should be in my aunt's *Ladies Home Journal.*

"Twirl, Mommy, twirl. Make your dress do circles." I screeched. I had transported to fantasy world and had escaped the momentary displeasure of her choosing to go out for the evening instead of being with me. We were so happy being together, but our moments were few and fleeting. I ached for her to stay.

She turned and picked me up and we started to dance. "Someday you will have such a dress just your size and we'll go out for a grown-up dinner just you and me." She grinned and left my cheek with her big red lip imprint.

"Oh, Mommy. You're the prettiest mommy ever. I love you."

"I love you, too, Sweetheart. My little Valentine."

That evening in March marked the beginning of the Lila-Dex twosome. They went out regularly for a year before she brought him around. My resentment of her going out with him never waned. Because he took her away from me, he would never win. He was up against tremendous odds, my stubborn resistance and resentment. I refused to accept his intrusion into my precious and limited time. Why must I share my mommy with some stranger?

I told my aunt I did not like this man called Dex. She said you don't have to like him, but you do have to be polite. My aunt appeared to be on my side briefly when she mentioned she might not approve of him either, but he wasn't any of her business. Then she winked at me and said, "Let's be kind to him for your mother's sake. He's a passing fancy. She works hard and deserves to have some fun, okay?"

Mother made the introductions. I didn't want to look at him. I thought he must spend a lot of time outdoors. He had brown, wrinkly skin and was tall and lanky. He didn't look anything like I wanted him to look. He did have pleasant blue eyes that twinkled with softness in stark contrast to the rest of him, which appeared harsh. I thought he might be kind despite his roughness, but who can tell?

"Hello, Valentine Monroe. I'm so glad to meet you. Your mom talks about you every day. She says you are her dream come true."

I said hello in my whisper voice and did not look up. I shook his extended hand as my aunt had taught me. But then I was done.

My voice abruptly returned full force. "Can I go to my room and play with my new doll?"

My aunt gave me the evil eye. My mother gave me a nod no. "Stay and visit with us. You look pretty in your dress." She knew how much I detested being dressed up at home, so going to my room was code for permission to change out of my dress into my comfy PJs.

Visit? I wasn't sure what visit meant. To me, visit meant listening to the three grown-ups and their boring stuff. I had been instructed to listen and, if they asked me a question, I should answer and not volunteer anything else and that was the extent of it. This Dex fellow had a husky voice and I didn't like that he smelled like cigarettes. I resented the whole idea of it. My mother worked long hours, leaving little time for me. Then this stranger imposed himself on us uninvited. He interjected between the love of my life and me. Another big thing irritated me. He wasn't attractive enough to be with my mother. It bothered me what my mother saw in this Dex character and why she thought we needed him (or any man) in our lives. She and I were perfect together. We didn't need anyone else except for Aunt Nona *sometimes*.

Aunt Nonie struggled to make chit chat and asked the obvious, "What does 'Dex' stand for?"

Husky voice said, "Dexter. It's just easier for folks to call me Dex, and I like it better than my full name. Speaking of names, I knew some Monroe's down in Louisiana. Do you all have kin down that way?"

"Yes, but our closest relatives are in East Texas and Mississippi. A lot of my cousins who are in Louisiana are distant cousins. We don't see each other often." She had drawn her imaginary line in the sand of her possible discussion with stranger Dex. Time for Lila Jo and her date to be on their way. Aunt Nonie didn't fool me. She wasn't crazy about him either.

I pleaded again to go to my room, and Mother gave in and nodded yes. I had worn her down. "So yes, go ahead. You can put on your pajamas. I'll tuck you in before I leave."

Minutes later, she came in and sat on the edge of the bed and saw my pouty lower lip. My mood had not improved. "Valentine, you don't need to worry. The bad stuff is behind us now. We will be fine. Dex and I are good friends and we laugh and have some fun, that's all. So quit being such an old soul. You fret too much for a young thing. Be a good girl for auntie, and I'll be home before you wake up. I love you to the moon and back, my precious."

"Mommy, why did he call me Valentine Monroe? My name is Valentine Lucca."

"He got confused because Aunt Nona's name is Monroe. My mother was a Monroe before she married a Devereaux. They were sisters. Now do you understand, my darling?" All of it seemed perfectly understandable to her in spite of my confusion. She continued beaming and happy and not annoyed by the name confusion, so I accepted her explanation for now. The future shows itself in the subtle.

The best way for me to describe her warmth, glow, and joy is that my mother punctuated with a smile. I needed her to be near. "Mommy, please don't go. I'm scared for you. I don't want anything bad to happen. You have to stay here, please. Please, don't go!" Whatever dread expressed in my childish pleas appeared so nonsensical as to not be worth considering. My preoccupation with what I wanted seemed easily dismissed without question. Mother looked into my eyes begging me for her freedom.

"You'll be asleep before I get out the door, and I'll be back before you wake up. You'll hardly realize I'm gone. Besides, I have a surprise for you. We will do something special this Sunday, I promise."

She hugged and kissed me, and then she twirled her skirt around rippling a breeze across my face, blew a kiss, and vanished into the night. I lay still listening to the quiet and saw Aunt Nona turn off the lights except for one small lamp. Maybe if I fell asleep, the hours would fly by and soon I'd hear the creaking of the front door. I closed my eyes and gave in to dreamy sleep. Then the suffocating stillness of my night of horror returned without warning. I heard my tiny voice pleading within. "Hurry! Wake up before the dream comes." But it was no use; I was powerless. Among the dark clouds, I floated back to my little room in New York. I must be quiet and not make a sound and stay in my room. My babysitter Angie was in the next room cuddled up with her bad boyfriend and a bottle of wine. I hated it and wanted to run away when he showed up. The first time she brought him here, he tried to be my friend. The next time he did bad things. I should tell my mother, but

9

he said he would hurt her if I told our secret. Sometimes he came into my room when I took a nap. When he drank, he got mean and mad and liked to make me afraid. Suddenly I heard him hollering my name.

"Get in here. Will wants to see you. What 'cha doing in there? Remember what happened before? I should come see if you need your diaper changed. You liked that." He laughed so hard he started coughing. "Get me some more wine. What in the hell's wrong with you? You can't piss without me telling you to. Get the wine. I'm dry as cotton."

"Oh for God's sake, Will, she's just a little girl. I told you last time when I caught you in her room you better leave her alone. Every time you drink you bring us down. Her mother will find out and you'll have nowhere to hide. You'll be back in jail."

"Shut up. Don't tell me what to do. I can't stand you trying to boss me around. I ought to knock your head off. There's no way for her to find out unless you tell her and unless you're that stupid. You don't want to be stupid and dead, or do you?"

I ran into the living room, terrified. He raised his hand as if to hit me and I jumped, startled. He threw back his head and screeched with laughter, showing bright white teeth and his streaked blonde hair flew across his forehead covered in beads of sweat. When he drank, who could tell what would happen, but it would be bad. I started walking towards my room. If I could only get out of here.

"Come back here. I'm not done with you. You remember what happens when you don't do what I say. I ought to give you what you need or I'll beat you blind."

I started to whimper and cry.

"Shut up. Shut up, I said. You pitiful little used grease ball. Don't even know who your daddy is. You're useless, only good for one thing, and not much good for that, *yet*. Sleep and eat and still shit in your pants and have to wear a diaper. Stop staring at me! Why don't you *do* something? I can't stand the sight of you. Get out of here!" I turned to look at him as he continued his rant. Wine slobbered out of the corners of his mouth and down his chin. I froze in fear.

Angie edged towards the telephone. "Will, you're drunk. Now stop it or I'm calling the cops."

10

He grabbed her by the hair and slung her onto the floor. "Don't threaten me. You're not calling anyone. It's time to party. You're nothing but a cow to hump." He sat on top of her and started ripping at her clothes, tearing off her blouse and jerking up her skirt. "I've got what you need, just need to calm down, bitch."

"Oh, Will, don't, not in front of her." Her pleas were useless; she was helpless and overpowered.I got under the table and made myself into a ball and tried to hide my face in my lap, covering my ears with my hands. I desperately wanted to climb into my dress and never come out. I was not small enough. The dark shroud of evil cloaked the room. I was in Hell with no one to save me.

I saw his bare feet with long dirty toenails as he stumbled to the chair, and I heard Angie in the bathroom crying with the water running. I raised my head. When she came out, her eyes were red and puffy. She had bloody scratches and whelps on her arms and legs where he had grabbed her.

"If you know what's good for you, you'll keep your mouth shut." He grabbed her around the throat and suddenly slung the back of his other hand across her face so hard she lost her balance. "I've got a good setup here, and I'm not going to let you spoil it with the kid. I might just cut you up and throw you in the river where no one would ever find you. Sink to the bottom, eh? You're good bait for the bottom feeders. Hey, what have I got to be worried about? No one would miss you piece of crap. You're so damn ugly; your face needs a sack." He threw the crumpled brown paper bag at her.

His laugh gasped to just above a whisper as his voice cracked and sounded more like a cackle. "Look at the ball of shit under the table! Scared of little Will, ain't ya? But I'm not little. Don't you see what I mean, girlie? You know how big Will gets, don't you? I'll take care of you later when I take care of your mother. Two for one special!"

He laughed so hard he spit wine all over his white t-shirt. I only wished it was blood. I got up slow and almost fell but was careful not to turn my back. As drunk as he was, he wanted to do bad things. I felt lucky, but he had to be stopped. I didn't understand what I'd done to deserve this and how I could get away.

My small body vibrated and exploded with overpowering hate. Suddenly I felt huge as a giant and not afraid. I edged towards the front door. Before I knew what I was doing, I screamed, "I hate you! You're mean and no good. I'm telling my mother when she comes home."

I turned and ran to the door. It was not locked. I ran into the hallway and continued screaming over and over until my voice gave out. "Help. Help. Somebody please help me!"

There were eyes peering through the slits of several barely opened apartment doors. People were curious but would not interfere in family disputes. The old lady in 4-D peeped out and motioned for me to come quickly. I ran to her, never looking back. Off balance and slow to react, by the time he made it to the hallway, I ran inside 4-D with the door shut. Furious, he started to screech and yell blood-curdling obscenities over and over until his voice gave way to a whisper. His hysteria echoed through the deathly quiet of the dark hallway. The old lady put her fingers to her lips for me to be quiet. She whispered I should stay with her until Mother came home.

"You can't hide from me. I told you. Your mother can't save you. Do you think anyone wants a stupid nasty maggot named Valentine who still wears a diaper?" He slammed the door so hard the flimsy walls shook and the floors vibrated. The old wooden green door crumbled away from one of its hinges knocking a piece of the doorframe to the floor. *Then a death knoll of silence.*

I sat in apartment 4-D trembling. What had I done? The old lady tried to be kind and gave me a glass of milk and a cookie. I sat there looking at the milk and cookie as if it were poison. My mind whirled faster and faster, making me dizzy. I didn't care what he said. I felt guilty because I didn't want Mother to get hurt. My hate and resentment rose like a fire out of control. Irrational and insulated from fear, being beaten was the least of my worries. I was more afraid of living like this and too scared to do anything or tell anyone. No one to stop him. I had to tell my mommy. I'd seen the look in his eyes that he planned to do something worse than I knew how to imagine. He wanted to hurt us or even kill us. I shouldn't have threatened to tell on him and then run away. It was my fault for making him so mad.

The old lady wanted to help me, but she wasn't sure what to do. "Are you okay? Is there someone I can call?"

"Mommy's at work and will be home at six o'clock."

"Okay, honey. Where does she work? Someone needs to call to tell her where you are. You can stay here until she comes for you." I shook my head. It was a big factory in New Jersey.

We sat and watched the big red clock on the dingy tan kitchen wall for the rest of the afternoon. I prayed for Mother to hurry and take me away, but I dreaded we both had to go back into that apartment.

At 5:30, I heard Mother calling my name frantically in the hallway. She ran in the old lady's open door and picked me up and squeezed me so hard I could hardly breathe. "Oh, Valentine, are you okay? I was so worried. I got here as fast as I could. We have to hurry."

"Please do we have to go back in there?"

"Yes sweetheart. Angie called me and told me what happened. She called the police, so he's probably in jail by now. We must get our things. Don't worry, we will be all right."

She got out the suitcases and started to pack our clothes. Suddenly the broken front door burst open and Will filled the doorway. He turned and slammed the door.

"Where in the hell do you think you're going?" He slung a sack of groceries on the table and packs of *Camel* cigarettes flew onto the floor. A bottle of wine splattered open, spewing pools of red over the concrete floor, seeping into the cracks. He grabbed an old wood kitchen chair and wedged it under the door knob. His rippled arm muscles bulged and his wide shoulders towered over his 6' frame. He exploded into a titan overpowered by anger and fueled by alcohol who wouldn't be stopped.

Mother continued to throw clothes into the bags. "Go to your room, Valentine. We're leaving. I won't let you hurt Valentine. The cops are looking for you, there's no way you're getting out of this."

His face grimaced, turning bright red. "Look at me. What do you see? Some little wimp you think you can wipe your feet on? No, you worthless bitch. What makes you think I'll even let you live? Don't you get it? You and your retard daughter are dead or I'll make you wish you were. You're not even smart enough to figure out what's happening."

"Why are you doing this? We've never done anything to you." Mother's face drained to pasty white, and about to collapse, she held onto the kitchen table. Tears of terror streaked down her cheeks.

His anger erupted like an earthquake through the small apartment. Every wall shook as he threw the cheap furniture around like sticks. "Ask your precious Valentine. Too bad she can't keep her mouth shut. You're one crazy slut if you think I'm letting you out of here to run to the cops. I ain't rotting in some stinking jail cell. Here's something else, dumb ass. You'll go when I say so and when I'm done with you and not one second before. She's old enough to get her share so don't think you're taking her anywhere."

As I peeped through a small crack in my bedroom door, he saw me. I could not have made a more critical error. He charged at me hitting the door with such force it seemed to fly off the hinges. Mother ran after him begging him to leave me alone. He turned and knocked her to the floor and kept charging toward me. His eyes glazed over in a trance and glowed with fire. He grabbed me by one arm and slung me full force against the wall. Mother fled to the kitchen and returned with her one knife--a giant butcher knife she used to cut up chicken--and charged toward him with full force blade glistening. My body hit the floor, and I blacked out in peaceful quiet. I floated away to the quiet of puffy white softness surrounding me in peaceful sleep. Then a suffocating smell. "Get it away, I can't breathe." I was soaked in alcohol. The nurse whispered, "She's coming to from her surgery. She will be fine."

I sat straight up in a soaked bed. Booming thunder and torrents of rain banged against my window. The nightmare had returned. I ran to Mother's room. She was not there. I needed to change out of my wet underwear and nightgown. But all I wanted to do was cry. I needed to be quiet. I was safe here with Aunt Nona. I had my mommy, and she had me. There were no more babysitters and bad boyfriends, hitting and yelling and threats and no one to hurt me. I kept repeating to myself, "I don't have to be afraid. I'm safe with Aunt Nona." Must not go back to sleep. The dream will come back. Streaks of lightning flashed and sounds of distant thunder bounced off the walls of my bedroom. I lay awake to the pounding rain praying to hear the creaking of the front door opening and my mother coming home.

∞

CHAPTER 2
FADE TO BLACK

The night of fun for Lila and Dex on March 23, 1951, had a heavy price. The rain-slick roads and the fast driving after a night of drinking proved once more to be a deadly combination. *Formula for disaster*. The driver lost control of the pickup truck as it skidded and rolled over, throwing the occupants like rag dolls to the wet pavement. Both died within minutes of the accident. I heard the rrring, rrring of the doorbell and the repeated rapping at the front door. I had been awake for hours, unable to stay asleep. I kept checking her room, and each time was the same. Mommy was not here. So when I heard the ringing doorbell, in a twisted way, it was relief. Death--the hand of the eternal dark abyss snatching us into its swirling blackness--called. My aunt arose out of a deep sleep to greet the early morning visitors from the police department. Her niece Lila Jo was dead. Aunt Nona had to go downtown. I heard her call the babysitter as the police tried to console her. I heard her sobbing as she paced in circles, and her shoes clicked against the old hardwood floors. The floor creaked and groaned in agony, about to give way under the weight.

I laid awake the rest of the night until I heard my aunt tell the babysitter she could leave. I prayed my aunt would not come into my room. I finally had to hear the words. My beloved mother was gone forever and this unimaginable nightmare night was only the beginning.

I was consumed with guilt. I begged her not to go out because I knew something bad would happen, but she didn't listen to me. It's quite an impossible task for a child to command the attention and demand adults listen. I experienced what grown-ups called a *premonition* or a child's foolish whim. Why didn't *someone* do something besides dismiss me? I begged to die. I knew something bad would happen. Everything was going too good for us. We weren't supposed to be well and happy like everyone else.

Grief and shock overcame my aunt. She adored my mother. These days of having Lila Jo live with her had been the happiest and most fulfilling of her life. I did not come out of my room for two days and arose from my bed only to go to the bathroom. No reason was good enough to entice me outside this room. I kept my head under the covers, crying uncontrollably. I held onto my quilt for comfort so tightly my fingers ached. My mother's picture beside my bed lay turned on its face. The pain of looking at her called me but I refused. After repeated attempts to coax me to eat, my aunt left my milk and food on the tray and retreated to her room and her private sorrow.

On the day of the funeral, I painstakingly dressed in my navy blue pleated skirt and white blouse and carefully buttoned the top pearl button of my pink cardigan sweater. Mother loved me in this outfit she called my Sunday clothes. Her precious Valentine was ready to go bury her beloved Mother. I moved through this continuing blackness on instinct. I was a child on a mission as grievous as it was simple. I refused to allow them to bury my mother without me. My aunt offered me the option to stay home. *Miserable choices, neither of which offered me comfort.*

The spray of bright pink Stargazer lilies on my mother's casket was as bright as neon against the background of gray. Everything else I remember (the sky, the weather, the hearse, faces) was gray or black. There were six other people besides us at the graveside — the undertaker, the grave digger, the preacher from auntie's church, the owner of the BluePlate, another waitress and another unidentified man dressed in a policeman's uniform who somehow seemed familiar. The preacher read a brief story about my mother.

Lila Jo 'Dynamo' Devereaux Lucca, born June 14, 1920 in Baton Rouge, Louisiana, was preceded in death by her parents Anna Estelle Monroe Devereaux and Joseph Thomas Devereaux. She worked as a public stenographer for several years in Baton Rouge before she answered the nationwide call for women as America entered World War II when she joined over a million women to help the war effort. In 1942, she traveled by bus to the Northeast and settled in Brooklyn, New York. She took a job in an aircraft manufacturing plant in New Jersey and then worked for several department stores in New York. She married Anthony Lucca, a pilot in the U. S. Army Air Forces, killed in the line of duty on November 9, 1943. On February 14, 1944, she gave birth to her answered prayer, daughter Valentine Estelle. She and Valentine recently moved from New York to live with her Aunt Nona Emmaline Monroe. Lila Jo leaves a legacy as a loving mother and niece devoted to her family and to her country. She had a strong sense of adventure, patriotism and devotion to others. She will be remembered for her strong and loving spirit as someone who loved her family and her fellow man. Those she leaves behind in their sorrow are questioning why Lila Jo's life was cruelly cut short leaving her young daughter. To the grieving family, I reach out to reassure you. She is a beautiful child of the Lord called home, and I pray you are comforted. She is with her Heavenly Father for eternity.

. . .

The minister read a passage from the Bible about preparing for the hour of our demise, and then he offered my mother to the Lord, praying for her soul. He also said something about we all need to be ready since it's unknown when the Lord will come for any of us. I struggled to stand at attention. After all, at any moment I would be awakened from this bad dream by the smile and warmth of my beautiful mother. But I knew what death meant. *Snatched from me in the darkness.* I would never see my precious mother again as long as I lived. I was seven and an orphan. Where do they send a seven-year-old? I wondered what would become of me. Who would auntie pass me off to? Perhaps an orphanage would take me. I needed to be with my own kind.

The policeman in the blue uniform came over to my aunt's side after the service. He said some kind words and gave her his card with the phone number of the police station. I heard him say if we needed anything to be sure and call. Then he kneeled down and stared straight in my eyes, "Valentine, you have a friend if you need me. Okay?"

As he turned and walked away, I looked up at my aunt. "Aunt Nonie, who was that?"

"He's the policeman called to the scene of the accident who came to our house. His name is Officer McShane." She stopped short of telling me the rest. The policeman was the last person to be with my mother when she took her final breath. I instantly felt close to him, although I had no idea why. But he was more than a stranger.

We drove home in silence. My aunt intently and carefully inched her car into the small garage. She gathered her Bible and her coat and gloves and helped me inside. I saw the slightest thing took her tremendous effort. Even the simplest task required every ounce of her attention and strength. Once inside the small kitchen, Aunt Nonie made hot tea and took cookies from the pantry and placed them on a crystal plate. She asked me to please sit down and join her as she poured me a glass of milk and waited while her tea brewed. I stared at the steam from the spout splashing into the cup. Just a vapor, poof and gone. Just like my mother. What a terrible thought. I stared at my aunt with tears welling up in my puffy eyes. I'm just too pitiful. What would auntie think of me if she knew my thoughts? I must think good things but how do you do that when all you know that is good is gone?

"Valentine, I can't imagine what you must be thinking. All this pain and sadness and you must be confused and wondering what will happen now. I hope I can ease your mind. I would like us to plan where we go from here. Okay?"

"Auntie, do we have to do it now? That sounds like a lot. I'm so sad I just want to go to my room."

"I feel the same way, my precious. But if we have this talk, maybe we both can feel better."

I nodded, silently dreading what was to come. I felt helpless and hopeless, so it didn't matter much what she said. I was only a child who had no rights or say about what happens. I resented everyone and everything interrupting my thoughts and my visions of my beloved mother. The thought of forgetting her terrified me. Never again to hear the throaty voice calling my name or see the face that lit up when she smiled and her luminous brown eyes that sparkled and danced and looked right through me. I closed my eyes and smelled the clean sweetness of her shiny brown hair and its softness against my cheek. Her slender loving arms and hands holding me close in their warmth. I was not afraid to be alone now. The opposite was true. When I closed my eyes, I saw her so real before me I reached to touch her. I remembered everything about her. I smelled her clean freshness. I heard her throaty voice calling my name. I heard her laughter. I felt her touch and could see her hands. Her comfort surrounded me. My aunt's voice rudely jolted me back. I resented being here. I wanted to be alone, to remember, and live within myself to find solitude, comfort, and peace.

"I want more than anything in this world to adopt you. I hope you will live here with me until you want to be on your own. Your home is Morningstar for as long as you want to live here."

Tears welled up. Sadness filled every hollow of my heart and soul with no space for any other emotion. But I did recognize this as a gigantic leap of faith for my aunt. She was 65 years old. Her life could not have become any more difficult. I felt guilty and sorry for her. I looked at my tiny body. How could anything so small cause so many problems and be such a giant complication? It seemed my whole life caused unhappiness and disruption. *Would there ever come a time when I brought joy?*

I looked toward her as if asking for permission and then hugged her. I desperately needed reassurance she had some feeling for me other than an overwhelming sense of obligation. "There, there, Valentine. We will be just fine but it will take both of us making some big compromises. I want you always to remember your beautiful mother as you last saw her. I'm not trying to take her place. I want you to live here with me so I can take care of you. I'll always be your Aunt Nona who loves you. Do you understand?"

"Yes, Aunt Nonie. I will be good and help you just like Mother would have wanted. I will make good grades and stay out of trouble and make you proud of me." In my child's mind, I made the singular promise I knew my aunt waited to hear, a small price to pay for her unselfish commitment.

"Valentine, I want you to have your mother's Bible. She treasured this gift from her mother. I remember when my sister gave it to her on Lila Jo's tenth birthday. I hope you will cherish and keep it near always."

She handed me the small black Bible, now worn around the edges. I touched it tenderly. My fingers were touching the same leather binding my mother's fingers touched. My eyes burned, severely irritated, red and raw from days of constant flowing tears. Mommy used to read me verses at bedtime. She said the words were called scripture and came from God. These words were important because they were God's teachings.

Aunt Nona tried not to cry. She kept clearing her throat and looking out the kitchen window. She was struggling. Struggling to understand why Lila Jo was taken, struggling to accept her niece was gone, and struggling to find words, composure, strength, and courage. She tried to reassure me, but I wondered. Who would help her? She loved Lila Jo like a daughter. Just because Aunt Nona was a grown-up didn't make her hurt and grief any less. In that instant, I vowed to be Aunt Nonie's rock someday.

"We need to go through all your mother's things in the coming weeks. I thought we would donate her clothing, but you are welcome to keep whatever you like."

I began to panic with the thought of someone touching my mother's things. "Oh, no, please don't. That's like throwing her away. It's all I have left. We don't have to do that now, do we? Please, auntie."

She hugged and tried to reassure me. "Oh, Valentine. I'm so sorry. I shouldn't have mentioned it. My mind is going a mile a minute and I'm not thinking clearly. I'm just like you. I'm in shock and not sure what to do. So don't you worry. We'll keep everything until you are ready.

There's no hurry. There is one more thing. You and your mother had extremely hard lives. It will be hard to forget those days. But you have to replace those dark memories with the bright days ahead. You and I will make a good team, trust me. I'll do everything I possibly can to help you make a good life. Auntie might be old, but she loves you more than you can ever know. I'm new at this auntie thing so you'll have to help me and keep me up to speed. I can never take Lila Jo's place and will never try. I intend to be the best auntie ever, and don't you worry, all this doesn't mean you'll grow up to be like me. Heaven forbid!" She grinned.

I appreciated my aunt's dry sense of humor, but back then I didn't see much humor in the midst of overwhelming confusion. What in the world did all this mean?

At breakfast the next day, a small gift appeared on the table wrapped to perfection in shiny blue paper with a gold bow. She handed me the small package.

"Go ahead, you may open it."

I carefully opened the package. A little gold heart locket shone on a gold chain. I held my breath. If only there could be a picture inside. My mind raced and my uncoordinated fingers fumbled. I looked up, bewildered. Aunt Nona showed me how to open the locket.

"Such a beautiful picture of Lila Jo. But we can put whatever picture you want. It's your locket. Let me help you."

She gently draped the chain around my neck and fastened the clasp. I ran to the bedroom mirror to see. "I'll wear this always. Now Mommy is close to me all the time. Thank you, Aunt Nona. I love it. I can see Mommy's face anytime I want to. I'll just open this locket. She's smiling like she always did. It's perfect."

"Valentine, this is a good opportunity for you and me to talk. You've had a lot of unhappiness in your young life. You are already sweet and smart, and I don't want you to change who you are. But there will come a day when you will be out in the world and have to make your way. There are people who will do their best to show you as inferior and beneath them. We won't let that happen. I want you to be prepared for life and live as an independent and confident young lady. Your mother was like a daughter to me. She wanted the best for you and wanted you to be the best no matter what the task or job. She wanted you to excel and not just get by. Do you understand?"

I nodded, but auntie hardly noticed; she was so anxious to continue. I guess she had a lot she needed to say. I was lost as a goose. But I needed to listen and try my best to remember.

"We cannot afford a private school like other young people attend but you will be competing with those same youngsters. You're still a child, but it's best from an early age to do your best to succeed. It's hard work and sometimes means sacrifice. You are smart, Valentine. I hope you'll always remember you can be anything you want to be with no limitations. *You have to discover the truth and wonder of you* so you can pursue your goals and make them a reality. God made us all special; we each have our talents. We are all His shining lights."

She hesitated for a few minutes and stopped to take a deep breath. Then she began again. "Your mother was smart. Even though she was a waitress at the BluePlate, she was capable of much more. She once worked as a stenographer and excelled at her job."

I smiled faintly and shook my head in agreement. It bothered me about what all she thought was wrong with me that she was determined to fix, and I didn't understand enough even to ask questions. I was sure of one thing. I accepted everything my Aunt Nona said as truth and for my own good. *I knew my Aunt Nona would never say or do anything to hurt me. That feeling felt so good.*

Even though I listened when she said someday I would understand, inside I trembled. I tried to be brave, but fear of the unknown consumed me. I shuddered. How was I supposed to think about things I didn't understand? If I had a thought, it included my mother. How do you stop your brain from thinking thoughts that can make you sad forever? I placed Mother's Bible in the drawer of my bedside table, but first I carefully wrapped it in my mother's favorite red, green, and navy blue silk scarf. Mother called it *nautical* because of the colors. This Bible would be my most valued possession. I said my prayers and thanked

God for Aunt Nonie. How did I get so lucky? I touched my new gold locket and opened it to see the brightness of my mother's smile. How would I live without her? I didn't have the faintest idea of how I would get through the next day, much less all the days and nights ahead. Nevertheless, the long, twisted road coiled before me like a giant snake of endless foreboding.

∞

CHAPTER 3
McSHANE

My aunt invited him to have an early dinner with us on Wednesday evening. Even though I understood somewhat his continuing connection and why he might be invited, I dreaded the evening. Yes, I wanted to see him again but the whole idea of talking to him about that fateful night horrified me. My head continued to spin with the thought. He was the last person to be with my mother. There had to be something special about this stranger God had selected to be with her. I decided my reaction was natural and therefore acceptable that I wanted to be connected to him. I received my aunt's instructions which were short and sweet: be polite. He arrived promptly at 7 o'clock and not in uniform. Today was his day off. He wore a long-sleeved blue shirt starched and pristine and khaki slacks. His shoes were freshly shined and his camel color socks had flecks of blue. Struck by his good looks and how well-dressed he was, I tried not to stare. The clean woodsy scent of his aftershave softly whispered in the air. I wanted to be near him and wished my mother could be here.

For some reason his good looks made me sad and uncomfortable. Why? He would always be a reminder of that night. I helped my aunt get the meatloaf and mashed potatoes and green beans on the table and made sure everyone had a glass of iced tea or water. Anxious to slam down my food and then go to my room, I could not bring myself to ask my questions. I didn't want to cry and embarrass myself and Aunt Nonie in front of a stranger. I wanted to talk to him and at the same time leave the past in the past. I saw the situation as too painful and horrific to hear about her and what happened.

Officer McShane and my aunt made some easy conversation about the usual—the weather, how we were getting along and if we needed anything. Then he turned to me.

"Valentine, how are you doing? I have thought a lot about you over the past couple of months. How is school?"

"Fine. I like school."

"I have a daughter about your age and she goes to the same school. Do you know her? Her name is Jessica McShane."

Jessica was the one girl I liked in my class. Odd she didn't mention her dad.

"Yes, I know her. She and I sit by each other and play at recess."

"I'm glad to hear you two are acquainted. You have a lot in common. Maybe Jessica has told you or not. It's hard for her to talk about. We lost Jessica's mother a couple of years ago."

"No, she didn't tell me. We don't talk much about our family. We just go to school and play. The other kids don't have much to do with us. We're not like them."

He bent down and again I caught a whiff of his after shave. He smelled clean and fresh like the outdoors after it rains. I liked the way he smelled and looked. My heart ached. I wished he and my mother could have been together. I would have picked someone like him. His voice was soothing, not too loud and not too quiet. And he was good-looking, just like my mother. They would have made a beautiful couple. Oh, Valentine, you're stupid. I caught myself and quickly stepped away. What makes me think thoughts that can never be? I imagine a world of make believe to escape a world of heartache. I should grow up. Life is not a fairyland.

I looked into his vibrant blue eyes as he took my small hands in his. "I hope you and your aunt can come over soon and have dinner with us. Valentine, you and your aunt can always come to me if you need anything." Aunt Nona smiled broadly and shook her head in agreement so I could go to my room.

Officer McShane and my aunt cleared the table in the kitchen so they could talk while they did the dishes. Aunt Nonie washed and he dried. He never banged a dish. I didn't hear every word they said, but I heard bits and pieces and put together the rest. I heard him say, "She said a few words before she died. I didn't understand some of it. She was weak and couldn't talk above a whisper." I started to cry. I didn't want to hear anything more and closed my door. Try as I might I couldn't help but think of my mother when I looked at him. They were linked for eternity. *The one to be with her when she took her final breath.* I wondered what she said to him. How strange life works. She lay dying on a cold, hard wet pavement spending her last precious minutes comforted by a stranger, a policeman doing his job at an accident. Can any human be closer to another?

He stayed about an hour after dinner and then my aunt appeared in my room. "Valentine, I want you to make a special effort to befriend Jessica. She will be a good friend for you."

"I already am. She's the nicest person in my class and spoke to me the first day. She and I are best friends. She makes me laugh."

"Wonderful. Jessica and Officer McShane have gone through heartache, too. Friends who care about you are important, Valentine, especially when they have experienced the same things in life. Good night, dear. Be sure and say your prayers."

"Auntie, what happened to Jessica's mother? Why did she leave or did she die?"

"I don't have all the details, Valentine, just what Officer McShane told me. She got sick with cancer for a couple of years before she died. He and Jessica have had some sad times. You must not mention anything to Jessica about her mother. Let her be the one to tell you about it when she's ready. Okay?"

"Yes, I understand. Thank you for telling me. Goodnight, auntie." I felt even closer to Jessica. We had a bond and now I understood. We both faced life without our mothers and our hearts ache. We face each day with sadness we hide. I still wondered. What did my mother say to Officer McShane? I should ask tomorrow or another day. I did not want to ask about anything more tonight.

The next morning on the way to school, I could wait no longer. "Auntie, what did my mother say to Officer McShane before she died? She said something, and I want to know what it was. He is special to me. He was the last person to be with her, wasn't he?"

My aunt looked at me bewildered. She knew but hesitated to tell me. "Valentine, your mother was weak. Officer McShane could barely hear and understand her. She said something about she knew she had to leave you, and she asked him to promise to see about you. She loved you so much her dying thoughts were about you and your wellbeing. That is what he told me." Aunt Nona fought back a flood of tears. She felt the fresh hurt still raw and deep.

For the first time, I felt reassured. Mother wasn't left to die alone in the dark of night on the cold, wet street, my worst nightmare. I knew God was with her and took care of her, but I also felt reassured she knew the caring presence of another human being in her last moments. Even if he was a stranger, Officer McShane was kind. I thought he was our *angel in blue*. I wondered about so many things but mainly I ached for her. Please God, I begged from my heart, let me know she wasn't scared. I couldn't imagine her last breaths of consciousness on this earth so alone. I spent the school day in the restroom crying but relief did not come. Jessica told the school nurse, and she called my aunt to come get me. I cried myself to sleep that night and begged God to help me. *Give me peace.*

∞

Chapter 4
Jessica and Me

The first time she spent the night with me she brought her favorite doll Monique. It was in fact her only doll. Monique was a beautiful angelic creature with features perfectly chiseled in creamy porcelain. Her eyes were deep ocean blue almost black, and her deep reddish brown hair cascaded in soft waves and curls halfway down her back. She arrived prepared with her personal overnight case complete with built-in mirror, comb and brush, pajamas, slippers, and toothbrush. Jessica explained the doll was as perfect as possible and therefore was a Parisienne model. Monique the model was designed to be exceptionally beautiful when wearing the latest fashions. Appealing as she might be, she was not the rubber-squeeze baby that wet and cried--the only doll worth my time. Peering down on us with untouchable beauty and unreachable perfection, Monique was intrusive. Jessica said she wanted to be *the* model Monique when she grew up. There had to be more. Why would she want to *be* Monique? Not to worry. Jessica and I knew how to disagree and not get upset with each other. We might not part our hair the same but we looked beyond our differences. We were strange little girls, and we knew it. We naturally gravitated to each other and were magnetized by impenetrable trust almost immediately. We spent the first visits getting acquainted exploring our everyday interests--what each other liked to eat, our favorite colors and flowers, the kids in our class who were weird or nice, and what we thought was funny or sad. We eventually grappled with the hard core *inner* core. She was first to broach the subject that hovered and dominated even though not discussed. We both felt the emptiness of a giant void. Acknowledging the hole in our hearts was another matter heretofore kept in our private place.

"Valentine, my dad told me about your mom. I'm sad when I think about us and our mothers. We both have to grow up without having a mom and the other kids think we're pitiful. It makes me so mad. They don't have any idea what it's like. I've heard some of the girls whispering about us like there's something wrong with us because our moms died, like we're to blame or we've got the plague. How stupid. What are they afraid of? Just because they have moms and we don't. They think everyone has to be alike."

"It's true what you're saying, Jess. I try to ignore what they say, like we're strange. Most of them like being mean and making us feel bad. They laugh at me because I limp. They've never had something so bad happen to them that they wake up sad and go to bed sad every day like we do. My Aunt Nona says caring people are sensitive to other people, something about walking in other people's shoes. If you've never had anything bad or sad happen to you, how would you know how it feels?"

"You're right. I wondered what happened to your leg but didn't want to hurt your feelings. They should just keep their mouths shut. My mom died from cancer. It was a bad time, and I had to help my dad get through it. Sometimes I wanted to stay in bed and be sad, but I had to be brave for him. He was strong for her and for me. I don't understand how he did it."

"Aunt Nona and I tried to help each other but sometimes you just have to be sad and cry. There's nothing else to do but get the tears out and hurt. It's nothing to be ashamed of when you grieve because that means you care about someone. Think how sad if you never love anybody."

"Valentine, promise me, cross your heart, you will never tell *anyone*."

"Jessica, I promise. You and I love each other like sisters and more. We won't blab our secrets and hurt each other because that's betrayal. Even if we get mad at each other. There's no reason good enough."

"Okay. I agree. It's so hard to keep some stuff inside, and it's even harder to let it out. But I'll burst if I don't. I want to tell you because you'll understand."

"You can tell me anything, Jess. There's nothing too bad or too sad I won't understand and keep in my heart forever."

"My mom had breast cancer, and it had spread when the doctors found it. They didn't have a way to save her. They had to cut off her breasts. I still remember all she had to go through. She was sick and in pain for a long time. And my dad suffered, too. They loved each other so much, and there was nothing he could do to help her. He told me he felt helpless. He still can't mention her without crying. He's guilty, too, because he didn't help her." Jessica's beautiful crystal clear blue eyes clouded over, and tears spilled onto her cheeks. Her heart was broken.

"I struggle to remember her without my heart breaking. She was sick and dying for so long, but I have to remember her beautiful and happy."

I couldn't comprehend or compare their sorrow to mine. We both had the heartache of loss and understood the need for comfort and kindness, and before I knew what was happening, Jess and I were holding each other, and the tears and heartbreak took over. Jessica was trembling, and I held her close to me. How could two girls so young be expected to carry this load? I knew there was no comforting or even acceptable answer. It was just the way it was. My mother was snatched away quick. Jessica's mother suffered long. Unexpected and expected--the circumstances of our losses were different--but the result was the same. We were robbed.

Jess looked straight in my eyes. "You don't have to tell me anything, Val. But I wondered where your dad is. It's got to be so hard not having a parent."

I sat in stunned silence. What should I say to someone who has my heart in her hand? She was the only one in the world besides Aunt Nona I would ever trust.

"Jess, you have to understand. I've never talked about him. Not even with my Aunt Nona." Jessica put her arms around my shoulders. We sat in the quiet synchronizing our breathing so we would be together as one. "I love you Valentine more than I can say. Just remember God sent you to me when I needed you the most, and I'll never let you go."

"It makes me sad because he died before I was even born. I asked Mother constantly to tell me about him. And she would tell me the same story over and over. I loved to sit and listen to her especially when she described him and how they met. It was their love story. Her eyes would sparkle and dance when she talked about him. They were only married a year when he left to fight in World War II. He was an immigrant from Italy who came to America when he was 14 with his parents and grandparents. Mother loved to boogie and drink beer at the local dance halls filled with servicemen on leave. She and her friends loved to dance and let their hair down after work so she didn't really have a boyfriend. But everything changed when she was working part-time at the department store where my father was a model and his father was a tailor. She was headed to the basement to the office, and he was coming up the stairs. He asked for her phone number but she wouldn't give it to him. He kept trying to talk to her and didn't want to let her go. But Mother said it wasn't in a scary way. She was interested in him but was playing it safe. Finally Mother said she would have coffee with him at the drugstore across the street after work. They must have fallen in love instantly because they started dating and were married in six months and then she got pregnant with me. Oh, Jess, it's so sad but wonderful in a way. He died in the war and was a hero and got a medal."

Jessica looked quizzical as if she was not quite sure but she didn't question me. Even if she wondered about my story, I knew Jess. She had a glorious innate ability--when to pursue and when to let it go. Either way, I never knew him and made up details to satisfy my curiosity and to create my story.

"Mother had some tiny black and white pictures of them together on a picnic in an apple orchard in upstate New York. He had on his uniform with what's called a flight jacket. He was a pilot, and that's how come he was shot down during one of the battles. I would give anything to have his leather jacket, but I guess he died wearing it. It gets cold up there flying so it wasn't just for looks but he was so good-looking in his uniform. Mother said he was so proud to be an American and serve his country; that jacket was his favorite thing to wear. When Mother met him, he was a civilian and said he was wearing a white short-sleeved shirt with sleeves rolled up over his muscular arms and tucked into his gabardine pleated trousers. He was very particular. The shirt had to be starched and ironed to crisp perfection. He wore Italian loafers and carried his cigarettes in a sterling silver monogrammed cigarette case-- he knew how to dress in style from years of modeling for the large department stores. He was very good-looking with dark, curly hair, and dark brown eyes. You've never seen a cuter couple than those two. They were meant for each other. Mother said I have his brown eyes."

Jessica's face lit up. I knew she wanted to hear everything I knew to tell her, made up or real. No problem. I had often imagined what life was like for them before me. "When they first met, he was still modeling and they would stay out all night. They loved to go dancing to the big orchestras like the Dorseys and Wayne King. Back then, there were dance contests for couples to stay on the dance floor for the longest, called 'still standing'. Sometimes they would dance all night and then go to work. They'd have breakfast with their friends at their favorite diner called the Sunny Side Up after dancing all night. One time Mother fell asleep at the counter after an all-nighter, and my dad couldn't stand to wake her up. He carried her in his arms to their little apartment in Brooklyn which was eight or ten blocks away. He was so gentle she never woke up until the next morning. He was so young and strong. They lived in a tiny apartment in Brooklyn which had the bedroom, living room, and kitchen all in one room, called a studio. Mother called it their love nest and said it was just perfect for them, they didn't need a thing. They loved to go to tango bars to learn to tango and to party. New York had lots of them back then. It was just a different way of life, romantic and intense in a way. You were young and had your life in front of you, but the War was the dark shadow of uncertainty whether you would come back home alive. So you crammed your days and nights full of life and thought twice about putting something off until tomorrow. Can you imagine feeding and entertaining twenty people every Sunday? His family had family dinners on Sundays with scads of people eating and drinking wine and having fun for most of the day. Mother said she had never been part of such a clan and eaten such delicious food mostly cooked by his grandmother. His family thought Texas was still wild like the movies where we rode horses and lived on big ranches and fought over land. My father loved my mother so much and called her 'Dynamo'. That was her nickname. She loved to dance and have fun and had all this energy. She hardly slept. I saw a letter from my father signed *amore* which is Italian for love. She tried to speak Italian but said it was hard and only learned to say a few words and phrases." I paused, breathless. Once I started I didn't want to stop.

Jessica's eyes were as big as saucers. "Oh, Val, your mom and dad are the most romantic and beautiful story. I can see them. It's just like the old movies about how every part of life was affected by the war and people counted every day as precious. It seemed people loved each other more then."

"I daydream about them sometimes when Aunt Nona catches me squandering my time as she calls it." There was more to the story, but it was a good place to stop on a high note. I liked to think my mother and father had the best experience of their young lives even though their time together was cut short. They made the most of everything they had. I saw the three of us together even though it never happened.

Truth be told, his family was not wild about either one of us. They preferred he had married within the circle--a family friend's daughter perhaps or at the very least someone of his background and religion. After my father's death, Mother said she never heard a word from them. They weren't the least bit curious about me and never inquired about our whereabouts and how we were getting along. We were on our own in Brooklyn with no family and no one to help Mother. I had to go to preschool for a couple of years, but on those off days when I was sick or the school was closed, there was no one to watch me while Mother worked. Angie had been my babysitter with no problems until she hooked up with Will. My face turned dark. Even though she reassured, Jessica was too young, too gentle and too good for me to contaminate with my woeful tale of despair. When we're older and I'm hardened to life in the ditch, I'll share my story. For now, I was content to keep the nightmare that tried to define me tucked away. It was too much to burden Jess with. I only knew one way to recount my memories, and it wasn't pretty. *Uncensored.* I should keep the ugliness to myself. Those Brooklyn days were still painfully raw and close to the surface. No, I wouldn't tell Jess. I loved her too much to load her down with my past. Besides it was over now anyway, and I should make my story to suit me. Mother would understand.

We sat and held each other. There was no one in my world but Jess who felt my pain. As long as I lived, she would be my soul connection and an extension of my being and beating heart. No matter what else happened, our bond would not be broken not even by death. We had been blessed as well as cursed. We had a rare friendship of unspoken trust, strength and understanding. My life would forever be brightened by the light of Jessica McShane. Her insight and perception would be a Godsend throughout my life. She knew me from the beginning. I never felt I came up short in her eyes or was compelled to explain myself to be acceptable and accepted by her.

"Valentine, I don't want to make you feel bad. You have your hurt, but sometimes I'll explode with all this bad stuff going on inside. Just because someone dies doesn't mean feelings and memories die. It seems impossible sometimes, but I try and remember my mom like she asked me to. She was so beautiful and sweet, so it should be easy to remember her. The bad dreams and sadness that take over need to go away."

"I have those bad dreams but seems like they're not as bad as before. Don't ever be sorry to tell me anything. We're so lucky to have each other and know we don't have to explain why we feel a certain way and not be afraid to tell each other whatever we want to say. We have to remember our moms the best way we possibly can. I remember my mom the way she smiled and smelled and looked and even her voice. Remember, no one can ever take away our beautiful memories. And anytime you're sad or you want to talk, you go right ahead and I will, too. We're okay not to be fake smiling all the time."

"Valentine, let's make a pact. We won't ever let anyone, not even a boy, come between us or separate us, ever." She looked around the room, searching.

"We need that special something to show we're part of each other."

She jumped off the bed and opened the top drawer to her dresser. She spent several minutes shuffling through her trinkets, retrieving a beautiful red velvet heart box holding a simple pearl necklace. "Oh, how perfect."

She came back in a few minutes with scissors in hand and cut the string connecting the pearls. She let the pearls slide into the box. "Here are your pearls." She counted out half of the pearls and placed the pearls inside a smaller heart-shaped pink box and handed it to me. "The pearls are like our friendship. Each is not complete with the other. Someday we can have matching pearl bracelets made. These pearls belonged to my mother, and she wore them on her wedding day. I remember her telling me her mother gave them to her as a wedding present. They are the most special possession I have and I want to share them with you."

"Jessica, are you sure you want to part with these? They're priceless and these pearls can't be replaced. No one could ever give me anything that meant more. I promise I won't let anyone ever come between us. There's no one in the world more important to me than you and Aunt Nona. I will treasure my pearls always. Thank you. No one can break our bond."

"I can see us friends forever even when we're little old ladies with blue hair and shriveled wrinkly skin. I never saw an old woman with a giant silver pony tail hanging down to her saggy butt. Guess I'll be the first." She made me laugh. Jess was funny even when serious.

∞

CHAPTER 5
TEMPTING FATE

A untie was having church ladies for Bible study in the afternoon, and I was underfoot and on her last nerve. I tried to set up the tables and chairs, but all I did was make more work. She scurried around setting out snacks and drinks and making sure the house was in order before the church ladies arrived. I asked to escape outside to ride my bike, but Aunt Nona had other plans. Auntie made sure I was sheltered close to home and confined to our neighborhood with one exception. I was entrusted occasionally with doing the grocery shopping with a bonus. And today seemed the perfect day. She needed me to be busy but with a purpose. She was no more anxious than I to get me out of the house. The vision of a disorderly afternoon with me and the church ladies under the same roof was cause for panic.

"Valentine, you better not ride your bike. If you go to the movie, you'll have to leave your bicycle and someone might take it. You'll have to walk and carry the groceries. Do you think they will be too heavy for you?"

I looked at the list. There were five things. I could handle it. "I can carry those things, Aunt Nona. It's fine."

"Okay. You better be on your way then and come home as soon as the movie is over. You should be home by 3:30."

I was excited to be trusted with such responsibility, even though my not being underfoot was the main urgency and the grocery errand was an afterthought. Aunt Nona was overwhelmed. We were both working hard to adjust and to be accommodating, but sometimes our efforts were in vain no matter how hard we tried. Sharing her life and her house with a child continued to be problematic on occasion, and this day was a prime example.

Down the street from the grocery store was a small theater and my reward for the errand. Inside the cool, dark theater I was thrust upon a giant screen of bigger-than-life characters to an exciting (even exotic) place as I anxiously awaited exciting exploits and fantasy. I was eager to escape to another time and place and leave my sadness behind for a few hours. A beautiful young girl behind the glass said I shouldn't enter the theater without a ticket. A ticket cost ten cents. I looked as pitiful as I knew how and still be functioning. I desperately wanted to see the movie, but I also wanted to keep my allowance. My dimes were hard to come by, and I became a hoarder and conniver of how to keep and increase my stash of coins. After the movie started, I lingered outside and carefully plotted my plan to sneak in. In the middle of my maneuver, after the lobby emptied of the moviegoers hurriedly getting their popcorn, sodas, and candy and had taken their seats, unbelievably, she called me to the window. I watched anxiously as she separated a ticket from the huge roll and handed me the purple stub. I could go in but be quiet. I can't say why she was so kind or soft-hearted; maybe she felt sorry for me and wanted me out of sight and out of mind. It didn't matter why I had to rely on someone else's kind nature. I loved the movies and if need be, I would spend my own dime to go. But I also knew how to take advantage of my good fortune. I did not allow pride to get in the way of my accepting the beautiful stranger's charity.

I loved the Westerns easily marking the bad guy being caught for his deeds. You get what you deserve in the western world, a welcome fantasy from the real world. I was a part of the movie. I rode just as fast and hard and cleaned up the town of the bad guys. And the horses! Oh, the thought of having a horse and learning to ride with the wind so smooth and fast with mane and tail flying! I would glide along the back of that beautiful pulsating creature as we floated across the land and over the rushing rivers. It was my dream. But I was fickle. When the musicals blared across the screen, they held a special mystery and enticed me with their outlandish costumes of feathery headdresses encrusted with sparkling stones so top heavy I sat in amazement how any human neck supported such weighty splendor—all in amazing Technicolor. Beautiful girls strutted over the screen, flinging their long, shapely fishnet-clad legs high in the air while singing and gazing into the eyes of the leading man. He had a bevy of beauties to choose from as each girl flirted and teased him to choose her. This romantic rather risqué interlude added some relief from all this razzle dazzle of glamorous screen props resulting in a delectable escape from the humdrum world of gray in which scores of us function. My afternoon on my own bolstered my confidence I was growing up but climaxed unpredictably into a situation much more than I bargained for and more than I was prepared to handle.

After the movie, I made one of my first independent decisions. On that summer day, I felt peculiarly responsible and threw caution to the wind. I wanted an escapade to rival the one I had just seen on the big screen. Why shuffle along the same sidewalk, along the same old street that offered nothing new, unusual or exciting? I wanted to see different houses and yards lining a different street. Why not take another way home? It was August and steamy hot. A shortcut coming from town on a hot summer day carrying groceries seemed smart and adventuresome. The usual way home my aunt insisted on, boring and predictable. I had never been home that way and imagined the fun of exploring. I loved the heat even the relentless summer in Texas. The rippling hot waves rising above the ground were hypnotic, and my bare feet stirred up dusty clouds of swirling smoke with each step in the dry, powdery Texas clay. The Johnson grass was still and high, and the quiet of it all startled me back to reality. I found myself lost in an unrecognizable neighborhood of vacant lots and rundown houses. The familiar neighborhood of modest houses with mowed lawns and colorful beds of flowers had been replaced by knee-high weeds and trash and the stench of rotting garbage. There were signs of neglect all around me. Didn't anyone care about anything around here? Abandoned cars and equipment were left to rust and rot. Houses were dilapidated with peeling paint and yards filled with litter. I had no idea where I was, how I got there or how to get home. The magnitude of my careless attitude and thoughtless decision hit me full force. I started to panic and looked anxiously for someone to help me.

I glanced up at the old brick house and rusty tractor in the yard. An old man came from around the back of the house. His overalls were dirty and sweaty, and he bent over as he shuffled along with shoes untied, spitting tobacco. I quickened my step, but too late as he looked up. "Where are you going in such a hurry? It's too hot to rush around." I did not speak. Something about this old man scared me. Gruff and frowning, he saw I was ill at ease and forced a grin. Quickly he said, "How about some lemonade on this hot day?"

I did want that lemonade; it sounded so good. But I didn't really want it from him. Today was like a furnace fueled by the unrelenting sun and I was beyond thirsty. "Okay, but I have to hurry. My aunt is waiting for me to bring home these groceries."

He ambled inside to get the lemonade, and I sat down in the shade of a huge old oak tree. My head was pounding, echoing through my ears, and my heart raced faster and faster. I should not stay here. Something was not right. Soon he came out of the house with two glasses of lemonade. I felt his piercing eyes burning a hole through my cotton sundress. I was uneasy and uncomfortable in this dress. My white ruffled straps kept falling down on my shoulders. I shouldn't be here. He smelled bad, and his overalls were sticking out in the front. He kept touching himself. I was trembling and terrified. Why had I been so desperate for this lemonade? He kept leaning toward me trying to get closer to me, but I kept moving back at arm's length. His teeth were as brown as if he had been eating dirt, and his breath smelled like sour throw up. I noticed a wet spot on the front of his overalls like he had peed on himself. I had one thought; I must get out of here and fast. I was determined not to panic.

"You're a pretty little thing. How old are you, little girl? I'll bet you'd like some cookies with cold lemonade. I have some in the house, and it's cool in there."

"I'm not little. I'll be in fourth grade." I took a gulp of the sour lemonade. "I don't want..." He was moving closer to me and cut me off in mid-sentence. He did not want to hear anything I had to say. He was intent on *me*. He looked like a dog slobbering over a bone. There was no one to help me. I knew I had to run for my life. This old but familiar stranger had reappeared. *Evil.*

"Let's go inside and get some good oatmeal cookies with our lemonade. It will taste so good, those cookies, and lemonade. I have games inside you will like. We'll have fun playing. I get lonesome sometimes, don't you? It's too hot to be outside in this heat. You could get heatstroke. You look like you need to cool off *inside.*"

Nothing he described sounded the least bit appealing. I was ready to make my move. I didn't understand exactly what he was after, but my instincts took over and I knew I was in big trouble. I started to plan my next move. I had to be smart, and the only way to get home since I was lost, was to re-trace my steps.

"Wait! You're not leaving yet. I've got other plans for you, little one." Just as I started to pick up the groceries and start on my way, he grabbed my arm and started dragging me toward the house.

"No, no, let me go!" I was petrified, frozen with fear. Terror ran through my veins and my brain electrified. Every cell was on overload. All I could think was not to panic and use my wits to get away from him before it was too late. I jerked my arm away with all my strength and must have caught him off guard. That was one time being skinny was an asset. My sweaty arm slipped through his gnarly fist as I turned and kicked his leg squarely in the knee. My arm throbbed with pain as though it had been jerked from its socket. The grocery sack tumbled over and groceries rolled to the ground. He tripped, still struggling to snatch me with his last effort and lay flat on his grimy face, holding his knee. I heard him yelling at me, but I concentrated all my power and energy on one thing. This was my chance to escape.

I ran at full speed, hopping and skipping as fast as my legs would go. I was hindered by my short leg, but I kept going at full pace and never looked back. I ran and skipped and ran and did not stop until I got to our yard. Hot tears filled my eyes and streamed down my face. Breathless, my heart pounded desperately as if to escape outside my chest. I saw my chest flip-flopping as my heart struggled to beat faster and faster. I tried to gain my composure before I went into the house.

My thoughts made no sense. Should I tell auntie? I was to blame. I should have come straight home and not wandered into unfamiliar territory. I was stupid and asked for trouble. I could not tell my aunt. She would never let me go anywhere alone again nor trust me to use good judgment. How could I fail a simple errand of bringing home the groceries? I knew better. It was my fault I got into trouble with the old man. I didn't want to disappoint her. I wanted her to trust me.

"Child, what happened? Why are you so out of breath? Are you all right?"

"Oh, auntie. I'm so sorry. I tripped and fell, and the groceries rolled all over the sidewalk and into the street. Then a car came and ran over them and smashed them all. I tried to pick them up, but it was mush." Tears rolled, and I was soaked in sweat. I felt dizzy and thought I would pass out. She told me to never venture away from home, to stay on our street and in our neighborhood. I knew our route to the store. What I did was against the rules.

"Valentine, come sit down and I'll get you some water. Everything will be all right. Don't worry about the groceries. The important thing is you're not hurt."

I lay in bed with the image of the repulsive old man hovering over me. I couldn't get him out of my mind. He wasn't just in my thoughts. His vile essence penetrated my room and this house. I yearned for the warmth, comfort, and security of my home as it was. I closed my eyes and smelled his nastiness around me. I opened my eyes and saw his depravity. He threatened to harm me in ways I tried to forget yet didn't understand. I was urgently in need of help. I wanted to tell someone what had happened to me. I was a child. Didn't I have a right to be protected? Looking around in my world, I hesitated to tell the one person who loved me enough to protect me with her life. *Aunt Nona.* No, there was no way to tell her without upsetting her. She would be frightened because I had done a bad thing by straying from the neighborhood. Yes, it was my fault the old man had come after me.

I knew this was a disaster in the making. Nasty old man had big plans for me and I got lucky. I learned a valuable lesson about deliberately inviting trouble and not listening to your instincts. I had never felt more vulnerable. I could not shake the horror of being under the control of the horrid old man. Some things do not have to be spoken like when someone is bad and when a situation is bad. I might have recovered from the incident, but the memory haunted me. I never forgot his face and his eyes. He reminded me of someone else so long ago with his same intense look as if he didn't see me at all but was looking through me. Why and what about me attracted evil?

I laid there for hours trying to be calm. I started to cry. Oh, Mommy, why did you have to go to Heaven so early? I need you here. She would know what to do. I reached for my locket to see her face. Before I reached to touch my necklace, I couldn't feel it. My heart quit beating. I couldn't breathe. It was gone! I jumped quickly out of bed and looked on and under the pillow, on the sheets, blanket, on the floor. No, it was nowhere to be found. My deepest dread was true; it had come off during my tussle with the old man! There was nothing to do. How would I explain to Aunt Nona? I cried myself to sleep and then awoke with a start. I remembered the strangest thing. *Officer McShane*. He once told me I should come to him if I needed anything. I thought about him and his kind reassurance; I repeated *Officer McShane* over and over until I quit struggling and gave in to the quiet beckoning of peaceful sleep.

∞

CHAPTER 6
MINI BOOT CAMP

A unt Nona was patient and understanding when I told her I had lost my beloved heart necklace. I explained I had taken it off to take a bath and had trouble with the tiny clasp when I put it back on. It had come off sometime while I was wearing it, and I had looked everywhere and didn't find it. She didn't scold because she knew children are sometimes careless even with their favorite possessions. Losing one of the rare pictures of my mother was another matter. She asked me to please be more careful, and if I was having problems with the clasp, I should have asked for her help. I hated myself for lying about the irreplaceable heart necklace and picture of my mother and for not telling Aunt Nona the truth. But no matter how frightened I was, I must not upset her and admit my wrongdoing. She would be scared and upset and there was no need since it was over and I had not been hurt. My decision whether right or wrong had been made; I felt it was the right one. We were in the process of adapting and learning each other's ways and didn't need another complication. In many instances, we were walking on eggshells. We were trying not to offend or hurt each other and at the same time build a life together. I tried to please her but there were trying times even for her high tolerance.

One of the first things I noticed, Aunt Nonie was opinionated and strong of conviction, even in the small details. Our generations were separated by countless differences and generally caused no problems and were accepted as expected generation changes in social behavior. Aunt Nona did not like our affection for nicknames. Jessica was Jess and I was Val. That was a given. I noticed Aunt Nona called people by their full names. Not Susie but Susan or Suzanne, not Jim but James. She never corrected me when I called her Aunt Nonie. She was much too polite and gentile to embarrass me into smallness. But she did grimace or recoil when I called her Aunt Nonie. She had been patient and understanding, but clearly I needed to grow up and give up my baby ways. I spent the early years inside myself as small, sad, and lacking (void of interest in the world) and lost. But somehow, someway I had to change and become a caring person. I needed to think about what is important to the other person, not just what is important to me. I heard Aunt Nonie refer to a certain person as sophisticated and cosmopolitan which conjured up visions of folks in fantasy land, the movies. Not according to my aunt; I could become exactly what I envisioned. Even more exact, I *become* what I envision. So she insisted; it's my choice. Why not strive for excellence and my full potential? She shrugged as she explained the obvious choice. *Ordinary vs. exceptional.* And one of her first rules although simple was paramount. People like the sound of their own names not some made up nickname or shortened version unless they tell you to call them by a nickname. I remembered my recent experience that Dex had been one of those people who liked a shortened version. From now on, I knew my aunt should and would be Aunt Nona.

And I was Valentine Monroe. Since she had adopted me, I assumed my aunt's last name. Another early rule: church every Sunday with no excuses. The pattern of our lives had been set in motion and in stone. For the next ten years, I went to school and to church, helped with the housework, laundry, and prepared simple meals. In exchange, my aunt provided everything I needed. I had a safe, comfortable home, clothing, and personal essentials and medical and dental treatment. But of the intangibles, the treasured gifts she shared were her wisdom, knowledge, and experience. She was understanding and I could confide in her. But she didn't mind revealing a definite impatience. My sloth tendencies were not tolerated. There were days early on when I just wanted to stay home, lie around and basically wallow in my misery like a fat, pink pig in a pen. I felt I had a right to my indulgence. I had been significantly wronged. My aunt agreed we had suffered a great loss, tragic and sad, but so do others. So she never passed up a chance for a character-building session, especially when my behavior was called into question. We had our time to grieve and now it was time to look ahead, not in the past. Busy people are happy people; idle hands are the devil's workshop sort of mentality. The more productive you are, the less time you have to dwell on everything that is wrong in your world. Succinctly put, she would not tolerate dwelling on the negative. There was no way for me to tell auntie about my troubled past. I was forced to put some emotions on the back burner where they smoldered for years; ultimately I had to deal with my unresolved sticky wickets. She meant well, and I fell into line, followed her rules, and benefited from her wise guidance.

When I was about ten, she grew weary with my self-indulgence. When pushed, she responded making her point clear, sharp and precise. "I hope you'll think about something, young lady. Look around and you'll see suffering and misery. Then you might begin to understand how fortunate we are. Being grateful is the first acknowledgement of God's goodness and blessings. The thing about pity parties is they last too long and the guest list is too short. I'm sorry to break it to you, Valentine, but living means coping with heartache."

Her eyes clouded with sudden sadness. She astonished me with her resilience. She was as tough as a boot and as soft as a marshmallow. Her loving essence and goodness overshadowed her staunch discipline almost certainly because she had taught school for forty years. I never questioned that she had my best interest at heart. I felt her kindness even when I was in trouble. She was not a task master but she did expect me to toe the mark. I would compare her to a matronly version of Maria in the *Sound of Music*. Aunt Nona did not fit the description of a drill sergeant, but she became a stern headmaster if pushed. I learned to limit those occasions and thereby improve my quality of life appreciably. Even with her occasional sternness, I never felt isolated or estranged. The error of my ways was distinctly understood. Most of my problems stemmed from my morose attitude which she would not tolerate as selfish, short-sighted and indulgent.

She gave me an allowance from the age of ten for helping her around the house and noticed with approval I saved my coins in a jar. She often teased me and asked if I would lend her some money. She showed me her bank book and how she kept the balance and suggested we go to the bank and open a bank account for me. It was one of my memorable grown-up moments of my young years. I kept my bank book in my bedside table cache as one of my treasures.

At the age of fourteen, I got my first job as a babysitter for a neighbor. Then at 16, I began working part-time as a sales clerk in a retail clothing store. Jillian Jamison owned *the* stylish dress shop in town. She thought highly of my aunt, and it was up to me to convince her I was her best asset on the sales floor. I practiced before the mirror for hours perfecting facial expression and voice inflection. For some unexplainable reason, this job was everything to me. I convinced her to give me a chance even though I had no experience and dressed simply and conservatively. It was obvious; I was fashion stalled but I wanted that job more than anything. I knew I would be good at it because I wanted it so badly. My lack of experience seemed irrelevant; I knew Jillian's store was the place for me. Many teenage girls applied to work in the shop but few were hired. She hired Jessica to do some part-time modeling and to fill in for the other sales clerks. There was no variation from the schedule. I arose at 6:30, made breakfast, got dressed and was at school by 8. Three days a week after school, I worked until 8. Then I came home to do my homework and up again each morning to repeat same. Until age 14, my aunt insisted I save my money and I not pay for any other expenditure. She provided for my needs as before I had a job. She wanted me to learn the value of earning and saving a dollar. Accordingly, I was slow to let go of my money. Occasionally, I splurged on a special dress at discount from the shop or an exceptional pair of shoes but seldom. My aunt made her preference clear; extra expenditures were for emergencies, not baubles. Once I became 16, I started to buy my personal toiletries and a few clothes. I still saved the major portion of my earnings and kept my bank book as proof I was worthy, a hard worker, and a saver. Not having money meant being powerless and dependent and its impact struck early and stuck with me. I understood no one was obligated to save me or fund my existence. I had been lucky once and the odds of it happening again were nil or at best unlikely. Depending on windfall again was foolhardy. How many Aunt Nona's come along in a lifetime?

By the age of 17, I had been promoted as the assistant manager of Jillian's which meant basically I did whatever the manager didn't want to do, but I also occasionally accompanied the owner on weekend buying trips to market. I was fascinated by the choices of inventory and took careful note of how the owner made her selections for our shop. She explained how and why she made her selections and pointed out the items that caught her expert eye according to price, style, fabric, quality, and quantity. She was unfazed by the array of choices. She focused on the contenders with laser precision based on our market, its customers, limits of acceptance of style and price. Every aspect of the fashion and retail world fascinated me, from the captivating colors and styles to the before and after transformation that a beautiful outfit translates into confidence. How could I have been so lucky? This was my opportunity to build a career I envisioned as my place in the world. I was determined and invigorated. The hard work, long hours, and competition did not scare me. I took advantage of this stepping stone and aimed for the top.

In the years following my mother's death, I confess I spent much of my precious time thinking about myself. I racked up hours in sorrow for myself and my circumstances, and then more lost time in soul searching and heartache. Ultimately I faced the fact I was in charge of my future. Aunt Nona said only losers find something or someone else to blame. I imagined and began taking small steps to become the type of person I envisioned. If I became moody or overly melancholy and pessimistic, I cut it off instantly. I had made up my mind early on to accept and deal with tragedy as part of life. My mother was my world, and yet I was left in this world to function without her. Instead of being the victim, I understood I was in charge of my attitude and the type of person I could be. I also knew the sequence of events although tragic might have been much more complicated and difficult. There were days I hated the thought of doing anything (predominantly school) and might simply have convinced myself lying in bed was my obvious preference, but I blasted my way through the dark moods concentrating on school and then later work. Initially, commitment provides distraction but also provides the path and offers the opportunity to a full life. My aunt instilled in me being productive was the best antidote for feigned maladies, not the least of which was a depressed outlook. Clearly, pitying myself did make me the #1 most pitiful person I knew. Gradually I looked beyond myself to see what was going on with other people, and from experience, I felt better by thinking better thoughts. Thankfulness reinforced how blessed I was and gave me strength and resolve to overcome. But it wasn't easy; I often resisted feeling better. For some reason I do not understand, it becomes easy to take comfort in feeling bad. The more I practiced being pitiful, the more negative I became. I made a conscious decision to be better and stronger. From continued practice, I blocked out the experience of the old man and refused to shoulder the blame. I already carried a great amount of guilt and rejected the notion I somehow had invited the old man's advances. Being a child in a world inhabited by evil people as well as good was part of the territory. *Evil preys on the vulnerable.*

Officer McShane was not a frequent visitor, but he did drop by occasionally to see how we were doing. As the months passed, I didn't understand his particular interest in us. Maybe he felt a professional obligation because he saw two alone females. As a child I knew he was kind-hearted, but I also knew it was a cold world with few caring people. To make me feel safe, I did hold on to the belief he would rescue us if we were desperate. I hoped someday to ask him questions that continued to haunt me. In the deepest and darkest part of my soul, I ached for my mother and was plagued by thoughts she may have suffered. My aunt and I never discussed the details surrounding the accident because we both felt there was no benefit to re-opening a wound that remained partially healed at best. Officer McShane's promise to my mother somehow had become hazy to me, but not to Officer McShane; he took his promise to heart. Years passed before I understood and accepted his role in our lives and why God had chosen him to be our guardian angel.

I learned to drive at sixteen along with my peers, many of whom already had cars. The significance was not in my learning to drive but *the* car I drove--my aunt's beautiful 1946 maroon Cadillac. It was outfitted to the hilt with tan leather seats, a cream leather and wood steering wheel, and glistening dash of burl inlaid wood and shining chrome. Every time I got into auntie's car, I breathed in all the luxury—enticing soft leather seats that cushioned like a glove, the swirling design of burl wood, the breath of springtime freshness of the showroom new. She took meticulous care of her car. The same service station had maintained it since new and no other mechanic but Earl Parsons was allowed to touch it. The fact she allowed me to drive her car (accompanied by her, of course) was the epitome of trust. I adored that car! Most of her friends had long ago traded in their antiquated cars for the latest models, but not my aunt. She had worked for years to save the money and had driven an old '36 Ford until it practically crumbled in a heap. The Cadillac was her baby. At least once a month, the Caddy had a standing appointment at the corner of Main and Oakmont to be washed, polished and shined with oil changes and maintenance at regular intervals.

My activities after school were limited. I was determined to excel academically and had to work hard for good grades. I was neither exceptional nor brilliant, but I did have a good head on my shoulders and the necessary determination which was all I needed. I had few friends and no boyfriends, not that I wanted one. Other than Officer McShane, I had never had a positive male influence in my life and doubted such a thing existed. My aunt reinforced my theory. I knew she wouldn't mind if I followed in her footsteps and became an old maid something but a schoolteacher would be best. I looked forward to working at the shop and loved fashion and going on buying trips with

Jillian, but working for someone else the rest of my life was not at the top of my list. The fashion world was cutthroat competitive and owning your shop took more money or borrowed capital than I could accumulate. We could not afford the cost. I had to find my path. We could manage the cost of community college to take a few basic education courses transferable to state college if I decided to go for a degree. For now, I had to make my living at Jillian's shop. I was indebted to Aunt Nona beyond my means to repay, but being a permanent liability was not an option. She used her resources creatively so I was educated, well-adjusted and comfortable in social settings. She worked hard to prepare me for whatever path I chose, including the obstacles. So I dreamed within my limits.

∞

CHAPTER 7
BEHIND THE BARS

N ona and Valentine Monroe for lunch with Imogene Larson." The speaker was silent.

"Aunt Nona, the secret password is 'open Sesame.' Let me say it, please." The thought I held the key to magically open the massive iron barrier to the land of enchantment was irresistible. She grinned but shook her head no.

"Be patient, child. We're entering a private club. They have to check to see if I'm on the list of visitors. You must either be a member or the guest of a member to enter."

Then without warning, the CCCC separated into CC and CC as the two gates swung wide, allowing (although not actually inviting) Aunt Nona to guide the Caddy into this favored world. The massive swirls and curls of the thick black wrought iron made me dizzy. I wondered what was so valuable it was protected behind gates fifteen feet tall and fences twelve feet high with black spike wrought iron bars. I hoped it would be easier to get out than it was to get in. It seemed to me if they wanted to lock people out, they might want to lock people in. But that didn't seem right to me either; that would be more like prison. I was still trying to figure out the new environment and its trappings, but I was excited to experience these new surroundings where some people were accepted and others were not. I had never been in such a place or even considered such places existed which had to be the reason it was important to Aunt Nona I accompany her to a fancy lunch at a private country club.

As we drove along the paved driveway, rows of bright red tulips, daffodils, paper whites, purple iris, and leftover winter pansies lined the emerald green grass. Aunt Nona edged her way into the rows of parked cars. I had never seen such an extensive and expensive display of exotic automobiles. There were Ferraris, Mercedes, and Jaguars, and the more common Cadillacs and Buicks. She parked into a space allowing plenty of room for us to open our doors.

"The restaurant is inside. Let's go find Imogene." She motioned toward a long pink brick building with white columns that looked like a house but much larger.

People in golf carts darted about, giving us irritating looks to insure any doubt we were in the way and out of our element. Golf seemed to be more urgent than any other activity on the grounds, and we were holding up the game. It was odd they didn't seem to be having much fun playing this game of golf. Most of them scowled and darted about with urgency as if they were late and stressed. I had second thoughts about golf as a game and should be fun.

"Aunt Nona, this looks like a house. I thought you said it was a country club."

"It's called Carillon Creek Country Club. Isn't it beautiful? It looks more like a mansion than a country club, such a lovely Southern traditional."

The huge frosted double glass doors had gold swirls and curls just like the gates. The shining marble floors were white and polished to perfection. A blond lady with her hair in a bun asked if she could help us find our party and then led us to the dining room. The aromas hit my nose like a blast food furnace of unidentifiable concoctions. I hoped they had hamburgers or meat loaf, but Aunt Nona had already warned me not to be picky. We were guests at a private club. This was my first ladies luncheon, and I was to be polite and on my best behavior. I hoped I wouldn't spill anything or knock over my glass or, what would be worse, knock over someone else's glass. I didn't want to draw attention and certainly not that kind. I was nervous. The environment was unfamiliar, I had never met Imogene Larson and her granddaughter, and I felt awkwardly out of place and conspicuous.

Imogene and her granddaughter Emily were seated at a table for four. She introduced us and gave me a gentle, warm hug. Emily did not speak but managed a half-moon smile. She did not seem happy to be having lunch with us. I asked what school she attended, and she replied, "I don't think you've heard of my school. It's a private school called Sweetbriar. It's a girls school and very exclusive." She tossed her head and her silky chin-length blond hair swung in unison as she turned to show her perfect profile--high cheek bones, chiseled chin and a small turned-up nose. She had good genes or breeding as Aunt Nona put it, but poor manners and personality. She got away with being rude whereas I could not. I might be young, but not too young to observe how the world worked.

I looked at the menu for something I recognized. I was curious about the soup du jour and wanted to ask what kind of soup that was, but decided against it. I was on guard not to embarrass Aunt Nona or me. "Aunt Nona, I would like some soup. You know what I like, so if you don't mind, would you order for me?"

I saw Emily's disapproving look. I prefer to think it was my imagination, but I heard under her breath, "What a baby." As if on cue, her grandmother saved the day.

"The split pea soup is tasty and comes with a grilled cheese sandwich. How does that sound?" I liked the way Imogene took the initiative to be helpful. It was obvious she wanted me to be comfortable and enjoy my lunch. Emily should have taken the subtle hint from her grandmother's good manners, but that would not happen. I was too far beneath her and not worth the effort.

"Oh, thank you. That sounds perfect."

When the waiter came, I spoke up right away. "I'd like the split pea soup with the grilled cheese sandwich please."

We had a table next to the window with a view of the golf course and the ponds surrounding the 18th hole. It was amazing to think people took delight in hitting such a small ball over and over. No wonder they were in such a bad mood and took them so long to finish a game! I thought I might like to play but knew it was a sport for rich people. I couldn't play most sports because of my shorter leg, but I imagined it was possible for me to play a sport where I walked and hit a ball. Gazing at the lushness of the golf course put some high-flung ideas in my head, plus offered a pleasant distraction from Emily.

Aunt Nona and Imogene talked about the Garden Club and the activities planned for the coming year. Emily sat stiffly in her chair, staring out the window. She never smiled or spoke. When the waiter asked whether we were having dessert, she spoke freely, "No, we don't care for dessert today. I have an important appointment."

Her grandmother stiffened in her chair and gave Emily a look of disapproval but immediately softened with acceptance. She was accustomed to her granddaughter's brashness. "Not so fast, young lady. I would love to have a piece of coconut pie with my coffee. It reminds me of my mother's pie. Nona and Valentine, what would you like? The chocolate cake is excellent also."

The chocolate cake called to me and Aunt Nona had the lemon chess pie. Later, Aunt Nona laughed and said Emily had the humble pie. She explained. I thought that was funny. We savored our sweets and ignored Emily. It was beginning to dawn on me why Aunt Nona brought me here. She wanted to broaden my horizons, and the trip to the country club qualified.

I didn't spill anything on the white tablecloth. In fact, when my dish was taken away, there was not one spot or splatter of food. I was proud I got through my first fancy lunch in style. Aunt Nona winked and smiled when she saw me looking down to inspect the tablecloth.

I thanked Imogene for such a delicious lunch and for inviting us to her club. I looked at Emily and smiled, "I am so happy to have met you Emily. I hope we didn't make you late for your appointment. My friend Jessica and I are learning to play tennis. Jessica is a good player and I play doubles with her. If you would like to play and bring a friend, it would be fun."

"I don't think so. I play in tournaments at the club and come from a family of tennis champions. My dad played on the Davis Cup team and still plays. My tennis coach says even at my young age I have the potential to be a great tennis competitor. He wants me to play in some city tournaments just for the practice. He says I probably wouldn't have much competition but it would be good for my confidence."

As Aunt Nona and I drove away from the pink mansion and out the gates, which swung open without delay, we looked at each other and smiled. "It's a nice place, isn't it Valentine? You were a delightful luncheon companion. You understand from today's adventure that being rich or well-to-do doesn't mean you have to be a snob. Let's hope Emily will grow up to emulate her grandmother's kind and courteous behavior."

"What did you think about your experience today? Any thoughts or learn something new?" Aunt Nona was a master at getting inside my head.

I sat quietly, thinking. There had to be a gentler way to say what I thought.

"Aunt Nona, I wonder. Do they want you to feel like an outsider?"

"I'm not sure what you mean when you say 'they'. The club has a responsibility to its members." She knew what I meant but was testing me to explain.

"The country club (even Emily) but not her grandmother. From the time you get to the club entering the big gate and all, it seems you are reminded you don't belong."

"There will always be obstacles of some kind to overcome and not always physical barriers such as walls and gates. Life is riddled with social, economic, and professional hurdles for most of us. What's the saying? Life isn't fair or some such. What it boils down to is awareness and preparation. None of us need to expect easy sailing. The demographic experts like to rank us according to our income and amount of wealth accumulated. As pitiful as it may sound, we are categorized into classes like upper, middle and lower class. Some live privileged lives while others struggle and barely eke out a living and others fall somewhere in between. Bottom line is you and I are not entitled and don't expect to live as they do. We are blessed to make our way. Valentine, independence is a gift to be cherished. Time and talent best used and not squandered. Our family has a strong work ethic. We want to achieve and excel, and we are willing to work hard to reach our goals. We can use the resources we've attained to help others, not as fortunate for whatever reason. If anyone has experienced life's challenges, you have Valentine. There's no reason to expect life will take an easy turn any time soon. But all in all, today was a success and a treat for us. I enjoyed the afternoon and hope you did." She brought me to the country club for a life-enhancing reason. My Aunt Nona never did anything without a reason. Even though it would be years before I understood, she did her best to instill the difference between believing in yourself as worthy and the yardstick of the world, which was not always an accurate evaluation or guide.

"Thank you for bringing me, Aunt Nona. It's exciting doing new things and going to different places. I want to be accepted and comfortable like I belong. I hope someday I can fit in anywhere, even in some fancy club or in a room of fancy rich people; like you told me, socially acceptable. What's the word you use, like posed?"

"You mean poised?" Aunt Nona's cheeks were pink as a raspberry. She was impressed I remembered somewhat; I actually listened.

"You do fit in, my sweet. I'm proud of you. Remember, you never outgrow kindness and courtesy no matter how much money you have. In fact, the more socially prominent a person is, the greater the responsibility. There are a lot of good people who belong to the country club and do good things for charity and for the community. Successful and influential people gather just like any other group. We are social animals, aren't we? Oh, by the way, I've never seen you eat split pea soup. In fact, you seemed to enjoy the soup. I have noticed you turn up your nose when I suggest having it at home."

"I guess I thought I didn't like it--just the thought of smashed peas. But guess what? It was good. I liked the ham in it. I bet you can make it better. You're the best cook ever."

Aunt Nona beamed all the way home. It was a good day.

∞

CHAPTER 8
TRAIN TRYST

Straight A's stood as my marker of school. Now as a senior, I felt restless and yearned for some fun. I had spent my school years on the sidelines. Although we were a large class, the luxury of a senior trip was offered as a benefit and privilege of the graduating class. We had class-sponsored, money-making projects during our junior and senior years for a trip to Chicago. On the list of school-sponsored projects were car washes, bake sales, yard work, and house painting and cleaning, window washing, and any other grunt work no one else wanted to do. It was strictly voluntary. Always full of surprises, my aunt was the one who suggested I go. She encouraged me to work to earn the money and to take advantage of an opportunity of my once-in-a-lifetime trip to see Chicago and travel first class on the train. She passed up the chance to give me the customary lecture on how to behave on my first trip alone away from home. As was typical of my aunt, she made her point clearly and succinctly. I'm sure she felt my training under her tutorage gave me the necessary insulation to resist temptation and relieved her of the necessity to fret about whether I was prepared to behave properly when left to my devices. Accordingly, it would be a test of my upbringing.

Jessica would accompany me and be my bunk mate on the train. This was our first grand experience, and we were excited beyond words.

We were actually leaving the city limits for the adventure of our young lives. Her dad was not excited for her to be out of his sight for a week but accepted the time had come for him to release his little bird from the nest.

Jessica told me the one piece of advice he gave her was hilarious. "Old folks are funny. They want to say something wise but try and be cool about it."

I was curious, but she lost me. My aunt had no problem saying it straight arrow. Jessica's dad was a policeman. I figured he had no qualms about just saying it. But then again, a dad having a heart-to-heart with his daughter is slightly more complicated.

Jess continued. "Get this. He said, 'Here's food for thought. Have as good a time and all the fun you can imagine without regrets the next day.' What does he think I'm about to do?"

"Well, we better not venture there. That's good advice. He was trying to be understanding. You want to have fun, but he wanted you to be careful, Jess. Let's give him a break."

Since losing Jessica's mother, he was slow to accept her independence and extremely protective. I was leaving the security of home, my aunt and my familiar surroundings. So we both would be on our own for the first time. The Saturday after graduation eighty of us climbed on the Texas Flyer for seven days in the Windy City. We were well-supervised with eight chaperones and two sponsors. Most of us had never traveled beyond the city limits which meant our keepers had their hands full. Most of them were adept--heads on permanent swivel and sleeping with one eye open-- which was preferable to the chaos we could cause when unsupervised.

Not that sleep was on our agenda. We took over the club car converting it into our personal casino headed by mini dealers who fanned and flipped cards, shuffling and dealing in rhythm. These kids were no strangers to the game table and could hold their own with the best of them in Vegas or Reno. I had entered into another gaming world. My card experience consisted of Old Maid and Go Fish and an occasional gin rummy game with my aunt as a secret pastime not to be shared with the church ladies. I stood with my mouth open in awe as cards flipped off the table and flew in the air. Someone yelled, "Hey Valentine, over here. This seat's not taken."

"I'm not great at cards. Need to keep my distance from the card sharks." Could I sound any more stupid? I couldn't *join in* for a game of cards? I had responded on instinct before I fainted. Rowan happened to be of the in group, popular and an outstanding baseball player. His other major distinction appealed even more; he did not have a regular girlfriend. Did I hear him call me by name? How did he know *me*? The very idea sent me tumbling into *Never Never Land*.

He stood up. "Did everyone hear what I heard? Someone actually had the nerve to say no to me."

"Yeah, sure says a lot—for HER!" His best friend Greg was slapping him on the back relishing every minute. Rowan had his pick of girls and was not comfortable with someone saying no to him.

"C'mon Valentine, have some fun. You only live once and then you're old or die or somethin'." Rowan was intent on winning what he viewed as a challenge.

I was embarrassed and not used to being in the spotlight. I decided it was best to join the party rather than to continue the commotion. I slid into the booth next to Greg. "What 'cha drinking?" Greg was quick to be polite. I was nervous and shaky. I felt awkward and lost being in the company of males but there were other girls at the table so I forced myself to sit and stay. I felt this strange sensation; I wanted to be part of the group and have fun. *What was going on with me?*

"Just a soft drink is fine, thanks." After several minutes Rowan left and came back and slid into the booth next to me.

"Cool move, man." Greg winked and nodded toward me. "Watch out, Valentine. He's slick for a southpaw."

"Yeah and I'm argumentative but I can't argue with that." He made no effort to disguise it. Rowan wasn't satisfied unless he had the last word.

Greg wasn't fazed and continued to pick away at his friend. "He thinks he'll be a lawyer, Val, better watch out. I've seen him squirm his way out of some sticky situations when he has to."

"I have to have something to fall back on if baseball doesn't work out." Rowan looked at me and shrugged.

"You mean you have to have a way to make a living when you try out for the big leagues and they kick you out on your can!" Greg brought the house down and had no plans to slow down, he was gaining momentum. "Rowan Rossi is the perfect name for a baseball card, but hey man, what else you got to offer MLB? Hey, shortstop, we're waiting."

"Where did your friend go? We were just getting acquainted." Greg was trying to deal the cards but messed up and cards flew.

"Her name is Jessica, twerp. She smelled a loser, so she scattered." Rowan payback as he obviously knew Jessica. "I've seen her around. She was in the city tennis finals played some uppity chick from Sweetbriar and beat her bloomers off."

"Oh, yeah, wiped up the court with Emily Larson, hilarious. Match was supposed to be a slam dunk, but Jessica blew her off the court." Greg seemed satisfied his latest target was worthy of his attention. He left the table noticeably intent on finding Jessica.

I smiled, but inside I was laughing my butt off. Tennis champion bloodline, Emily. What goes up must come down. Splat! Now I was next to Rowan joined by my companions terror and panic, but I was determined I would be cool. I decided to join in the fun for once in my life instead of looking on from the safety of a spectator seat.

The crowd started to thin out, leaving Rowan and me alone at least temporarily. "What's up with those eyes of yours?" He slid closer to me so he could look straight into my face. I struggled to remain calm in the aftermath of overcoming sensuality. I had never allowed myself to sit this close to a guy. He was in my personal space and heretofore not acceptable.

"What do you mean? You've got some haunting greenish-gray peepers yourself." I was confused.

"Don't change the subject. Yours are big and brown and speckled with black. They're great eyes but they are spooky, kind of dark and brooding in a way. It's my mystery to see what's hiding behind those dangerous and gorgeous eyes."

"Thanks, I think!" Now I was officially about to faint considering I was experiencing what is commonly called 'coming onto you.' Never in my life did I imagine someone would do that to me. I wasn't sure it was a compliment, but it was an attempt anyway but the way he looked when he stared into my eyes is what just about did me in. In a self-conscious motion, I reached up and combed my bangs with my fingers to make sure they covered my forehead and my scar. I fought the fire within; Rowan was interested. My aunt's words rang in my ears. I had to keep my head; keep my cool and act like I do this all the time. He hasn't proposed, made a move, or jumped on me. Try not to be alarmed. It's called friendly conversation. Males and females do this when they interact, or so I hear.

I saw spots. Someone snapped a shot with their flash camera. "Got it! Now I have evidence." Greg grinned at me. "Want a copy? It'll cost you."

I shrugged. "Free is good or no deal." I could tell Greg liked me. But then tonight, I was riding high. I imagined everyone was in love with me.

At that point, our classmates re-joined the table. "Hey, you two, we're back in case you hadn't noticed. Deal the cards!" Greg and the card sharks were refreshed and ready to continue the marathon. I laughed more than I ever had in my young life and momentarily lapsed into being part of the group. Then it was over as quickly as it began. My fantasy night was interrupted by the annoying scratch of the loud speaker. Our arrival in Chicago was scheduled for four hours and twenty minutes.

"Hey Val. I'd like to look you up later when we get to the hotel. Let's sit together at the game. Should be a fun one."

"Sounds great. Talk to you later." I was on a puffy cloud of delight, and I was not in a hurry to come down. I made my way to our sleeper berth to clean up and change clothes. Jess awoke just enough to be assured it was me. "Where in the world have you been all night?"

"Oh just me and fifteen mad hatters at the party of my life."

"You better hurry and get some sleep, or you'll be dead on your feet. Don't you remember? We're going to the Cubbies game this afternoon when we get to Chicago."

"Yeah, I was reminded." I said dreamily. And I thought of the certain someone I envisioned sitting next to me. "Jess, you probably think I'm making this up, but Rowan mentioned he wanted to go to the game with me. I'm still floating."

"I understand. Now go to sleep, Cinderella."

I sat on the lower berth and, for the first time in the eight hours on this train, the clickety clack across the rails grabbed hold of me. I gave in to the hypnotic rhythm like a baby being lulled to sleep as the pumping adrenaline took a well-deserved break. I should lie down for a few minutes. It takes energy to have this much fun, and I was ready for the challenge. I had experienced the most invigorating evening of my life and survived. I was exhausted! Sweet dreams, Valentine.

Beginning to experience what dreams are made of, I had six more days to see where this adventure was going. I wanted to let myself let go and experience new freedom. There were some mighty attractive benefits yet unexplored to being eighteen. Without warning, it dawned on me--having fun will never be any more okay than right now. *Within limits.*

∞

CHAPTER 9
CHICAGO WHIRLWIND

We were instructed to check into the hotel, get our room assignments, unpack and be in the hotel lobby by 2:00 to board the bus for Wrigley Field. My attempt at being inconspicuous did not work. Jessica didn't ignore my obvious distraction. "Valentine, what's going on with you? Your head is spinning around like a top. Who or what are you looking for? As if I didn't know."

"Well, we haven't had the chance to talk, but I had fun last night and hoped I might see some of the gang I was with."

"Like someone in particular, Miss Valentine?"

"Actually, Rowan." How brazen I had become in a day.

"Oh my gosh, Val. You're serious!"

"No, I'm not, but maybe he was. When we were in the club car, he did mention something about seeing the game together."

Jessica and I got on the bus and took the next available seats close to the front. The bus had few remaining seats, and we had to wait for the stragglers—Rowan, Greg and their three buddies. As they passed us, Rowan gave me a nod and headed to the back of the bus.

Well, Valentine, there he goes. Think again about your big afternoon at the game with Rowan. Jessica was a good friend and said nothing. My disappointment was short-lived as I realized where I was and the chance I had for a fun-filled day. We were seeing the Cubbies at Wrigley Field. No way we wouldn't have a fabulous afternoon, so to heck with Rowan what's-his-name. We oohed and awed over the sheer magnitude and beauty of the stadium and filled ourselves with hot dogs, popcorn and all the soft drinks we could hold. It was a day to remember even though the Cubs lost.

I fell asleep on the bus and scarcely made it to our room. The night before had caught up to me. I fell into bed with my clothes on and didn't awaken until 7 o'clock the next morning to the persistent ringing of the telephone beside the bed, our wake up call.

Today was another tour day of Chicago with breakfast served until 9 and unbelievably we would be late. Auntie taught me to be on time every time. She would not approve. As I dressed for the day, I decided to go for comfort--tennis shoes, aqua pedal pushers and matching shirt. I pulled my hair back with a white and pink scarf headband and decided to forego the makeup. I fought the urge to dress to impress some guy named Rowan who evidently had forgotten I was alive. Jessica was more fun anyway.

The next few days we saw as many sights as the chaperones dared schedule. We toured the Northside, the Loop, Lake Michigan lakefront, and downtown, including taking the elevator to the top of Sears Tower. We toured the Frank Lloyd Wright home and studio and several museums. After all, this was an educational as well as a recreational trip. But to Jess and me, the winner hands down was *the* department store that defined Chicago. Two clothes-crazy teenage girls let loose in Marshall Field's for the day fulfilled our wildest fashion dreams.

Jessica looked at me and grabbed my arm. "Val, take a breath. Take it in."

I was stumped. "What?"

"You've got to be kidding. Don't you get it? Life in the fairy tale lane."

Totally off guard, I spit all over myself. I almost choked on my saliva. "Jess, if you ever do that to me again, I'll, I'll--"

She just laughed her head off. "Oh, you'll be all right. Let's do a tour. But we better be quick or you'll have to inspect and touch each piece of clothing and, of course, the price tag!"

"And you, Miss High and Mighty Model of the Year, of course, would not be caught looking at a price tag just the designer label!"

I'd never seen so much marble, shine and sparkle. I wanted everything. *Sensory overload.* The mannequins were dressed and accessorized to perfection with clothing from the finest designers and fashion houses. Step into the world where money is no object. In our town, Jillian was adamant her customers have value above all else. She did have a few designers for her high dollar clients (like Rowan's mother) but the majority of her customers were working women. Jillian's was not couture. This department store exuded upper crust. We rode the elevator, took the escalator, explored every floor, oohing and aahing our way through every rack affirming this might be Heaven on earth! Alas, sad but true, our one afternoon to spend in the Promised Land came to an abrupt and cruel end at five o'clock and brought us down to earth--time to catch our bus. The last night, we were having a dance in a hotel ballroom at 7 o'clock. I was seriously considering passing on the dance when the phone rang. It was Rowan.

"Sorry I missed you for the game and all. Guess I kind of overslept and just made the bus. You probably noticed."

"Oh well, at least you made it. It was a good game and a fun day."

"Sure been better with you. Wonder if you'll give me another chance. I hoped we could get together for the party tonight."

I was quiet. What should I say? I hoped he didn't hear my heart beating as the blood throbbed through my head like a bass drum. The seconds zipped by while I froze. I had to speak up.

"Jessica and I are going. We should be down at the ballroom by 7:30 if you want to get together then." My attempt to sound casual mixed with unbridled exhilaration and serious doubt he thought I was indifferent and only mildly interested.

"Sounds great. I'm holding you to it. I'll be looking for you."

I hung up the phone, shaking like a leaf. Jessica was patiently waiting but knew without asking. I looked up amazed; this striking creature was my friend. Her good looks demanded attention; she was impossible to ignore. You *had* to stop and stare. Every inch of her statuesque 5'9" frame was flawlessly proportioned, topped off by a face meant to grace the cover of the most notable fashion magazines. She was wearing her new outfit, all in hot pink. Her makeup consisted of lipstick to match her outfit. No need for paint on this perfect palette. What's there to conceal or improve on a perfect face? Her long blond hair tied back in a ponytail swished back and forth over the back of her neck and shoulders. How anyone her age could have this ease and natural elegance — simply stunning! It was as if I saw her for the first time. How I took for granted her outstanding beauty was almost as amazing.

I was wearing my favorite dress in navy blue with small polka dots and a full skirt and a sweetheart neckline. It showed off my small waist and camouflaged my hips — a trick from my aunt. I felt good and resisted the last critical look in the mirror. Mother would have loved me in this dress. I had searched for a dress similar to the one she had and finally found one at Jillian's. I slipped my freshly manicured blush pink toes in my white ballerina flats and grabbed my white clutch bag. Jessica and I locked arms.

"Look out, suckers, hope you're ready for us. Let's go, girl. Dance up a storm and close down this ballroom." Jessica grabbed and hugged me. I might have tingled with excitement with Rowan next to me, but the warmth of Jessica's friendship filled me with happiness and light. *Soul connection.*

∞

CHAPTER 10
CLOUD 9

Rowan and Greg met us at the ballroom door. "Wow. You two look amazing!" Greg's enthusiasm couldn't be more obvious. He grabbed Jessica by the hand and took off running. Rowan laughed. "Greg's not wasting any time, is he? Looks like he's afraid someone might snatch Jess away from him."

"Well, I guess. He has an eye for perfection." I suspected Rowan felt cheated.

"She's okay, tall and all. But I've got the one with the beautiful face." He did have a way, smooth and easy. But I doubted he meant half of what he said.

As he took me by the waist, he snuggled his face in my hair and whispered, "Your hair is so soft and smells so sweet, I should have gotten flowers. Imagine a big white orchid in those shiny brown curls. Someday, Val, I'll give you the most beautiful flowers any girl could ever want."

"Oh, I didn't expect any. Orchids are magnificent but just a giant Stargazer lily if you please."

He looked puzzled for an instant. Then he grabbed my hand. "Okay, Miss Valentine, whatever you say. I have no idea what that is. I'm not making any promises, but for the record, it's still an orchid, so there."

We danced the first dance and every one after whether fast, slow, in between. It didn't matter. We were caught up in a whirlwind of delight and didn't want to come down. The dance floor glittered in lights reflecting the magic. I was not the same girl who got on the train. His good looks magnified, diminishing everyone in the room. His short brown hair and hypnotizing green gray eyes accentuated by a set of perfect white teeth were Hollywood ready. I was spinning in our world where each moment was filled with discovery. One minute we were bursting out laughing and giggling and then the next we were staring into each other's eyes. As our hands and cheeks touched, our young wildness begged to be unleashed. We were discovering each other. Rowan's dad was a lawyer with one of the largest law practices in town and planned for Rowan to go to law school after college. There was no doubt. His dad expected him to return to his hometown and join the firm. I knew there was no denying we both felt the chemistry. Then, as quickly as the evening had begun, the end came rudely and abruptly. The disc jockey's muffled warning, "Okay, all you love bugs, last chance, and last dance."

I floated in his arms and softly sang the words to one of my favorite songs of the day as *You Don't Have to Say You Love Me* played. Rowan was holding me tightly. I felt the music between us. "That's a good one. Maybe it's our song. Although being a frustrated sax player, I go for the big band sound, Glenn Miller's *Moonlight Serenade or Dancing in the Dark* with Artie Shaw works for me. Okay, so I'm an old-time romantic, our secret; could ruin my cool." He snuggled me closer.

I snuggled back. "You're full of surprises, a bona fide Renaissance man. I'd love to hear you play. I'm not into 40s music. I like the new stuff. Doesn't get much better than Dusty Springfield, I say." It was hard to envision being so free with a guy I hardly knew. What had come over me? The real kicker, it was easy being with Rowan; I was meant to be in his arms.

Then the music stopped, the couples begrudgingly parted, and the glare of the overhead lights came on. All the debris and trimmings of the night covered the tables and floor. My fairy tale was coming to an end. We closed the place down at midnight. He took my hand as he walked me to my room. He was at my door holding me and looking in my eyes. Now the full force of my aunt's admonition had meaning. The thrill of being captivated by another's charms hit me full force with my head spinning and heart racing. The impenetrable wall I'd built was beginning to crumble.

"You're an okay dancer for the quiet type. Not saying you're a shrinking violet mind you but does make me think I have my work cut out--lots of layers to peel back."

"Really? You make me sound like a rather large yellow Vidalia onion." He laughed and squeezed my hand. He liked my making him laugh.

"We make a good pair, Val. I can feel it in my bones. Too bad I have to ride off into the sunset just when we're getting to know each other."

I smiled and looked up at him. There were no words. I nodded, not sure what to say, but I knew what he meant.

"Did you hear what I said? Or are you relieved the night's about over?"

"Don't be so defensive, Rowan. I'm just enjoying our last moments so I can remember us. How 'bout them apples?"

"Isn't it a shame? Oh, well, I guess we'll just have to be content with what I consider a perfect evening. I'm heading to college out West all the way to California. And I've got a lot of stuff to do in the next few years. I guess it all works out for the best. I won't be coming back home except for Christmas and spring break. We can get together when I'm home or you can come for one of my games next summer. But for future reference, I see in my crystal ball two very happy lovers. That's what I say about your apples, Miss Monroe."

"Oh, speaking of eating, what's your favorite grab and go or sit and eat?"

"What a strange question out of left field. How'd you like that, baseball whiz?"

"I love it. I hope that's not all you know about America's pastime. You haven't answered my question. It's important. There's only one right answer, kid."

"Hmm. I'd have to say, easy answer. Chili dog, Texas style." I knew it had to be a hot dog although if push came to shove, to me burger was best.

"Little lady, you win the grand prize. Me!"

In the elevator, he gently put his arms around my waist and pulled me close. I felt his lips slowly brush against mine, and then his lips met mine fully and completely. I knew. He did not want to let go. "Val, I had a blast this trip. I wish we could've been together more. I'd noticed you in the hallway at school, but you weren't friendly. I wasn't sure whether to approach you. We may have something here, but we're both so young and all."

The elevator door opened. The inevitable wouldn't be denied. This was our floor, and the chaperones were waiting. Our mystic mood might be interrupted but not ended, yet. While the grown-ups were busy patrolling the hallway and watching only the person assigned to a room entered that room, we were intent on finishing our evening our way.

"Rowan, I guess I'm kind of a loner so I am surprised you noticed me. We do have something special; it's more than an attraction. If we do, it'll all work out. I had a magical evening. Good night."

He took my face in his hands. "Take care of yourself, Val. Not all of us are bad. Some of us deserve a chance. My advice to you, fasten your seatbelt for a bumpy ride. Life's full of surprises."

"I'll be sure to make notes to myself."

"One thing's for sure. I'll be back, so don't you even think about forgetting me!" He flashed me his smile of perfection. His dazzling green eyes inspected me for approval. Then he turned and disappeared down the long hallway.

I fumbled with the key, stunned. Something about Rowan felt forever. Stupid girl, Valentine. Your heart is overtaking your brain. Get a grip. I was having second thoughts about telling some of my past to someone I hardly knew. Rowan had been incredibly easy to talk to and before I knew what was happening, he knew more about me than he should. Why had I told him? It seemed natural and effortless. I shrugged my weary shoulders and decided I had to worry about something and my confessional was all there was to second guess about this charmed evening. What was so difficult about being in dreamland? Nothing.

Jessica was already in bed, so I tried my best not to disturb her. Too late, she turned on the bedside light. "Have fun much?" She grinned.

"Not too shabby. How about you? Saw you and Greg tearing up the dance floor."

"Yep. He's okay. Just a one-night stand, you understand. He's going to college in California with Rowan." She giggled.

"Same here. I forgot those two are joined at the hip. Rowan got a scholarship to play baseball at Stanford so he'll be scarce."

"Too bad they'll miss out. Call us late bloomers but I say we're making up for it. We've had more than our share of fun on this trip, Miss Val."

"You're so right. I couldn't have had a better friend to share it all with. Now I guess we have to go back to reality, but it will be good to be home. Good night, Jess."

The train ride home was quiet. We were all exhausted and glad to catch our breath, just to take in the scenery and savor all the memories of our Chicago experience. Jessica and I sat quietly staring at the countryside all the way home. We had shared an unbelievable week full of firsts and memories. We knew without speaking our experience happened once in a lifetime. Our bond was stronger, our memories sweeter, and our understanding of our friendship deeper. We were together to experience our first step into the bigger world, and blessed to have each other.

Aunt Nona was at the station waiting to take Jessica and me home. "Okay, girls, you look like you enjoyed yourselves but I'm more concerned about Chicago. Did you leave it standing or blame it on the wind?" Her wit made me smile and during our years together, as my rough edges began to smooth, Aunt Nona's edges also softened.

We hugged her. "Oh it was just fabulous, and we hardly left a dent on the place." Still on Cloud 9, I needed to clear my mind. I was grateful I had the chance to experience a date but yet did not have to be alone with Rowan. I needed time to discover men. I should take it slow. At least I was open to the idea all men were not a threat. Aunt Nona was studying me carefully. I wondered if my new experience was showing. Did I look different? I felt different.

Aunt Nona was obvious. She had missed me. "Welcome home, sweetheart. It was eerie and quiet without you. Too much creaking from the old Tudor and not enough rock and roll. But now you're home, I say let's continue the adventure—Valentine, you drive. Away we go then. Let the horses run, girl."

"I beg your pardon. I've had the best driver education available in a 1952 Ford. I can shift without stripping the gears, no riding the clutch, brake, turn on a dime and parallel park in three moves."

I slid into the driver's side and felt the luxury of the beautiful old Cadillac. As I drove through our town, the message glared as if set in neon lights, how small our town had become and how *comforting*. What a revelation to come home after a week in the big city. Perfect! I was as happy to return home as I'd been excited to go away. But I was a different girl.

∞

CHAPTER 11
LOFTY GOALS

O ne old maid in the family was enough on some days, but I knew there was a genuine possibility there might be two. I was young and impressionable and unsure of where I was heading. At the present, I was enthralled by the exciting world of fashion, and I thought any other job was boring and not worth my talents. Tomorrow I might wake up in another world. Some girls bragged about college as a means to an end--marrying well, settling down to fabulous lives as well-endowed wives with families. Others set out to be schoolteachers and nurses. Others had endured school with no thought of continuing education. Graduation was the signal many waited for to marry a lifelong sweetheart and have a family, as foreign a concept to me as jumping blindfolded off anything. Few of us had work-related goals. I had no interest in complicating my plans by marrying or joining up in double harness as my aunt called it. Living with my aunt was the economical and comfortable way for the both of us. Aunt Nona was aging well, but I knew the day of her needing care was on the horizon. It was not merely a sense of obligation; it was my love, respect and gratitude for her unselfish and heartfelt devotion. Our roles were changing, and I felt responsible for her. Thinking over the last ten years, I was overcome with nostalgia; the bold realization I was no longer a little girl flowed over me without warning. I should get serious about my future.

As I drove up to 4112 Morningstar Lane, I stopped abruptly in front of the storybook house with the sharp peaked roof. I had grown up in this house. The dark red brick 1920s Tudor was the only *home* I remembered. The small dark front porch hidden away under the brick arch seemed cozy and welcoming rather than dark and foreboding as I first remembered. *Creepy.* Back then, I preferred to come in through the back yard, which was easy access from the detached one-car garage. The dark recess of the front porch was the setting for nightmares. The large wood medieval oval door with heavy metal handle opened straightaway into the living room, reflecting shiny wide plank hardwoods throughout the house. It was the perfect size house--three bedrooms and one small room used as a study, with my aunt's books stuffed in every corner and cubby of the built-in shelves. I spent hours in the nook which enveloped me in warmth and comfort, offering me escape, entertainment, enlightenment, and knowledge. Early on, my aunt cleared off a shelf reserved for me and my books. We did not have a television until I was in high school. My aunt encouraged me to spend my leisure in productive pastimes reading or drawing and painting. Frittering away hours listening and watching mindless dribble was not on her list of preferred activities. Although I had nothing to contribute when my friends discussed the previous night's programs, what I missed by not having television could hardly be considered being deprived--countless passive hours spent with entertainers catering to the masses. I was loved, nurtured, and enriched by special guidance. My mother and I appeared without warning on my aunt's doorstep; mother and child on the streets without a home. Aunt Nona provided a sanctuary with whatever I needed without question or restraint. As the years passed, I became more and more devoted to her and thankful for her generosity, wisdom, and guidance. I recognized the day was approaching when I must return the favor and repay her kindness.

And to do all this, I needed to continue my education and my career. I was a working girl on a tight budget and needed to upgrade my wardrobe. As fate would have it, my innocent appeal to my best friend to step onto the runway was merely the beginning and whether my instigation was wise is questionable. My perception with hindsight confirmed, let others chart their course. I had my hands full trying to plot my way. In retrospect, I was struggling to focus on my goals. Shifting my attention to arranging Jessica's future seemed more fun and much simpler with nary a thought of the implications and responsibility.

I was scanning the newspaper ads for bargains when my eyes riveted to a full-page ad by our largest and most prestigious department store advertising for aspiring models. I just happened to be best friends with a perfect someone. I ran to the phone. The deadline was Monday; there was no time to waste. The fierce competition meant the chances were slim even in our town, where if you were a girl in your teens, you were an aspiring model. Jessica hadn't seen the ad and at first called me crazy. What a responsibility to be the one to convince her of her potential. Is there something wrong with this girl's vision? All she has to do is look in the mirror and see the fabulous creature looking back at her. After an hour of persuading, cajoling and even coercing, she agreed to ask her dad if she could go. Then it was Jessica's turn to do the persuading. Eventually he relented. She was allowed to go to the interviews for modeling at the local store but no New York. Her dream was to model in the Big Apple (farfetched and elusive), so we both knew this was her chance.

She cautioned me against getting my hopes too high. "Val, there is something called 'the look.' These people are after a certain face and body, a type. It's a cattle call for every tall, skinny girl with cheekbones."

"I get that. You don't see me making a beeline for the mall to fill out an application, do you? I mean, I'm not unconscious. I look at the magazines. You have as good a chance as anyone else if modeling is what you want. Hey, I'm just trying to help. I thought you wanted a career in modeling. You've been dreaming of schlepping down the runway since you were a tadpole."

Once we arrived at the mall, I saw what she meant. The flood gates had opened. Countless aspiring young models within a radius of 100 miles flooded into the mall. There were 200 other beautiful girls who had the same hopes. Undaunted, she spent the afternoon being interviewed, walking the catwalk numerous times and being photographed from all angles. She made the final cut and was to return the following day for a more microscopic examination. The next evening, after another long day, she called me to say she'd been given a chance to model for the department store and to apply to New York. She had to have professional photos taken and then send her portfolio along with her application for a chance to be interviewed by several modeling agencies to see if she was their type. She had to be stamped for approval by the head of the modeling agency who had the reputation of being a witch and impossible to please. You never knew what she wanted as it changed at her whimsy. No model was signed without her okay. For now, Jessica would wait until the agencies made their decision whether they wanted to interview her. The immediate result was she had a job modeling locally which would look good on her résumé. I knew Jessica was the complete package. All she needed was the opportunity to spread her wings. If only she had the confidence I had in her. Instead, she questioned her good fortune and shrugged off her assets. I had started Jessica on her quest if she wished to continue the adventure. Meanwhile, I was stuck with no aspirations. My aunt had some ideas I should continue my education and expand my view of the world. I had no clue. I was much more interested in imagining the modeling adventure of my friend than zeroing in on my reality of setting mediocre, dreary and weary yet out-of-reach goals. Jess was extraordinary with a thrilling future without limits. Fantasy wins again.

∞

CHAPTER 12
BROADENING HORIZONS

Unbelievably, Jess didn't make New York first. I spent my nineteenth birthday in Manhattan. Instead of being suspended in euphoria with my feet never hitting the ground, my delight was dwarfed, shadowed in dread. I had not been back to New York since my mother and I fled over ten years ago. Trepidation set in, bolstered by the bad thoughts of my troubled beginnings. Would negativity control me forever? Once invited in, fear takes root and takes over. Angry and impatient because I was preserved by a shield of never, I wanted to change. Phobia sucked the life out of me and I was the culprit–– lone prohibitor and prime originator of limits on every positive aspect of life questioning whether to enjoy, to experience, to indulge, to live freely. I decided, no matter how dark my past, I had to let the light of promise shine through. I had to experience, discover, and make my judgments and mistakes. I was lucky to have someone who cared enough to show me a wonderful time in one of the most exciting cities in the world. The least I could do was to open my mind and heart. Self-pep talks do work. Enjoy yourself, Valentine. What have you got to lose? Just a lot of excess stink baggage. There's no way I would miss this opportunity to give New York a chance. Excitement took over the fear; curiosity in place of anxiety.

How predictable, at the exact point when I was satisfied I had Aunt Nona figured out, she threw me a curve. I never imagined such a thing! Thursday after work she picked me up in the Caddy and headed to the airport. I truly wondered if she was all right. This was beyond extravagant not only for us but for most people we knew. And Aunt Nona didn't do extravagant. She managed to justify the trip to New York in her budget under the heading of education.

"I've already packed your bag, Valentine. I hope you don't mind. You have everything you need and a couple of outfits. Of course, we can't go to New York and not shop, so we'll have to explore until we find the perfect something you can't find at home. I don't think it will be difficult, do you?"

"But Aunt Nona, are you okay? I have classes tomorrow and all. We've never done anything like this, kind of scary." I was stunned, confused and worried she was not well.

"All true, sweetheart, but altogether not a good thing either. We need to break up the routine in our lives and this is one of those times. We will have fun. It's a combination late birthday and high school graduation present and early college graduation present. I've already told your professors you will be absent until Monday. So don't you worry. You are officially excused from class. Now all you have to do is sit back, celebrate, and enjoy your trip. We're on vacation to take a great big bite out of the Big Apple."

I sat back in the leather seat, amazed. "Aunt Nona, I don't want you to spend your savings. I would be happy celebrating at home. Correction, I *would have been* happy with cake at home." She smiled at how quickly I was adjusting to decadence.

"Simple is good, most of the time. But trust me, this is not that time. Don't you know me better by now? I wouldn't spend money carelessly. I've never actually splurged on you. So let me have my fun. You deserve a special birthday and you will have it. You're turning nineteen, a milestone. So no more chatter about anything but having a--what do you kids say--blast on our trip, okay?"

I looked at her disbelieving. Can we say alien? This woman definitely could be an imposter, but I was willing to go along for the ride. What fun! "Okay, Aunt Nona. What about when I turn twenty-one? How will you top this? Shall I let my imagination go crazy? It's never too early; I guess I should start planning our trip to Italy or Greece. You've created your personal monster niece." I started laughing and leaned over to kiss her on the cheek. How could anyone be this dear?

"Sure, sure. Let's put it this way. Don't ask questions. Cherish your trip to New York as it will most likely be *the* trip. I don't have a travel budget, so you don't have a travel budget, young lady. At least not until you earn your own, which I have no doubt you will." She grinned, and her eyes twinkled at me over her sunglasses.

We settled into our airline seats. "Aunt Nona, I almost forgot, I was so excited about our trip to New York, my first time on an airplane, should I be nervous?"

"You will love it, so sit back and enjoy the view. Trust me; flying is the only way to travel."

The cabbie pulled up at E. 55th at Fifth Avenue. I looked up at the astounding sight as the doorman welcomed us to the St. Regis. "Aunt Nona, can this be happening? I should wake up, but I don't want to. I've never seen such a magnificent hotel."

Aunt Nona was way ahead of me. "Thanks to John J. Astor IV, my dear. Come along, Valentine. We must check in and then freshen up before dinner. Our reservations are for 7:30 sharp at Tavern on the Green."

Our room was lavish, and the bathroom was covered in Italian marble, including the bathtub. The monogrammed towels were Turkish cotton and six inches thick. There were soaps and shampoos and sprays and toiletries not to be found in the local drugstore. There was no forgotten detail, merely finishing touches. The bedding was puffy and white and held you in a magic cocoon of layers of softest cotton. And the pillows! My head had never experienced such a luxurious cushion of downy perfection.

I was busy taking it all in, but the pamphlets on the table grabbed my attention. A myriad of tourist attractions looked equally significant and begged to be on the schedule. "Aunt Nona, how will we see it all? There are dozens of museums and monuments and stores and Central

Park and the Statue of Liberty. I can't name them all, much less see them all."

Aunt Nona stopped her unpacking, took a deep breath, and plopped down in the green velvet side chair. "Well, I did consider our options. The other reservation I've made--and I hope you will approve--are two tickets to *Funny Girl*."

Seriously, this was too much for me. My legs gave way, and I sank to the bed. "You mean Barbra Streisand?"

"Yes ma'am. She's the one. Saturday evening. I thought that would be the topper. You might say the cherry on top." She opened her handbag and waved two Broadway tickets.

"Do you have any idea what poor auntie had to go through to choose from all these great musicals? I wish we could have seen *Hello Dolly* and *Fiddler on the Roof*, but we made a great choice. Barbra is a legend you will remember all your life."

I hugged her. "Oh, Aunt Nona. Thank you from the bottom of my heart. I hope I can repay you someday. I would say our trip is a dream come true, but I never dreamed of anything so elaborate. It's pinch-me-can-this-be-happening time."

"Okay, you asked for it. Here's a little love pinch. Good, everything's settled. Let's go to dinner. I'm starved. Off we go to our customary Thursday night dinner overlooking Central Park." I doubted the dinner with a view would be worth the elevator ride, but I was mistaken. The dinner and the view were beyond fabulous; I was ready to go again.

Friday was our day to tour. We checked off the Empire State Building, tour of the Statue of Liberty, Ellis Island, and Staten Island. When we got back to the hotel late that afternoon, I practically crawled, I was so exhausted and having difficulty keeping up with her. I couldn't have been happier when she said room service. We watched some television and were in bed and asleep by nine o'clock. I knew there was too much to see on this short visit, but we were intent on making the most of it. My head was spinning, but I didn't want the weekend to end. The next day we were out and about by ten to the Guggenheim and the Museum of Modern Art. Aunt Nona commented on pieces of artwork and pointed out nuances such as brush strokes and use of color and hues even shapes to evoke emotion and to tell a story.

But she put it all in perspective. "We have no obligation to explain why a piece speaks to us. We like and appreciate whatever art attracts us. It's our opinion that matters. End of discussion."

We strolled along Fifth Avenue and then back to the hotel. Even though we were tired, our adrenaline kept us stimulated through a perfect evening. Broadway was shining; the lights led our way to a magical evening at the Wintergarden Theater with Streisand.

The whirlwind weekend could not have been any more perfect. Our plane thundered down the runway and lifted into the sky over the city, as snow blanketed the rooftops. "Not such a bad city after all, is it?" Aunt Nona gave me a knowing smile.

I kissed her on the cheek. We knew this was a giant step for me to get past the stumbling blocks. New York and I passed the test. No sinister city as I had conjured up since childhood. No renewed horror because I dared return to the place of my nightmare. The wonderment of the last three days instilled confidence and hope and reinforced my belief I could overcome my demons. Aunt Nona was already asleep. She had exhausted herself to give me the ultimate enchanted birthday a girl could only wish for. I loved her so much not only for what she did for me but for the person she was and for the love she shared and the hope she inspired in me. The dark foreboding of New York, a part of me for as long as I could remember, was fading and replaced by the bright light of hope. I felt blessed rather than jinxed. I yearned to continue the process. Shed the shackles; silence the dark voices I wasn't worthy or good enough; refuse to perceive the reminders of evil as those I had encouraged or caused. My precious mother deserved a daughter of brightness and hope. I renewed my resolve to live a life that exemplified spirit. Now my precious Aunt Nona with her encouragement had opened the door as she continued me on the pathway. I would not disappoint.

My nineteenth year marked a renewal of my spirit. I was bound and determined to fulfill my destiny. I owed so much to so many. Only Aunt Nona would have the wisdom and insight to make this trip a reality. She knew I would never have had the strength and conviction to return to New York, a city immortalized by my horrific beginnings. She would not have it. I was entitled to discover for myself the beauty and extraordinary magic of New York. Damn anyone who tried to overshadow my joy and rob me of my experience! When I think of New York, I can't quit smiling--once *noir* Naked City to now bright Big Apple! All my bad memories could have happened anywhere and are absolutely not relevant and not deserving of this magnificent city. Memories of the weekend in New York with Aunt Nona inspired and renewed my spirit throughout my entire life. She was the quintessential classy lady, yet unpredictable, uncanny, and wise--with a heart of gold.

∞

CHAPTER 13
REVIVAL

She did not make a habit of asking anyone for anything, but she had reached the age she hesitated to drive half way across the state. I needed to drive her. The celebratory weekend was again approaching and Aunt Nona had been talking about it for weeks. There was no doubt we were going. Timed to coincide with an even bigger event of summer revival held at the local tabernacle, the Monroe family reunion was held in August. The prospect of spending my entire weekend as a lost soul sweating it out in a hot tabernacle seemed dreary at best, but I tried to remember one lone weekend out of my life wouldn't kill me and would be another first for me. I would anticipate this experience as an adventure.

We had the Caddy serviced and ready to go that Friday for our three-hour drive to Nona's cousin's house in east Texas some twenty minutes from the closest town. On our way, we passed a strange-looking open-air wood structure with a crisscross beam roof and bench seating, choral platform, and preacher podium. "There in all its glory, Valentine, is the tabernacle. I was saved at my first revival there. Look at this breath-taking country! I have so many wonderful memories but just a word of caution. The Monroe's can be a little rowdy when they all get together but we're basically harmless. Revivals and reunions are the glue that binds our families."

"I tried to visualize what a tabernacle looked like but this wasn't it." I was disappointed. Ancient and dilapidated, the tabernacle had withstood its share of revivals in better days and looked painfully close to giving up and falling in on itself. But when you consider one hundred years of tambourine-shaking, blood-curdling calls to repent, and rafter-shaking gospel songs, the shaky old wooden structure looked amazing considering its age.

"The old tabernacle looks sad. I imagine it won't be long before the whole idea of a tabernacle will be extinct. When I was young, we raised the roof off this place with the preaching and singing. Those were rousing days of saving souls. I was saved when I was about eight at one of those summer revivals. I miss those days."

Cousin Etta lived with her husband Cecil and their three dogs down the road two miles from the tabernacle. The reunion Friday evening at their house comprised twenty or so of us in the form of ten cousins, several great aunts, and uncles and numerous children and then I lost track. But they all agreed the main event was the revival which they predicted could be the last one. The days of saving souls tabernacle style was at the end and soon to be a fading memory.

"There's something you need to understand about revivals. The point of all this hoopla is to save souls, all souls. Since we're all sinners, each person in the tabernacle must make the trip down the aisle to the front so everyone can witness their repentance. You will see for yourself, Valentine. The process and tradition doesn't change. I'm just giving you fair warning." Aunt Nona spoke with authority as one who knew from experience.

The service Saturday afternoon stretched into the evening. People brought their rations for the weekend. Everyone hauled picnic baskets full of fried chicken and coolers of water, iced tea, and lemonade. There were chunks of watermelon taken as the green light for children to eject mouths full of watermelon seeds at unbelievable speed at each other. Some folks stayed in the nearby camp grounds in their campers and trailers and didn't leave the compound for two days. The revival was a coming *together* of souls and of people seeking connection and fellowship through a common bond. The East Texas heat was sweltering and unrelenting day and night. Humidity took on a new dimension closing in on 100% without rain. But human spirit was not dampened by minimal discomfort, and the enthusiasm of the congregation actually gained momentum with the intensity and fervor of the service. Napping and nodding off was not an option (impossible unless you were deaf) and not tolerated.

A few large electric fans were scattered throughout the tabernacle and occasionally a hot cross breeze swept over our sweaty brows, but our paper fans never stopped. A piano was the instrument of choice although a few had tambourines and shook them full force with the music and then continued shaking as punctuation and endorsement of the sermon. A short, stout red-faced man led the singing with robust baritone tones and feet-tapping tempos. Dancing in the aisles was frowned upon but tolerated. The entire audience knew the words without hymnals to these old standard gospels songs. Anyone who needed a hymnal received a side glance of disapproval as a heathen who clearly did not occupy a pew regularly. The singing was as important a part of the service as the preaching and prepared the congregation for the preacher's message. The message was predictable and predicated on our fear of eternal damnation into the world of the devil to burn for eternity in hellfire and brimstone. The purpose of a revival was to save souls either first-timers or those who had backslidden into sin—all of us. The service lasted well into the evening. I was exhausted. I looked around and saw there were more empty seats than occupied ones. The majority had made the trip to the front even Aunt Nona. I was one of the stubborn few who had not. It was expected; the least you could do was bear witness.

During the continued call for witness and re-dedication, my aunt returned to her seat and whispered, "Valentine, do you ever want to get out of this tabernacle? Then you better get your butt down the aisle. It will only take a few minutes. It's important you benefit from the full experience." She grinned and winked at me.

I succumbed to her wise counsel, got up from the middle of the pew, excused myself for all the stepped-on toes until I reached the aisle and then made the long trip to the front of the tabernacle. Shortly thereafter, the congregation was released.

We were up early Sunday, had breakfast, and were in the pews by noon ready for the revival to start. We stayed until the service was over mid-afternoon for a brief respite and then the service started again in early evening. I was relieved and my aunt rejuvenated as we said our good-byes and started home. As we turned onto the main highway, Aunt Nona brightened. "Valentine, if you don't mind, I'd like to make one last stop. I have a little patch of land a few miles off the highway. I'd like to check on things. It won't take but a minute. There's not much to see. It would be a shame to be this close and not go by."

We turned off the highway onto a gravel road, across a cattle guard, and past a Posted No Trespassing sign. I saw familiar outlines of producing oil wells as well as others which had been capped. "Just stop the car along the barbed wire fence up ahead."

We sat in the car for several minutes watching the pumps pump. "Are those yours?" I was flabbergasted. My aunt was as naturally unpredictable as the weather, and she didn't hesitate to catch you unguarded. I'd be wise to remember she was her own person. Truly they broke the mold. You might say she took great pleasure in dashing any thought you had her pegged.

"Well, in a way. Actually the land is leased to the oil and gas company. They send me a pittance occasionally from their drilling, called royalties. You've seen the envelopes from Premier Energy. I hold what they call mineral rights."

"How large is this 'patch' as you call it?"

"Not much to brag about in Texas but land is precious, even these few hundred acres. Since the oil company found some oil, I'm happy I held onto the land. East Texas is rich in oil and gas resources so you can get lucky. At one time, I seriously considered selling it to some doctor in Dallas. Since I didn't raise cattle, I convinced myself it was a waste to keep the land. But turned out, holding the land was preferable. Sometimes we make a productive decision but not very often without that crystal ball. Even a blind squirrel finds a nut occasionally."

I giggled. "That's a funny one, Aunt Nona. Did you make it up?"

"Valentine, tell me you're kidding. It's as original as a cookie cutter." She was satisfied with what she saw and anxious to get home.

"Okay, Valentine, next stop Morningstar Lane and let the horses run, girl."

I heard not one more word from Aunt Nona, only the sound of her gentle restful snoring. She slept the entire way. I was relieved to be home but knew it could be my aunt's last trip to see her relatives and likely it was our last revival. It was the 1960s and the times were changing at record speed especially if you were of my aunt's generation.

Say what you will about revivals, the power of the experience cannot be denied. Every fiber of your being is affected by the sheer uninhibited intensity of the service—powerful music and singing that shook the rafters, the unleashed bring-you-to-your-knees fear of burning-in-eternity message from the preacher, the yearning of the human spirit for elevation beyond mere earthly satisfaction—all combined in a glorious happening not to be forgotten. All my life, I smiled when I remembered Aunt Nona and me at the tabernacle. True to prediction, the tabernacle revival was destined for extinction replaced by the mega church.

∞

CHAPTER 14
CHRISTMAS BOMBSHELL

R owan phoned in mid-December he was home until the beginning of January and said he had big plans for us. His parents' annual Christmas party was December 20. I should dust off the old taffeta standby or even better, buy a spiffy new one for the party of the season.

"Don't try to worm your way out of this, Val. We don't have to stay long but it's important you make an appearance and the perfect occasion so you can meet my parents. Besides I have hopes they'll get off my back. I made the mistake of mentioning what a great trip we had to Chicago. So put on your party shoes, girl. I expect you to wow 'em!" He was excited enough for the both of us. Parties didn't hold the same fascination for me. It was all about impressing and being seen.

I already knew about the party. Rowan's mother was a regular at Jillian's shop and had invited Jessica and then off-handedly commented I was welcome to come with Jessica. I had mixed feelings about the party. I wanted to be with Rowan, but I'd been just as happy for the two of us to go for a burger. It was obvious Jessica had captured Rowan's mother's interest, and she had already partnered up her son with my beautiful friend. When Caroline Rossi came into the shop, she wasn't rude but she made her preferences clear both about the merchandise and who was worthy of her son's attention.

"Rowan, it's the busiest time of the year at the shop, and I'll be working late trying to help Jillian. Her other sales people have taken off for Christmas so she's depending on me. Then Aunt Nona is in the hospital for a few days so they can monitor her. Her doctor had to change her medications. I want to stop by the hospital after work and check on her. Things are getting complicated. We thought she was coming home, but the doctor decided to keep her a few more days. I'm being pulled in every direction right now."

"Too many excuses. Number one, there's no reason good enough not to be with me, and number two, it's a Saturday night and the shop will be closed. Number three, you can stop by the hospital on the way home. Besides we have things we need to talk about. I haven't seen you in months. Phone calls don't cut it. It's our time and we have to grab it."

Since Chicago, he had called occasionally but we had difficulty making conversation. He was busy with college and baseball, and I was working at the shop and taking a few college courses. It was mundane superficial conversation at best. What we both were really after was time to discover each other. We had never had the luxury of getting to know each other beyond a brief chemical reaction.

"Your mother was in the shop and invited Jess and me to come to the party. I wondered if you knew. I'm not sure if she connects me with you or not. She is more focused on Jessica."

"Oh yeah. She's mentioned Jess several times. I'm pretty sure Greg's bringing her. He's crazy about Jess. Don't tell her I said so." He seemed unfazed by his mother's plotting. I imagined it wasn't the first time she had tried to arrange her son's social life. I was making a bigger deal out of her poking her nose in our business than I should. It was part of being an involved parent, maybe.

The day of the party was the coldest of the year, and it started to sleet in early evening. By seven o'clock, snow covered the ground. I fussed about my clothes. I knew the guests were the crème de la crème and the women were style setters. Not that I was foolish enough to compete, I was satisfied not to be a standout, "Good evening, ladies and gents, here she is, your token country bumpkin for the evening." There was no choice for outerwear over my satin dress. My practical (and only) wool coat won by default which was out of place and blatantly *bourgeois.* One advantage to being young is you're not held to the same scrutiny. I'd gladly exchange a few years for more glamour.

When the doorbell rang, I was not prepared although I had pumped myself up to overinflated. My new red satin off-the-shoulder dress with a giant bow in the back fit me like a couture dream, and my red peau de soie heels were dyed to match. A pearl headband held my long hair back from my bangs into a dark mass of curls to my shoulders. For once, my hair behaved for the occasion. I had no idea what I'd done differently, but I gladly accepted my good fortune I didn't have to spend hours controlling a wayward fuzz ball. I looked as presentable as possible. Nothing else I could do beyond cosmetic surgery to prevent my looking out of place. I was more concerned about what Rowan thought of the way I looked.

Rowan was decked out in a navy blue gabardine suit and a Christmas tie. "I see you staring, so stop it. You're supposed to stare at me, not my tie, Val. Guess whose idea?" No guess necessary, his mother of course. It was kind of cute in a way but definitely not his style.

"I like it. You look (grasping for words) festive and handsome." Who was I kidding? He could wear a potato sack and I'd be impressed. My memory may have faded of how good-looking he was but his Adonis good looks had not faded. He was dreamier than I remembered which did little for my confidence but did reinforce my questioning: what in the world did he see in me? He continued to explain the tie as if it mattered. I had already figured out Caroline Rossi was a power to be reckoned with and someone he rarely said no to even when it involved something as insignificant and harmless as a tie.

"It's easier to keep her happy than have her on my back. You don't argue with my mother. It's for our appearance at the party and then it's back to my old threads and no choker tie! You know I don't like to be restricted."

He grabbed my hand and tried to get as close to me has he could and still be an acceptable way to see if we could pick up where we left off. "We better get going Cinderella if I'm to have you home by midnight. Too bad we have to do this party thing; I'd rather take you away somewhere private."

Once we were out the door and onto the sidewalk, he stopped and turned to me. "I've dreamed about this but no more dreaming."

He held me close and kissed me softly and completely, taking my breath away, as I took in the sharp cold of the darkness, clean and invigorating. I felt alive. My pulse raced and my heart pounded in rhythm. There was so much more to us to discover.

"That's the way I wanted us to begin tonight, Val. It's all that and more than I hoped for. You look dynamite in the dress. You should wear more red, yeah!"

We drove through the snowy night to the other side of town to prosperous territory. Here *subtle* separation of economic differences shifted to *apparent* without pretext and with clear indicators. The streets were wider, the schools superior, the houses majestic and yards bigger, and the cars top-of-the-line whether foreign or domestic. The contemporary house screamed subtle sophistication, set up high off the street, brightly positioned to look down on those entering, with gleaming glass windows lining the front facade. The circular drive and the street were jam-packed with expensive cars, shined, buffed and polished to perfection. We spotted a prize—an unclaimed parking place in front of the house next door.

"Bingo! Must have reserved this one for us. The Millers are at the party anyway and their party guests don't hesitate to park in front of our house. It's part of the good neighbor policy."

Filled with excitement *and* dread, I wondered if we could go in the back way and miss the grand entrance and all those strange eyes. I might have looked presentable but inside I was a waif on parade. All those years of Aunt Nona's prep work were a mere dress rehearsal. This was the real thing, opening night.

Rowan sensed my reluctance. "C'mon babe, it'll be fine. What do you expect? I'll bet it's a lot of old folks dressed to the hilt acting like fools chugging eggnog. You'll knock their eyes out. They're all jealous of us anyway because we're so young and they're so old."

"Rowan, you're being mean and I doubt it. Besides remember we'll be old someday. I'd say they are sorry for us because we're so young and stupid and have so much to learn. And *some* of us think they know everything anyway."

He stuck his tongue out at me just as his dad opened the double door and dazzled us with a broad smile that was instantly recognizable. He and Rowan had the same smile. I felt the warmth of an exciting new world and silently gave myself a pep talk. *You can do it. Fake it and blend in for at least for one night.* Aunt Nona would look on this evening as another opportunity for a grand adventure to broaden my horizon.

It was *the* Christmas party of the Season. Jillian was there with her permanent boyfriend of ten years and Jessica and Greg were perfect as the holiday couple. I doubted if their arrangement was what Rowan's mother had in mind. Too bad the best planning doesn't always produce the desired results. The sound of posh celebration permeated the air. Constant chattering, chinking of ice in crystal glasses, spike high heels clinking on marble floors, and loud laughter as the VIP guests grazed from two massive tables of hors d'oeuvres and desserts accompanied by perfect Christmas melodies--tinkling by a pianist at a Steinway. Servers in black and white garb effortlessly balanced trays of champagne and tasty tidbits moving nimbly through the crowd. It didn't take long before some brave souls with renewed confidence kicked in by adult beverages felt compelled to sing along.

I could have been mystically transported to a Hollywood movie set. I had never been in such a grand house. Shiny objects abounded. The Italian floors glowed in the light. The glass windows towered toward the ceiling and glistened with white reflection from the snow. The creamy white walls soared toward the sky with no limits. I looked up and assumed ceilings were up there somewhere. Jess and I were giddy. We checked out the delicacies in the massive dining room and the luxurious living room with four white sofas and chairs and glass tables in conversational corners and still weren't satisfied. It was our chance to explore, and we wanted more. On the way to the powder room, we took a tour opportunity and got *lost*. The library and office was solid walnut with bookshelves on the back wall with two giant picture windows. The massive desk set atop a bright intricate Persian rug in browns, rusts, and turquoise with two overstuffed brown leather nail head-trimmed chairs opposite the desk. Two gleaming brass lamps flanked the credenza behind the desk. Photos of the family lined one shelf of the bookcase. We giggled. Both our houses could fit into this one room. The powder room was opulent with gold fixtures and textured art quality printed wallpaper and more Carrara straight from the pages of *Architectural Digest*. The flattering candle-soft lighting was addictive. Imagine looking like this all the time! Package the lighting and then who needs cosmetics? I looked at the flawless skin and chiseled features of my friend. Jessica needed no help in the face department. She was striking as usual in a black strapless dress with a full skirt and her long blonde hair in her signature pony tail. We peered in the mirror, rubbing our rosy cheeks together, making clown faces reflecting wide, toothy grins. We were two best friends in our prime with little thought of yesterday or tomorrow. We were giddy not from champagne but from drinking in the posh of unfamiliar up-to-our-neck lavish surroundings. It was a magical evening I didn't want to end but Rowan was anxious to make a getaway. He kept whispering in my ear, "Val, you're avoiding me. Let's ditch the old folks. I've got some plans for us. I'll take you to places you've never been and you'll never want to leave." Whatever Rowan had planned was his private mystical weaving while I held on by a golden thread to yet another fairy tale night.

I was shivering as he held me close under his coat. His hand was delicately beneath my right breast. We stumbled along kissing and holding each other finally making our way to the car. Two drunks would have been more coordinated. He was kissing me and caressing me all over and then gently took soft nibbles on my neck. I was suspended in a soft cocoon in dreamland but I had to keep my senses.

"Rowan, you're taking my breath away. We should slow this train down. Let's not rush it. We're still getting reacquainted." Acquainted is more accurate, I thought to myself. Our time on the Chicago trip might have been off-the-chart exciting but in retrospect was limited and restricted as we sought out our few private hideaway moments.

His green gray eyes met mine. "Okay, doll. Whatever you say. Party pooper."

"What is so hush-hush that's got you possessed? Whatever you've got to say has me curious; so stop your teasing and tell me."

"Okay, here goes. Are you ready for a cork popper? Are you ready? You have to be ready. I can't tell you if you aren't ready. You have to convince me."

"Rowan, stop it. You've been hinting at this for days. Now tell me. Just a warning; I could start to lose interest."

"Okay. No. I've changed my mind. You have to guess. If you can't guess, I can't tell you."

I crossed my arms in defiance. "No, I'm not going to guess. That wasn't part of the original bargain. You said you had something to tell me. There was nothing about guessing."

Rowan grabbed me close. "You are I are going to Aspen skiing with my family for ten days!" He was grinning from ear-to-ear and his green eyes were dancing in the light reflecting from the house. He held me close with my head on his chest. His heart was pounding in my ear faster and faster.

"Come on, it's freezing. Let's get in the car." He turned on the ignition and turned up the heater.

"Oh, Val, it will be fantastic. My parents have rented this huge house with fireplaces and five bedrooms and hot tubs and decks with mountain views that go on forever and ski runs out our back door. You will go out of your mind it's so gorgeous. You'll have a private room and bathroom fit for a queen. Okay. Okay. You're wondering what to tell Aunt Nona, etc., etc., no worries there. Everything will be entirely proper (my mother will see to it), at least while we're in the house. But we'll be free as birds with a mountain to explore. Ski, snowmobile, ice skate, you name it. We'll try it all. There's unending fun calling us. I see the look, Val. If you're thinking you can't ski because of your leg, you are mistaken. So no way out of this one, girl. I can teach you to ski, no excuses. When can you get packed?"

Silence. I swirled in gravitational pull back to Mother Earth. I was heartsick. How could I possibly go to Aspen and leave Aunt Nona before she was released from the hospital? Even then, I couldn't just leave her once she was home. She would need my care. Even more pressing was how to tell Rowan there was no way I could go. I hoped he would understand. But in his present state, how could he? Just stick a pin in his giant fantasy balloon and suck the life out of him. No problem, he'll understand. I felt guilty. Why did I have to be the bad guy? I had a sinking sensation.

"Oh, Rowan, I'm speechless. Sounds like a winter wonderland trip out of fantasy land. When are you leaving?"

"You mean, 'when are *we* leaving,' don't you?"

He stared at me, searching my face for a clue of what I meant. He had to realize something was wrong, but he didn't seem to get it. I struggled to have to explain it. Why didn't he get it? Now I had to be the bad guy out loud. It was up to me to ruin everything including this heavenly night. His well-orchestrated harmony just fell flat. Why couldn't it be our joint decision that the timing wasn't on our side? If I let him think about this for a minute, it'll sink in and he'll be receptive and reasonable. He's not stupid and seems to care about me; so what seems to be the problem? I yearned for his understanding. A minute or two dragged into an eternity and the longer the silence the more dread. I wanted him to take the lead; the timing was not right and confirm he understood. I couldn't stand one more second ticking by sucking the life out of us.

"Rowan, I'd love to go more than anything, but the timing couldn't be worse. You better take me home. It's getting late and I've got to be at the hospital early."

I thought he could connect the grow up dots with a hint. *Hospital, Aunt Nona, responsibility, priorities.* I tried to be understanding; he was having his plans thrown in his face. But it was hard to be concerned about him when I was in agony I had to say no. He made no attempt to console me. In fact, all he wanted to focus on was my apparent insensitive and selfish assault leaving him wounded and blindsided. Apparently he had no thought of how disappointed I was to have to say no.

"Val, is that all you can say? What's wrong with you? I've just laid out my dream with you. What is going on with you? Have I done something? We have to talk this over. This trip is not some off-the-cuff junket. You and I are meant for each other, but we need to spend time together and we have our chance to do that. You have no idea how important this trip is to me, to us. It's been planned for months."

His face had fallen to his feet. He revved up the engine and turned onto the street with the car slipping and sliding out of control on the snow and ice. His jaw was set and eyes straight ahead. His once supple body had turned into rigid, rigor mortis. My heart raced and my stomach tied in knots. The vision of Rowan and me together in Aspen for ten days could be our dream come true. But in reality, a fantasy. There was nothing I could say or do to fix the problem and make it happen.

The lull of the car engine was *the* sound for the twenty-minute drive to 4112 Morningstar. He pulled up in front and stopped but left the engine running. He looked at me impatiently as if saying "get out of the car." I didn't budge. He reluctantly got out of the car and obviously out of deep-rooted obligatory politeness, came around to my side and opened the door. He never looked at me. His eyes glistened red with tears. *Shattered.* Why had my enchanted night morphed into horror? I wasn't prepared for his hurt and disappointment. I had hoped he cared for me and dreamed he did but never knew until this moment. He could even love me. His intensity scared me. Our times together were few, and I wasn't sure how he felt about me until now. I still wondered if I was misreading his reaction. The thought lingered: did he care so much about me he was reeling from my rejection that ruined his plans or because his ego was slammed from not getting his way? The sidewalk was slippery, and I reached for his arm. He edged away and then obliged.

"Rowan, I need you to understand. I told you my history with Aunt Nona. How could I leave her for ten days when she hasn't been released from the hospital? Honestly, I don't have a choice. You're disappointed and lashing out. Please, I have to do the right thing."

"The *right* thing? What is the right thing, Val? The right thing for you, Val, or the right thing for Aunt Nona? She's doing okay. She'll be coming home, right? What about the right thing for you and me? Don't you care about us? I had big plans. You have no clue."

"Rowan, there will be other times for us. I understand you're disappointed and angry but don't make this situation worse than it already is. Think about what I'm dealing with and how I feel. I want to be with you more than anything. I'm torn apart and miserable but I have no choice. Can't you understand?"

"No, Val, you're wrong. There won't be *other* times for us." He turned and walked toward the car.

I sank to the cold ground. My warmth melted the snow now a cold puddle beneath me. Sleet was hitting my face. I yelled at him, "Don't do this to us, Rowan."

"I didn't. Get it straight, Val. You didn't just throw away our chance to be together. You threw away *us*. I should have listened to my folks."

"And what do you mean by that? What have I done to deserve a black mark from them?"

"Nothing. You've done nothing, that's just it. You're just a scared little rabbit afraid to come out of its hole." His voice trailed off into a whisper. He wanted to come back to me; I sensed his hesitancy. His pride won. He turned and I could see his green gray eyes were red, not from the cold, but from the hurt. Tears rolled down his cheeks. His voice returned full force. "Remember. I have options." I had been warned. He had turned from my dream to my horror. He honestly thought I was using Aunt Nona as an excuse not to go. How could he be so insensitive and misguided?

I screamed for him to come back. He never looked or turned, just kept walking and opened the car door and got inside. He revved the engine. Headlights glared angrily against the white night as he swerved and sped away. Don't worry, he'll come back. He won't leave with me sitting out in the dark cold. At the very least, he wants to make sure I'm safely in the house for the night. I sat there, waiting. *Pitiful girl grasping at her fluttering butterfly wish.* I wondered at my predicament. Did he care for me so deeply his disappointment blinded his good judgment? Or did he allow his anger to take over because he was spoiled and I had ruined his plans and damaged his ego? I was disturbed I loved someone who could be this selfish and this wrong. He should have appreciated and loved me that I cared enough for Aunt Nona to do the right thing. What a dreamer I am! Now I've elevated my position from understand I can't go skiing to worship me because I'm such a martyr and practically a saint. I knew my decision was the right one, but I wasn't comforted. What really concerned me was Rowan's reaction when I was beginning to take my guard down and trust him.

I was left to stew in my juices or in this case my puddle. The winter sky cleared and turned into the deepest, darkest navy blue dotted with millions of tiny sparkling diamonds. I looked up at the Tudor aglow with warmth beckoning me inside its safe shelter, as always. I pulled myself up out of the cold water weighing *my* options, as Rowan had coldly reminded me. I could go inside before pneumonia sets in. I could sit here in the snow freezing my behind off waiting for the spring thaw or for Rowan to come to his senses whichever comes first. *Spring thaw.* Get up, moron.

∞

CHAPTER 15
INTERLUDE

The sun showed no sign of mourning the night before. Shining its brightness and light on more than the melting snow, the sun appeared in the East without exception despite my miserable mood. My relationship with Rowan had sputtered into the outer limits of oblivion on our love rocket to the moon powered by a sparkler firecracker. A lot of instantaneous snap, crackle, pop and then inertia. I conjured up a myriad of rational reasons for our rocky relationship and why it stayed static whether it was geography, social strata, immaturity, different priorities, and goals, indifference (you name the complication) and our relationship suffered the consequences. The notion we were not meant to be was easy to accept today. I needed to be hopeful and looked inward and forward to the prospects for my future. Past time for me to consider my personal goals. Rowan didn't have the exclusivity on a desire for career achievement although his goals were more grandiose. I decided from now on, the complications of Rowan would not overshadow my thoughts and plans. I could hardly think such a thing; I faced a future however distant without Rowan Rossi.

Today was slippery when wet and a good day to leave auntie's Caddy safe and dry and take a cab to the hospital. I didn't need an accident to add to my woes. I dressed and put Aunt Nona's clean clothes in a bag. I looked at the clock, almost noon. I had overslept. I called the hospital and spoke to the nurse who answered at the main desk. Aunt Nona had a good night and hadn't shown any adverse effects from her new medications and was resting comfortably. Some welcome good news.

When I arrived at her room, I was amazed. She looked wonderful. "Aunt Nona, you must feel better. You look your rosy self today." I kissed her on the cheek.

"Hi sweetheart. Yes, I am much better and even slept some last night. I hope you can get me sprung out of here in the next day or two. A hospital is a place for sick people; I should be at home."

"I stopped by the gift shop and saw these. I had to bring them. They caught my eye and thought how perfect to brighten up the place." I set the small vase of red roses on the window ledge.

"Beautiful! You couldn't have pleased me more. I love flowers and these are exceptional roses for winter. These gray days can use some cheer and me, too."

"I want you home, too. As soon as the doctor gives his okay, we're out of here. They want to see how you do on your new pills. But I have it on good authority you'll be out of here in a couple of days."

She grinned and gave me her hand. "I couldn't make it without you, Valentine. I hope I'm not running you ragged. You've got your hands full trying to work and take care of an old lady."

"Nonsense, you're easy. You don't have a demanding bone in your body. Keeps me out of trouble and makes me useful. Besides, we both know who takes care of who here."

She cringed. "Okay, Aunt Nona. I stand corrected, who takes care of whom." She smiled approvingly.

"How was your party last night with all the fancy pants? Or should I say soiree?"

"Oh, it was fancy for sure, one of those must-attend events. Jess and I enjoyed the full experience and didn't miss a thing. It was grand, decadent and over the top just as expected. It was the evening to see and be seen. Too much of everything for me."

"How was your young man?"

"Well, Aunt Nona, seems like he isn't my young man, at least not yet." I winked trying to be upbeat. I wanted to make her smile, and it worked--she gave me a broad grin. She approved of my having a social life at last. After all, life is about balance.

"But Rowan and I are good friends. We knew each other in high school and have fun together. Nothing serious."

I hoped my feigned good humor hid my sadness. If there was one thing I didn't want to burden Aunt Nona with, it was my romantic dilemma. She was in her 70s now with heart problems and her health was the number one priority to me. I was concerned and wanted her to have the best possible chance for a complete recovery.

"We were in the same class in high school. He's on a college baseball scholarship and not in town often. He's got a rather large agenda. He goes to Stanford pre-law. His dad is a lawyer, and he plans to come back to join his dad's practice. His big dream is to play major league ball."

"He must be an excellent player. Have you seen him play?"

"Not since high school. Jess and I saw a game now and then. I have a tiny inclination of what's going on during a game. Hit the cover off the ball and run like the devil around the bases. I for sure don't have a clue about the finer points. He plays shortstop."

"What did you say his name is, Rowan? I knew an Andrew Rowan in school."

"This guy's first name is Rowan. Rowan Rossi."

My aunt's face flushed red. I was startled. "Are you okay?"

"Oh, yes. I just had one of my hot flashes. It happens when you're in the--what do they call it now--golden years. I'll admit the name brought back an old memory."

"Should I call the nurse?"

"Oh, no. I'm fine. I had a crush long ago on an Andrew Rowan in school. Silly old woman thinking about those years. Bet you never thought about your old Aunt Nona liking a boy."

"You don't fool me, Aunt Nona. You could have had any boy you wanted."

"Well, sweet of you to say. Girls weren't as forward and bold as they are today. We waited for the young man to make his move. But the times change sometimes for the better. You can wait too long."

"Did you date this Andrew?"

"Why, yes. We dated for a little while. Then he went away to law school. He was nice and came from a well-to-do family and higher in the pecking order than mine of course. Anyway, neither here nor there. The old brain reversed into ancient history when you said 'Rowan' so I digress. I'll just close my eyes for a few minutes until lunch is served. Why don't you see if they'll bring you a tray so you can eat with me?"

I took her signal she was uncomfortable and needed rest; I gladly paused the conversation. I'd discussed Mr. Rowan Rossi sufficiently to last a lifetime and too much for today. Aunt Nona had taken the pressure off me reminiscing about Andrew Rowan. She was full of surprises. I could count on one hand the times she mentioned her past. In a few minutes, the nurse brought in our trays. She ate her mashed potatoes, picked at her meat and vegetable but seemed to enjoy her milk and cookie. I noticed and mentioned her lack of appetite.

"Food doesn't taste so appetizing in a hospital. When I get home, I'll eat like a buzz saw again."

About mid-afternoon the doctor came in, gave her a brief check and looked over her chart. "Well, young lady, you're doing exceptionally well. Your blood pressure is stable and your lab tests look good. If you continue with your good behavior tonight and tomorrow, it's homeward bound for you."

"Thank you Dr. Stevens. Don't get me wrong, I don't have any complaints about my care here, but I'm ready to go home. Just say the word."

He smiled and continued writing in her chart and then he was on to the next patient.

I stayed for another hour and could see her growing tired. "Aunt Nona, I'll let you get some rest, but I'll be back in the morning. I need to do a little housekeeping to get ready for your homecoming. The house is well, past the lived-in stage."

She smiled a weary smile. "Love you and hope you have a good night." I bent down and kissed her on her soft pink cheek. Her complexion glowed without a smidgen of makeup, and her eyes were clear for the first time in weeks.

"Thank you, my sweet. I'll see you in the morning. By the way, have I told you lately? You are the light of my life." She blinked away a tear as her eyes closed.

I stopped at the nurses' station to make sure they had my telephone number and asked them to call a taxi for me. Dr. Stevens was at the desk making notes and instructions on patient charts. He looked up as I walked up and motioned for me.

"Good timing, Miss Monroe. I'd like to visit with you if you have a few minutes and go over your aunt's new medications. We have increased the dosage on her blood pressure drug and added a rather potent heart medicine in addition to the ones she was already taking. She's doing well but these additional medications are needed as she gets older because of her existing heart condition. Just be sure to keep a close eye on her for a few days. I don't foresee any problems. She needs to limit her excitement if possible."

I assured him Aunt Nona's wellbeing was my top priority, and I would do my best to take good care of her. I couldn't wait to take her home. Seeing her in the hospital was troubling and uncomfortable. The night before had taken more out of me than I realized. And I was worried. Her heart condition had become more pronounced as the years wore on. Dr. Stevens had given me a gentle wake up reminder. I needed rest and time to think about my plans for my life and especially my career. Jillian's shop had served its purpose, but I was standing still, treading water. *Time to move on.* I wanted to have some good news for Aunt Nona when she came home. She shouldn't be concerned about her irresponsible wackado great niece refusing to grow up. She deserved more than I was giving her. I needed a plan.

As the elevator door opened, I saw Pastor Leland. "Hello Valentine. It's good to see you." He extended his hand. "I was in the hospital to see some of our members and wanted to stop by and see your Aunt Nona. How's she doing today?"

"Oh, I'm so relieved you're here to see her. She's doing well but anxious to go home of course. You will lift her spirits when she sees you; she thinks so highly of you. She's already had lunch and might be resting her eyes, so don't hesitate to go in and say hello. She'll be happy to see you."

"Thank you Valentine. Great to see you. I miss seeing you two on Sundays and hope you'll be back in church soon."

I assured him we would be back in the fold as soon as Aunt Nona was well. He had a wonderful, soothing manner to be so young. The word that comes to mind is gentleman, accent on the *gentle*. I guessed a young 35 or 40 because his boyish good looks were deceiving. It's surprising he's single but then again he's been in seminary and focused on his ministry. He wasn't caught up like the rest of us heathens in the frenzy of the materialistic and transitory spinning our wheels.

∞

Chapter 16
Back to New Beginnings

I paid the cabbie, then slipping and sliding, made my way to the front door. I fumbled with the key in the lock and heard the sound that made me hold my breath. I hurried to answer the ringing phone hoping it wasn't the hospital. I was so relieved; I practically shouted into the receiver, "Jess, it's good to hear your voice. I just got home from the hospital. I heard the phone and hoped they weren't calling about Aunt Nona. How are you?"

"Fine but still recovering from the party. How about you? You and Rowan looked like you picked up where you left off."

"It was okay. Well, no it wasn't. We didn't end the evening on a good note, so when you have a day, I can bore you to tears with a whole different conversation."

"What's going on with you two, anyway? Greg called and said you two were on the outs and I was worried."

"Long story short, Jess, he asked me to go skiing with him and his family and I had to say no. Aunt Nona is still in the hospital. I couldn't just leave her. Rowan took it as a personal rejection. He didn't understand is the understatement of the century. We blew up in each other's faces."

"Oh, Val, I'm sorry. Sometimes the timing isn't right. Seems to me he should be more understanding but then again he must be accustomed to having his way. Think of him being an only child plus he's a baseball standout who gets constant attention. Can you just imagine how he's catered to? Never hears no would be my guess."

"You're right. But is it a free card for his behavior? He needs to grow up is my take on Mr. Rossi. I thought we had something special but not so sure now. Anyway, I'm trying to move on. It's becoming clear my future won't include Rowan Rossi. What's up with you?"

"Oh, Val, you've got a lot to deal with especially Aunt Nona and all, but I didn't want to leave without telling you. Greg and I are going to Aspen with the Rossi's. I'm disappointed you won't be coming but I hope you understand. I might never get another chance like this. Caroline has taken a shine to me for some reason."

"Don't apologize, Jess. There's absolutely no reason you shouldn't go especially not on account of me. I wish things could have worked out, but I'm not in control of this relationship. It's a two-way deal and the other half has chosen to act like a five-year-old, too bad. When are you guys leaving?"

"Tomorrow for ten days. Dad is not excited about my going but he has to push me out of the nest sometime. He felt more at ease after Caroline Rossi called him. He laughed and said she was taking me under her wing. Apparently she thinks I could be the daughter she never had. Anyway, her reassurance worked. He relented and is comfortable with me going since it's the Rossi's. Influential and upper class always seems to work. You know how protective he is."

My curiosity got the best of me. "Jess, you don't have to tell me, but I was wondering if Rowan is taking someone."

"Not sure. Greg mentioned something about a girl from Stanford meeting us in Colorado. It's someone Rowan dates occasionally. I'll give you a full report when I get back."

"Oh, no, you won't. I don't want the details. Do me a big favor and tell me not your concern if I ask. Stick to it, no matter what I say. Let's make this the last time we talk about Rowan and his girlfriends, his ski rendezvous, romances, or escapades, whatever. No more. Rowan made his position crystal clear the other night. We are done, kaput."

"For sure, I don't understand him. But I'll honor your wishes and protect your feelings. Guys are notoriously fickle especially at this age.

I remind myself constantly to have fun with Greg and not count on anything more serious. Besides, I'm too young and have plans. You do, too. Guys are just a giant distraction."

"True, true. Chemistry is not the culprit. If he had his way, we'd already done the deed. Anyway, I should see the flashing lights and red flags but what's past is over and done. He's a good guy deep down. Sad to say, any relationship with this much difficulty getting off the ground is doomed. I hope he grows up but chances are he won't have to. I'm sure he has his pick of girls who will be more than glad to tolerate and over-indulge him. But it won't be me."

"You're right, Val. I just hope he opens his eyes to what he's losing. Well, I've got to run. Got a million things to do to get ready. I'll see you when I get back in town. Love ya."

"Love you too, Jess. Have a ball and be careful on the mountain. On second thought, better be careful *off* the mountain!"

"Ha. Ha. Call if you need me. See you soon, bye."

I was deflated inside but wore a cheery cover-up for my friend. What did I expect? Life doesn't stop for me to catch up. I looked around the house, a mega mess. Aunt Nona would not approve. The sooner I got busy, the sooner I could pamper me. A long, bubbly hot bath was in my future. Besides, a thorough housecleaning is good therapy. I didn't stop until the bungalow was spotless. Floors clean and shiny, furniture gleaming, clutter stowed, kitchen and bathroom sparkling. As I filled the tub, the cleansing aroma filled the room. The nagging notion of teaching school would not go away. Perhaps because of Aunt Nona's influence or because I realized I would never be more than a glorified sales clerk pounding out sales for the owner. Teaching would be rewarding and a career I could be proud of. I could register for the spring semester and if I took full loads for three years, I could get my teaching certificate. Aunt Nona was generous, but I wasn't sure paying for my college was in her budget. She has to be stretching her teacher retirement funds thin. I could continue working at Jillian's part-time during the week and on Saturdays. If I put my mind to it, I could graduate in three years. It was an ambitious plan, but I intended to make up for lost days of poor planning.

I brought Aunt Nona home the next day. She was doing well on her new medicine, and her doctor had lifted restrictions except he reiterated she was to rest more and avoid stress. However you do that. I had to do my utmost to protect her from upset but I knew Aunt Nona. She mixes it up and can't stand not being involved whether it's her church, ladies group, my comings and goings. We should take the middle ground even though she was not one to take direction. My giving Aunt Nona orders or even gentle guidance on how to live her life could be a calamity in the making.

She felt well enough for me to return to work the next day for a few hours. Jillian had been supportive but now with Jess out of town, she needed me at the shop. She was running end-of-the-year sales to make space for new inventory. Spring fashions would arrive any day which meant extra time stocking inventory. It was a busy season of the year. I needed to keep my mind occupied and welcomed being at the shop. I worked through an entire afternoon without thinking of RR.

"I'm glad to have you back, Valentine. Aunt Nona must be doing well."

"She's doing well and looking good. She's happy to have her house back and relieved I would be at work today so I wouldn't be hovering."

"I thought today we should tidy up from Christmas. It was hectic last week, and I let things go more than I like to. Oh, by the way, I want to tell you how beautiful you looked at the party. You were a vision in the red dress."

"Thanks, Jillian. Listen, I can't thank you enough. I couldn't have been happier when you picked a dress for me. I would never have taken the risk, boring and safe me. Who knew I could pull off such a big bright sophisticated look."

"Nonsense. You underestimate yourself. You're a beautiful girl. The red dress was the finishing touch. I can help you with wardrobe to bring out your best but the confidence thing is something else. I keep hoping you'll learn to appreciate and show off your assets. If you've got it, use it, young lady."

We tidied up and re-arranged the inventory, putting out party dresses for New Year's and starting to organize the sales items. I looked outside, and it was dark. "Oh my gosh. I need to scat. It's six o'clock! The day flew by, huh?"

"You run along. I'll close up. Give my love to Aunt Nona."

I walked through the garage to the kitchen and to the smell of homemade potato soup. Aunt Nona was at her gas stove grinning. "Surprise! I cooked. Hope you're hungry. Did you have a busy day, Valentine? I wanted you to have something to warm you up from the cold and of course it's my favorite soup."

"Mine as well. What could be tastier on a cold day in December? Yummy. How was your day, did you manage okay without me constantly asking you how you were?" I hugged her gently. She smoothed her apron.

"Okay? I feel fantastic, my dear. I did some reading and made some phone calls and relaxed in my chair. Well, relaxed to the point I napped. Being home is the best medicine. We take for granted the everyday things."

I got the napkins and silverware and bowls ready and Aunt Nona's cup and saucer for her tea. She loved her tea, freshly brewed with lemon and sugar, but NO CREAM. She bowed her head and gave our Blessing. It was wonderful to have her home and well. I was grateful beyond my wildest imaginings. She was my rock. Despite the heartache and sadness, I felt warm and hopeful, the effect my Aunt Nona had on me. I acknowledged my bright optimism had a downside. She was human, but I refused to think of my life without her. Tonight was our time to cherish being together.

"What's new at Jillian's? Are you busy?"

"Always. You know, Jillian. She's got the spring stuff coming in soon and end-of-year merchandise sales. She loves the store like her baby and keeps it spotless. Today we cleaned up after the Christmas rush."

"I was wondering if you planned to stay at Jillian's or get a degree as you mentioned once. It's a wonderful place for you to work and you seem to enjoy your job."

"Aunt Nona, I'm glad you asked. I do like working at Jillian's but the fashion business is so competitive and I'm not sure it's for me. I was taken in by the excitement and glamour of the fashion world. I've worked in retail long enough to see the options are limited for me. In fact, over the holidays, I did some thinking and soul searching. I want to go to state college and get my degree."

Aunt Nona looked up from her soup. She was surprised but not flabbergasted. "Oh gracious me, Valentine, what a wonderful idea. Education is music to my ears. In today's world, it's a necessity."

"Oh, I'm finding that out. I need to work part-time and could continue at Jillian's or I might get something at a school. To make my goal, I have to take a full load of courses and go to summer school to graduate in three years. For once, I'm serious about my career. I mean I'm practically 20 already and ready or not I'll be 21. Good grief!"

Aunt Nona laughed. "I have been meaning to talk to you about that! Such an old woman at 20 and almost an adult so you better get busy. I admire you want to accomplish so much so quickly but what's the rush? Aren't you overloading yourself?"

"No, I can handle it. I want to start teaching as soon as possible."

Aunt Nona almost choked. She took her napkin and wiped her mouth. "You want to *teach*?"

"Yes, I do. I am drawn to teaching and to a career with meaning. I love fashions and always will but I need to separate delusion from reality. I need a tangible and rewarding career. Needless to say, your dedication to teaching has been an inspiration."

Aunt Nona was beaming. "Oh, Valentine, what wonderful news. You will be a remarkable teacher." I was transparent as she saw the questioning in my eyes of how I would pay for tuition, books and all the expenses of state college.

"I haven't made a big deal of it because I didn't want you to feel pressured to go to college, but I have an allotment for your education. I was waiting for your initiative as to what your plans were. I didn't want to put ideas in your head. What you do for a living is such a critical decision. But don't worry, the college expenses are taken care of. If you want to continue working at Jillian's, then it's fine if you can handle the load and it doesn't interfere with your studies."

"Oh, Aunt Nona. I wasn't hinting for you to pay for my expenses, and I have no intention of spending your pension on my schooling. You worked long and hard for your savings. I didn't intend for you to pay for college. I was excited to share what my plans were, finally."

"Nonsense. The money has been put aside for years, ever since I adopted you. I planned for this day and now it's here. Discussion ended. Your end of the bargain is to take advantage of the opportunity to reach your goals. So let's eat cake and celebrate!"

She brought two pieces of chocolate buttermilk cake with fudge frosting dripping down the sides to the table. "Oh wait. This cake is begging me for a glass of milk!"

"Well, then. You should have it." She set the cake on the table and returned with a glass of ice cold milk for me.

"You spoil me, Aunt Nona."

"And you, me. Isn't this the way it should be? We have a great thing going here." She looked rosier and happier than I had seen her in weeks. My heart was light as I sighed with relief and sang out, "Here's to my Aunt Nona the love of my life." *Dessert forks clink. Celebration of us.*

∞

CHAPTER 17
FAMILIAR STRANGER

W e need to hire a new yard man." Aunt Nona was yelling from the kitchen. "Spring is here and our yard looks pathetic. I'm embarrassed to pull into the driveway. Those high schoolers cut the grass but with zero yard maintenance. I had a man stop me the other day when I came home from the grocery store. He needs the work. He must have followed me. Anyway, he said he was looking for more yards to mow and gave me a fair price. He will lend a hand with the garden and keep it weeded and help me each spring with all the planting. The thing I noticed about him was his boldness. He gave me quite the sales pitch and must need the money. He startled me when he suddenly appeared in the garage out of nowhere. Guess he meant no harm, just eager. I never thought I'd say this, but this old yard is getting to be a giant pain in the behind and more work than I want to handle. I love the garden and I'm not ready to give it up yet. Don't ever get old, Valentine. It's for the birds, whatever that means." I could hear her familiar chuckle. "This old guy, named Angus, says he does other yards in our neighborhood so it would be convenient."

"I could do it, Auntie. Our yard is the size of a postage stamp. I could mow it in thirty minutes. We'd save the money and not hire a yard man." I heard the words but what was I saying. I hated yard work and being in the heat. Sun was for fun and the only working would be on my tan or swimming with my friends.

"No, absolutely not. You're busy with college and work and do most of the housework. Besides what would the neighbors think? I don't want you doing yard work, and you don't care much for gardening. I appreciate the offer but it's too much to ask you to keep the yard and the garden. It's settled. I'll hire Angus next week."

After work Monday, I walked up to the front door and just as I put the key in the lock, a shiver went down my spine, an eerie sense someone was behind me. I could smell him and hear his breathing. I jerked the key from the lock and whirled around. "I'm your new yard man. Remember me?"

I couldn't breathe. My throat closed and my mouth was as dry as if I'd swallowed a giant cotton ball. I couldn't spit if my life depended on it. "What are you doing here? Get off our property or I'll call the cops. You have your nerve."

"No, missy, you're not calling anyone. There's no one who can help you now. It's just you and me. I knew I'd find you someday."

He reached in his shirt pocket and took out a shiny gold object. I knew what it was before he even brought it out of his pocket. He swung the little gold heart back and forth like a pendulum. "Bet you'd like to have this back, huh? It's yours, and it's got your old lady inside it. I found it on the ground when you ran away that day."

His slimy brown teeth grinned oozing tobacco juice down the side of his mouth. I hardly recognized my heart necklace now covered in crusty filth, dull and scratched. As dear as the necklace is, I thought, since his grimy hands and fingers have touched and held it, I'm not sure I want it back. My mind raced to that hot afternoon so many years ago. How was it possible he recognized me and knew where I lived? His hair was white now but the rest of him had not changed. Foul, disgusting, and scary.

I was in the throes of pure terror and panic had taken over. "What do you want? You better get out of here before my aunt comes home." My shaky attempt to sound in control sounded ridiculous and made me even more vulnerable. This wasn't happening. He couldn't be the new yard man!

He edged even closer. His eyes were all over me. I knew I was done for. "Do you like your aunt? Let's put it this way. You be a good girl and nothing will happen. Do you get what I'm saying, little girl?" He grabbed and squeezed my arm. "You don't want to make me hurt you. Just keep your mouth shut and listen. There's nothing you can do now. You can't hide. I see everything. I see where you go. I see where your old lady goes. You and me are goin' be real close. Remember that. And I'll be back. If you think I'm kidding, there's one sure-fire way to find out, girlie. Just dare to open your mouth and she's a goner. Remember your old auntie means nothing to me. She's just in the way." He let go and flung my limp arm now numb and throbbing.

I felt weak and faint. I leaned against the giant wooden door. He turned and ambled down the sidewalk to his old red pickup truck parked across the street and slowly drove away. I knew the face of evil and hate and here it was again. I felt nauseous and couldn't get enough air. My head twirled and my legs were rubber. I was hyperventilating and could pass out. Get yourself together, Valentine. My thoughts ran wild. What was I going to do? Then the real terror set in as reality hit me. I had to think this through and not panic. This situation was bad, but I had to be careful not to make it even worse. Did I dare risk and call his hand? I had to protect Aunt Nona. I expected her home any minute from her meeting at the church. Inside the safety of the house, I went straight to the bathroom to douse myself in cold water. I looked into the mirror. My eyes were wild and my skin drained to ashen gray. This could be the new me. I've got to calm myself. My aunt is not easily fooled. She can smell trouble a mile away. I heard the purr of the Cadillac as she pulled into the garage. I was shaking and wobbly but I had to straighten up. I could hear her calling for me.

"Valentine, come help me. I stopped at the grocery store. We're having your favorite supper. Monday has to be the dreariest day of the week. Let's celebrate something."

"Here I come, Aunt Nona."

"How was work? Anything exciting going on? Did you have classes this morning? I'm still not up to speed on your schedule. You're either at Jillian's or have class. I guess as long as you keep up with yourself is what matters." She chuckled.

"Everything is fine, although I do feel like I'm running into or meeting myself. But it's okay, good practice for my grand entrance into the working world."

"As if you haven't been in the harsh world. She grinned and grabbed a grocery bag. "You're like me. You're as tough as a boot ready to handle whatever comes. I know you, Valentine. You'll be just fine."

"By the way, I called Angus. He'll start doing our yard next week. He's quite reasonable and seemed grateful to get the work. He needs the money."

I felt my body turn cold at the sound of his name. I started to tremble. "Okay, but we could handle this little patch ourselves. Seems like a waste of money."

"Valentine, are you okay? You look pale." Nona put her hand on my forehead. "You're not warm but a little clammy. After supper, I want you to go to bed and get some rest. You have a full schedule and you need to stay well and not overdo. Pace yourself, girl. There's a lot of year left on the calendar, and you need your strength. I hope you're not coming down with something."

I twirled the fork in my plate picking at mushy meatloaf and now cold green beans. Eating was not on the agenda for me tonight. I couldn't wait to go to my room and hide. I needed to think and calm down. My insides were churning. I knew this so-called yard man. He had not changed; just an older version. The dirty old man who tried to grab me when I had the groceries was no longer a fading nightmare. Those ten years had flown by, but the horror of him was happening again. A predator on a mission, to terrorize and maybe more. From this day, I knew our lives were not worth ten cents even if he turned out to be nothing more than a nasty nuisance. There was no clear way out of this predicament.

∞

CHAPTER 18
THE ARROGANCE OF EVIL

I finished the week in a daze. Jessica was suspicious something was terribly wrong in spite of my repeated assurances I was overloaded with school and work. She knew me too well and kept pressing. She was not one to be shrugged off. "Valentine, something's wrong. What's going on?"

"Jessica, trust me. You're my dearest friend. I confide in you. Honest. The whole thing of trying to work at Jillian's and going to class and getting my studies done is more than I expected. Becoming a responsible adult is not all it's cracked up to be. Where's the fun? And then of course the Rowan thing. It's not serious turmoil, just everyday dilemma, that's all. I'm distracted. I'll be fine." I sounded hollow and unconvincing. I hoped she wasn't insulted that I expected her to swallow such garbage. I had a serious malfunction; I refused to ask for help. There was no problem I couldn't handle. Pride, shame, guilt, confusion, lack of trust was a sickening cocktail of delusion. Hark back, if I'd handled the old man's attempt to grab me differently, I wouldn't be having this crisis. Should have, would have, didn't and I'm forced to deal with my mistake. It's the risk to Aunt Nona that's eating me alive.

Jessica shook her head showing her impatience and becoming out of sorts with me. "You can't help some people. I give up. You win. But if you change your mind, I'm here. Okay?"

I was consumed with guilt. How could I tell her the yard man is the pervert from that day ten years ago? She had begged me to tell her dad, my aunt, someone who could do something to stop him. I knew better and had all my excuses ready. Telling a grown-up was too upsetting and risky especially for my aunt and unnecessary since I hadn't been hurt. The old man would do something horrible to us and on and on. Right or wrong, I would be blamed. I did nothing and now here he is back in my life and, even more frightening, in my aunt's life.

I was no nearer to a plan by the following Monday when I arrived home and Angus was mowing the grass. Aunt Nona was already home. I tucked my head as far into my shoulders as possible and headed through the back door. It didn't work. Aunt Nona heard me. "Child, why are you coming in through the back door? You usually come in through the front. You startled me."

"Sorry Auntie. I didn't want to disturb the yard man. How often will he be here?"

"Once a week after he gets the yard presentable. He's got a lot of work to do in the garden because I've neglected it so long but he'll whip it into shape. He's a hard worker."

"What do you know about him, Aunt Nona? Where did he come from and did you get any references? I doubt if he even lives around here."

"What a strange thing to ask. He's merely taking care of our yard. It's nothing to be concerned about. Actually, he just appeared on the doorstep asking if I had any work for him mainly yard work. You sure seem suspicious of him for some reason. I can tell he's a good gardener; he works hard and is reasonably priced. The big reason: I can afford him. Valentine, it's not easy to find someone to do yard and garden work in this heat that lasts for months."

"Okay. I just wondered. It's no big deal. I'm sure he'll be fine. Guess I'm practicing to be an adult, turning into a worry wart. If you don't mind, I'm going to my room. They're pouring it on. Now my favorite pastime has become a chore. Reading is a dirty word. I've got to read three chapters in history and on top of everything else, I have to study for a biology test."

"Oh, before you go, would you take him some water. It's hot and humid out there and I'm not sure whether he brought any with him."

I looked at her in disbelief. How did I hope to get out of this? "Can't he drink from the garden hose?"

My aunt was mortified. "Valentine, how thoughtless and arrogant! What has come over you? Here take this."

I filled up the thermos with cold water. Too bad we didn't have any arsenic handy. I let the kitchen door slam behind me and marched toward him trying to remember I had to be nice even though he was depraved and dangerous. What could I be thinking? No soap strong enough or water hot enough so I'll be sure and trash the thermos after he's done.

"Auntie wanted you to have some cold water." I shoved the thermos towards him.

"Why, ain't you sweet." He grabbed the thermos with his sweaty hand trying to touch my hand and then gulped the liquid letting the water spew from his dirty mouth and run down his smelly undershirt and dirty overalls. I had to smell his clothes, so repulsive; my terror gave way to burning anger. For a fleeting second, I felt brave even invincible. Had I lost my senses? How could I win against this monster? Suddenly I realized how foolish I felt. My aunt being here didn't improve the odds. Lose the brave front, Valentine. He is not the schoolyard bully. He's desperate and preying on two weak and vulnerable females. *Easy pickin's. He sees you're afraid and intimidated and have no defense. Don't make him mad.*

"Here. Bring me more water so I can see you wiggle your ass in your tight skirt. You're invitin' it but we'll get to all that later, girlie. Yes sir, you're all grown up nice for Angus."

His tongue covered in thick yellow saliva broke through red, peeling cracked lips. My eyes sent back daggers. The more he threatened me, the more intense and determined I felt to get rid of him. My inferno of anger returned with vengeance. I scared myself; he pushed me to the edge. How far should I go to stop him? Suddenly, I found myself five years old in the shadows of evil threatening Will with my overblown ego and anger spilling over, drowning my logic. My progress wasn't much to brag about throughout the years.

"You touch my aunt, you slimy nut job, and you'll find out more about me than you can handle. Get your own water from the water hose." I steamed with hatred. I couldn't stand him and his nastiness. I spun around and headed toward the house. He flung back his scrawny neck and laughed out loud. "Full of spit, are you? Might want to save yourself for what I have for you." He stared with wide yellow grin looking down at himself.

"Go ahead. Show the neighbors, make a spectacle of yourself. The police will take care of you. You're crazy if you think you can get away with this. You leave us alone or I'll make you sorry you were ever born. You want trouble, you found it. I'm not afraid of your kind."

My head whirled as I headed toward the house leaving him laughing, coughing and spitting up. A lifetime of smoking had taken its toll and overwhelmed his lungs. He looked so small and scrawny and malnourished that he could crumble in a heap at any minute. I could probably take him if I put my mind to it, but his nastiness to the bone gave him the edge. Reality blazed through me. I was in for the battle of my life whether he was a real threat or not. I couldn't afford to take the chance.

My aunt took it all in through the kitchen window. "What were you doing out there? I asked you to take him water, not become his best friend. What in the world did you two find to chat about? Maybe that's good or not. You don't have to go out of your way and be friends with him but no need to be mean either." She shook her head puzzled, again.

"Yes Aunt Nona. I will try but I still think he's disgusting. I doubt if he's had a bath in this century. He smells to high heaven. I'm not sure we need him around here. We could find someone decent."

Privacy, please and quick pounded through my brain. In panic for a plan, I shut the door to my room so I could think. Who could I trust to help me to prevent my aunt getting hurt? I should handle this my way. If he enjoyed seeing me squirm as part of a game he played, he wouldn't actually harm us. Ridiculous! He came here for a reason. He intended to hurt us or worse. I hated myself for considering the obvious. Doing away with him wasn't a serious option but thinking about it had its advantages and made me less anxious--well, hopeful anyway. The problem might be serious, but the way I had chosen to handle it seemed more troublesome.

∞

CHAPTER 19
LIMBO OF TERROR

Over the next several days, I had to face a grim dilemma that would not magically disappear. What is it about problems like this? It's as if I'll just wake up one day and all around me will be hunky dory. Then I'm hit by a gigantic realization. I have to be just as tough as the problem. I had to take a chance and trust someone. A strong dose of fact tempered my arrogance I could handle the situation. I could get hurt or even more horrifying, Aunt Nona. He knew how to make me listen. He was reckless and hell bent to hurt or even kill her because she was his bargaining tool. He might be vile and disgusting but he wasn't stupid. I could be making one of those crucial mistakes from which you never recover.

I dared not think about what *could* happen to me and to Aunt Nona. His depths of depravity were too much to consider yet were the key to resolve the situation. This situation is out of my control and out of my capability. I will either wind up doing something I will regret that will haunt and/or ruin the rest of my life or he will proceed to make life a living Hell. I had to take a chance without frightening Aunt Nona. Someone else had to make the decision to alert Aunt Nona. I could not tell her. Aunt Nona wouldn't let anything or anyone stand in her way once she made a decision. She had the inner strength and grit to confront the devil. The longshot whether he was serious about his threats was a gamble for idiots. How obvious could a situation be? He was a criminal. Threats be damned; our only hope was the police.

My mind was made up. I had to find a way to confide in Officer McShane, but I had to be careful. I had to cover my tracks and make sure that Angus didn't know I was doing precisely what he warned me against doing. I should confide in auntie. She was smarter, more experienced, and wiser than I could ever hope to be, and I trusted her with my life. Why did I refuse to tell her we were in danger? Would she accuse me of inviting or provoking this intrusion by a deviant who was invading our safety and privacy? I listened to myself. Aunt Nona is as trustworthy as a human can be. I had to tell her and pray we could figure out a solution. If not, I could find myself in the big house. I hated my desperate thoughts. But to protect us, I knew I *was* capable. He endangered everything dear to me. He flaunted his conceit and blatant disregard of decency as a banner of deviancy to exploit and manipulate me without payback. To him, I was an amusement. Another stupid, helpless female easily intimidated. I suddenly became furious. Waiting for what? Disaster to strike? We must take the opportunity to resolve our dilemma.

"Aunt Nona, please come in here. I need to talk to you."

"Valentine, I'm about to start supper. Can't it wait for a few minutes?"

"No, it's important, please."

My aunt came into the study wiping her hands on her red and white checkered apron with the rather large red apple on the front. She smiled at me. "Gracious, child. You look like you've seen a ghost. What in the world is the matter?" She looked adorable in her apron and with no worries. I could hardly stand to ruin her day. How could I burden her? She had been out of the hospital and on her new meds for six months. She was doing well and now this. It could kill her. I organized my thoughts.

"Well, it's hard to begin. There has been something bothering me but I don't want to worry you. I have to learn to solve my problems. I guess this is as good a time as any."

"Nonsense, Valentine. We all need someone to confide in and sometimes just talking it out helps us figure it out. Now, what is bothering you? It must be serious. I've not seen your eyes look this dark in ages. Cloudy eyes, cloudy skies."

"Aunt Nona, you've noticed I don't like the yard man. No surprise to you, I'm sure. But I have a good reason. You better sit down for this one. It's straight out of a horror movie."

My aunt's face drained to ashy blue gray and her cherry cheeks deflated.

"Do you remember when you sent me for groceries and I came home crying and upset? Well, I never told you the whole story. I had a terrible scare then. I thought it would be fun to take another way home. I took a shortcut and got lost in a bad neighborhood. An old man came out and offered me lemonade and it was so hot, when I took the lemonade, he tried to grab me. The old man is our yard man."

My aunt seemed to stop breathing. She gasped for air. "Oh, no. It's been so long ago. You could be mistaken. Are you sure it's the same man? Did he hurt you or anything?"

"No, no, auntie. I ran away from him before he could grab me. And yes I'm positive it's the same old man. Remember when I lost my locket? He showed it to me the other day. The chain broke when we struggled. I honestly didn't have an idea what to do. I was so confused and didn't want you to be upset. Since I didn't get hurt, I decided there was no reason to tell you. Besides, I escaped before he could do anything. But now I have to tell you because he *will* harm us. He's desperate with nothing to lose and he's not afraid."

"We have to call the police."

"Wait, auntie. Please, listen to me. You can't just fire him. There's more to this, and it gets much worse. He's made advancements toward me and threatened he'd hurt you if I tell anyone. We have to figure out how to handle this to get him locked up. He must not know I've told you or he will do something to us. It's the evil in him; he's capable of doing horrible things. He might just be a slimy creep, but we can't afford to underestimate him. We have to be smarter than he is."

My aunt collapsed in the chair, her face pasty white. She struggled to breathe and came close to passing out. Everything I hoped didn't happen was happening right on cue. How could I do this to my beloved Aunt Nona? Then just as I expected her last breath, she partially recovered her composure. "Valentine, we won't allow anyone to do this to us. I'm calling the police." She started to pick up the phone.

"No, Aunt Nona, no! You can't. He's watching us and if the police come, he'll kill us!" I tried to get to the phone before her but I couldn't. I must not stop, I had to keep running, running--

I sat up suddenly with my heart racing and out of breath. I looked around and tried to get my bearings. I'd fallen asleep on the sofa. Beads of sweat dripped down the sides of my face and my blouse, soaked. I slowly gathered my wits, but I realized the reality of the nightmare. I could not risk telling Aunt Nona. Deadly shock would be on my hands and was not an option.

No, I decided. This will not work. I have to protect her. Telling her about the old man might just kill her. Even with her strong will, her weak heart could not withstand this jolt. I looked up. Aunt Nona had come into the study and was staring at me waiting for me to speak. She searched my face for a clue. What did I need to tell her? I was blank now.

"You said you needed to talk to me. When I came into the room, you were sound asleep on the sofa. You're exhausted and must have had a bad dream; you're covered in sweat. What is it, child? Are you okay? I'm sorry it took me so long but I was in the middle of cooking dinner."

"Oh, Aunt Nona, it's nothing. I had a nonstop day and Jillian's was pure craziness. Sometimes, it's just too much. I guess I just needed to complain, poor me. I love to exaggerate when I'm overwhelmed."

She didn't look convinced, but she did look weary so she accepted my explanation. "Okay, Valentine. Whatever you say. But if you change your mind, I might not have all the answers but I have great ears."

"Can't I even get a grin?" She smiled. "Come on, you get out of those wet clothes and we'll have dinner. Then straight to bed for you. You need a good night's rest, and I hope that's all there is to it, but I'm not convinced. You're not telling me something."

I hid behind a fake smile. Keeping my vow to protect Aunt Nona was getting more difficult by the hour.

CHAPTER 20
MONSTER MISTAKE

Jessica stopped by the next morning on her way to Jillian's. She had mentioned on the phone she might stop by today and show me her new outfits for her modeling interviews. New York liked her application and portfolio and had set up appointments for her to come to the Big Apple. She was getting herself interview ready. In a panic she would figure out one + one equals Angus. I saw her car pull in behind his old truck. As soon as I saw her through the window, I ran to the door trying to get outside before she got out of the car. Too late. Bam! There they were--two perfectly proportioned long, tanned legs as she opened the car door to get out. She had on pink shorts and a tight white blouse tied high. Guilt-ridden, I could see him eyeing her and drooling all over himself. Look what I've caused, my best friend on display in front of this Lech. What a disaster and it's my fault. I rushed out to meet her and practically knocked her down getting her into the house. Angus took a long, lewd penetrating stare that chilled me to the bone.

"Hey, Jess, what's going on? When did you become such an early bird? Come on, come on in."

"Yeah, well, I had a lot of errands and wanted to get an early start." She looked puzzled and uncomfortable and gave me the evil eye. She was in no mood for my excuses.

As we got inside the house, she couldn't hold back. "Where in the world did the creep come from? He's too scary to be in your yard. Now you have to run to my car and escort me in? Please tell me he doesn't work for your aunt on a permanent basis. This crumb bum is a walking time bomb."

"Yeah. Tell me something I don't know. I wish I could say he's not coming back after today, but she hired him to get the yard back in shape and to help her in the garden. The high schoolers cut the grass wham bam and they're out of here. This hobo is the king of yards and fertilizer and how to get the grass back, so he's here every week. He looks bad but harmless." I looked away to keep from facing my friend. She could see through me. I was barely holding it together.

"Val, look at me. Who is he and where did he come from? There's something big time wrong here. He's not only filthy, but he looks suspicious as hell and desperate. I saw him eyeing me up and down. Gives me the creeps." Jessica knew people, and she had him pegged. What she couldn't figure out was me. What was I hiding and why?

"He just appeared and asked Aunt Nona if she had any work he could do. He told her he liked to work in yards and gardens and needed the money. You know how soft-hearted she is. She felt sorry for him and hired him." I paused to get my breath. Now I had another innocent life at stake, and my attempt at a credible account of our predicament was as hollow as it was unconvincing.

"I've tried to get her to get someone else or even let me do it. The yard is no big deal; I could find the time. But she won't hear of it. She thinks he works hard and does a good job for not a lot of money. Nothing mysterious."

"What day does he work so I can avoid this place? I worry for you and Aunt Nona though. That guy's up to no good, trust me. I'm listening to the sound of my voice which should be an echo. You're smarter than this." Jess looked straight through me.

"Jess, come on. He's dirty and foul but I'd say harmless. He likes to look at girls but then what old guy or any guy doesn't?" I was trying hard to shrug off her concern, but Jess was no dummy. I felt the beads of sweat dripping down the sides of my face. I had to be radiating remorse. But there was nothing I could do. I had successfully penned myself into an impenetrable corner with three women's lives in jeopardy thanks to my fear and arrogance.

"He works Monday and Thursday mornings. But he also takes care of a couple of other yards around here and I've seen his truck on Wednesdays."

"Oh, not good. The area should be posted. *Enter at your own risk with bodyguards.* I'm telling you, there's a big problem, Val. But now he's infiltrated the neighborhood. What are people thinking? Even if your aunt gives him the boot, he's still around. Dirty business."

"You're making a big tadoo over a dirty old man. He works cheap and gets the job done. No one wants to work out in the heat. He does the work no one else wants to do for an unbelievable price. Let's change the subject to something pleasant, okay?"

She scowled at me. "Okay. But it's hard to think of lively conversation with that slimy freak at your elbow gawking at you. Plus you're hiding something. I'm surprised at you. You're usually so forthright and cautious."

"When do you leave for New York and how long will you be gone?" I sounded absurd in my continuing disregard.

"We leave next Monday and we'll be gone a week. But get this. Dad is definitely going with me. I thought I might be on my own. But he absolutely put his foot down. No way am I going to New York by myself. He's taking off work for five days. He said we needed to have time away together. At first, I was bummed about it, but I'm used to the idea. We'll make it fun. He's on the front line, and even in a small city like ours, he sees and hears all the bad stuff. The whole modeling thing puts him on edge. Since we're both going, he's more positive and I am, too. Remember when you and I were in Chicago with all our chaperones? We had bodyguards and felt grown but being plopped down in the middle of the Big Apple alone and not knowing my way around might be too much. Not to mention I'd stand out like I was wearing a 'Hayseed Warning Sign' with nary a soul to call if I got in trouble."

"I can't wait to hear about how it goes. I'm so happy for you. Beyond exciting, Miss Jess. But then you're already runway ready as far as I'm concerned."

"Okay, well, we can hope. But I have a sneaky idea I'll be cut down to size after this trip. Caroline says forget New York. She has contacts in San Francisco she wants me to meet. She insists I can get a contract with a major line and do magazine layouts. That's where the big money is. So if New York doesn't work out, maybe I'll take her advice and try San Francisco. Well, I better get going. Too bad my car's in front. Is he still out there?"

"Well, actually no. He's left. Good timing. I'll walk out with you."

I looked up and down the street--no Angus. Thank goodness. Another week of relief from him. I watched Jessica get into her car and go down the street to the stop sign and start over the hill. I thought I saw her car turn right which was odd. She usually turned towards town. Oh well, she possibly had some other stop to make or it could have been another car and not hers. Too much to wonder about.

I had housework calling me. I made my bed and had finished cleaning the tub from my bath when the doorbell rang. I thought to myself, "Oh, please, don't let it be the old man." Then I caught myself and realized how asinine. No ringing the doorbell, no warning. He would just break in.

Slowly I edged into the hallway and peered out the front window. I could see Jessica's car. What in the world? I ran to the front door and flung it open. "Jess, what--"

"Let me in, Val, quick and shut the door. You can't make this go away."

Jess is not one to lose her cool; something dreadful had her upset. It had to be Angus.

"Val, he followed me. He was waiting up there at a side street, so I for sure wasn't going home. I drove for several blocks just to make sure my imagination wasn't running wild. Trust me, he was following me. He stayed far behind me, but I recognized that old truck. Okay. I've had more than enough of being stalked by some spook. Spill it."

"Oh, Jessica, I'm sorry he's upset you. We'll have to stop him. Come in the kitchen and sit down. Let me get you some cold water. You're right. He's trouble. I'm so sorry."

"Finally! Are all your doors locked? Make sure and the windows, too. I'm thinking I should call my dad. What is going on?"

I checked the front and back doors and the bathroom window I had raised. But I knew if he made up his mind to get in, nothing I could do to stop him. This situation was coming to a head and my foolish notion I could handle him was blowing up in my face. What had I done? Now he was after my best friend. I had taken it upon myself to handle a situation way over my head and had entangled my best friend in his snare.

"Jess, this matter with Angus has gotten out of hand. I never imagined how far he's willing to go. There are things I should tell you about him." Jess scooted to the edge of her chair.

"Val, what are you keeping from me? I knew when I left here this morning something was terribly wrong. Quit pretending. For whatever reason, you're keeping a deep, dark secret from me, is spreading like a fungus. What's going on here?"

"Jessica, he's the same old man who tried to snatch me inside his house." Jessica's face turned pale. I could see her heart pounding.

"No, Val. No more stalling. You have to call the police. You have to stop him."

"He said he finally found me. He's been threatening me with his dirty, vulgar suggestions and warned me he will hurt Aunt Nona if I go to the police. He keeps saying he has plans for me. It's been a nightmare with no end and no solution. I have to protect Aunt Nona, and now with her heart and all, it's more than I can handle. Since the doctor changed her medication, she's felt much better but any scare like this might be too much. I'm afraid for her. It might just kill her."

"Val, it's been ten years. I wonder where he's been. Do you think he could have been in jail or prison? My dad could find out if he has a record."

"Yes, we have to call your dad and get him over here. I've waited too long. Now this worm has gone after you; he's desperate and has nothing to lose to make his threats real. I'm a believer. Distorted but I think he wants to get caught, and frankly, his wish coming true is overdue." A few minutes passed. "Jess, we can make that happen with your dad's help."

"Val, what about your aunt? Where is she?"

"She's at Bible study and should be home after lunch. Is your dad on duty? Do you think he could come over or would it be risky for him to come in his uniform and in the squad car?"

"Excellent. It's good she's at church. Dad's on duty. I should go to the police station and tell him what's happening, but I hate to leave you alone here."

"No, it's best to explain to him in person. He'll go ballistic when he hears this nut case followed you. Is there any way you can get hold of him and see if he can meet you at the station?"

"Oh, yes. I have a direct line when I need him."

"Okay, then. Let's get this plan in motion. I need to stay until Aunt Nona gets home and explain what's going on. She'll be home in about an hour. There's no time to waste. Angus is playing his hand and forcing a confrontation. He's never been this bold. Get going while you can and be careful."

No sign of the old truck so Jessica quickly made her exit. She was going directly to the police station to meet with her dad. Officer McShane was no stranger to undercover. He had done it all during his years as a police officer and had the necessary resources to handle Angus. How stupid I'd been. My dearest friend had to be placed in harm's way for me to come to my senses. How arrogant and foolhardy! I have no excuses; I am smart enough and old enough to figure things out. I said a silent prayer bargaining with God to see us through this unharmed and that I would never be this conceited again. He gave me the wisdom to ask for help; my arrogance was an affront to Him. Even a child can understand this. Well, a smart child anyway.

I paced and found busy work around the house. I continually checked the windows and the doors. An hour and a half later, I heard the old Caddy in the garage. I ran to the kitchen and helped Aunt Nona with a bag of groceries. "What are you doing home today? I thought you were working at Jillian's."

"No, not until later this afternoon, Aunt Nona. Come in. Jessica stopped by a couple of times."

"You look flushed, Valentine. What's going on? Has something happened?"

"Aunt Nona, come on in and sit down. I'll brew some tea if you like."

"Okay. We had coffee at Bible study and tea bags, and you know how I feel about those." She smiled.

I put the water on to boil and took care of putting away the groceries. I sat down at the familiar wood kitchen table where discussions from small to life changing and even problems of the world were solved. I sat there outlining the scratches and marks of our past with my fingers nervously waiting for my next inspired utterance. What a mess! Where should I start--at the beginning or with the latest threat. Anxiously, I considered how to proceed. I should start the story from the present, go backwards.

"Aunt Nona, there are some things I haven't told you in the past and now they've caught up with me. It has to do with the old man who takes care of our yard. He was here this morning when Jessica stopped by. When she got in the house, she said he stared at her and made her uncomfortable. But it was much more. I've never seen her so upset. She stayed for a while and then left to do her errands but returned about thirty minutes later. Angus was following her. He waited far up the street, and she spied him a good distance behind her, but he was definitely following her."

Aunt Nona looked dazed and confused. I wanted to reassure her, but I hesitated. I should wait for Officer McShane. I'll tell her Jessica had gone for him.

"Anyway, Jessica has gone to the police station to explain to her dad what happened. They are coming back here possibly in an unmarked car, I'm not sure. But Officer McShane will be coming here to check out Angus."

"Oh, I'm so relieved. You girls did the right thing. The police should be called when something like this happens. It's just asking for trouble to handle it alone. You girls used good judgment. It was irresponsible of me to hire him and despicable he did this. I should have checked him out more thoroughly. I asked the neighbors about him, and they said he did good work. I didn't ask about his personal background."

I didn't have the reserves to go on. I looked at my aunt trying to take all this in stride, but she was overcome with worry. I should wait to tell her the rest of the story when Officer McShane and Jessica arrived.

∞

CHAPTER 21
COUNTDOWN TO
SHOWDOWN

They arrived in an unmarked car but McShane was in uniform. I walked to the porch to meet them, and Aunt Nona ushered them in. She hugged Officer McShane and scampered to the kitchen to get his customary cup of coffee which he had yet to turn down. Jessica and I made our way to the kitchen and the tea and coffee. I whispered to Jess I had told Aunt Nona about Angus following her but that was all. I stubbornly resisted telling Aunt Nona the grisly details. I had no qualms she had the mental toughness to confront almost any challenge, but her fragile health was another matter.

"Val, listen to me. You're underestimating her. She's lived a long life and is fiercely independent. She's a tough cookie. I appreciate what you're trying to do but you have to tell her. You have to quit protecting her. He's dangerous and needs to be put away. I told my dad everything and didn't spare the details. He's running Angus through records to get his criminal history. This guy has got to be stopped and now. Your aunt would want that. Give other people some credit and some trust. You'll save yourself some grief and prevent complications."

I hugged her. "Oh, Jessica, you're right. Thank you, thank you. Can you ever forgive me? What would I do without you and your level head?" Bless her heart! On the verge of disaster and my precious friend stepped in. She has a lot more street smarts than I ever will but the real kicker is she knows me. For whatever reason, my screwed-up past and mentality, arrogance, conjure up a problem and I assume I can fix way beyond my capacity.

My aunt and Officer McShane were talking quietly. We served the coffee and tea, and then he began the discussion and took out his paperwork.

"I've ordered a full history on this guy to see what we're dealing with. It's a safe bet he's got a record, likely on probation. I've seen too many like him. Guys like him on the edge are capable and predictable, and his brazen behavior is a red flag of repeat offenders. I'd only be surprised to see he hasn't been incarcerated, but we'll see if he's got a rap sheet. Our main priority is safety, and if there's any threat, we'll get him off the street."

"His background will tell me a lot, but I need you to tell me what he's said and done, what you know about him, and as much detail as you can give me. Now is not the time for you to choose the information you decide to give me. Tell me as much as you can and I'll sift through it. Secrets protect the perpetrator, not you."

He looked at me to speak but I was dumbfounded. Aunt Nona broke the silence. "Go ahead, Valentine. Tell him everything. I realize now you've been uncomfortable and uneasy with Angus for a reason. I will be all right, go ahead."

"I'll try, Aunt Nona. I realize how wrong I was to keep it all bottled up. I thought I did the right thing because I didn't get hurt and didn't want you to be upset for no reason. I didn't want to disturb you. Who would have ever dreamed he would re-appear?"

Blank faces stared back. I would not get out of this easily. My time to tell all had come, long overdue. My deep dark secret needed to be told. "It all started one day when Aunt Nona sent me for groceries. I felt brave and grown up; I decided to come home a different way, and I got horribly lost and confused. I was surrounded by rundown houses and trashy yards, and I passed by a red brick house with an old rusty tractor and an old man out front. Right away, I felt something wasn't right, but he saw me before I could get away. He yelled out asking if I wanted some cold lemonade. It was blistering hot, so I said yes. I went into the yard and sat under a big tree just to cool off, and he went inside to get the lemonade. I kept thinking I should leave, but for some reason, I decided it would be okay. I'd just drink some lemonade and then I'd go. He came back out and said he had cookies and I should come inside where it was cool. He wanted to play games and give me cookies. He kept getting closer and closer and became insistent and impatient trying to persuade me. I felt afraid. I gulped the lemonade and started to get up. He grabbed my arm and started dragging me, trying to pull me inside the house. As he made a move to pick me up, his grip relaxed. I jerked away with every bit of strength I had. I thought my arm was being pulled out of its socket I yanked away so hard. My arm was wet with sweat and slipped from his grip. I started running as fast as I could and didn't stop until I finally saw my street and made it home. Angus is the same old man. I'll never forget the eyes--piercing with wickedness. He had plans for me, and I knew I was in terrible trouble. I've never forgotten that day." No need to share my familiarity with *the look*. Once imbedded, the memory of Will blazed with fury. He robbed me of my innocence leaving me contaminated. The piercing intensity of desperate eyes intent on evil was identical just different faces. In my distorted thinking, I connected that I was the spark.

My Aunt Nona was in tears. I put my arms around her. "I'm so sorry to burden you with this ugliness. I should have confided in you then but I was too afraid. I thought I was to blame. In some way, it was my fault. I had asked for trouble."

She started to cry and held me. "Honey, you didn't do anything wrong. There are bad people who do bad things. You were still recovering from your own hell so it's understandable how you felt. Too much, it was just too much. We can't go back and undo but we certainly can do something now. You were young and vulnerable to cope with this situation but you were amazing. You had presence of mind and took instantaneous action to get away from him. Don't ever forget or minimize your strength. But now we have the help we need to take care of the problem." She patted my hand.

Officer McShane asked me several direct questions about the old man and whether he touched me. He also asked what he had said and done since he appeared on our doorstep. I told him in detail all the suggestive things he said and did and the threats he made against me and Aunt Nona. I told him the old man said he had looked for me and finally found me. If I told the police or anyone, he threatened to hurt and likely kill Aunt Nona for sure. Officer McShane continued writing his report and started to ask me another question when the phone rang. The call was for him.

We sat in silence while he finished his call. He turned to his report and continued to write. Then he looked up and cleared his voice. "My hunch was right. He was convicted on an aggravated rape charge and served eight years and is on probation." Officer McShane explained our options--all of which were bleak, risky and dangerous. There were no guarantees, but he had a plan.

Shrouded in naiveté and fear, I had no inkling of the trouble I had brought to this house. In fact, I had shrugged the old man off as a nasty nuisance and not nearly as dangerous as I had remembered. I was a frightened little girl, and he seemed dangerous but couldn't a lot of what I feared been created by my imagination? There were no words to describe my guilty regret and my bad judgment. *Fear took control.* Angus had opportunity, but I had given him permission. It was up to Officer Michael McShane to bail us out.

Chapter 22
Covert Encounter

The plan had risks, but to get Angus, we had to get evidence. I would wear a wire. It was my job to get Angus' threats and innuendos on tape. Aunt Nona was against the whole idea at first, but after Officer McShane explained our limited options, she began to come around and reluctantly gave her permission. With some luck and gentle persuasion from me, we could get Angus where we wanted him. Without the recording, it was my word against his. We also needed him to be caught with the heart necklace. He must brag about it and flash it as he did once before. The gold chain and heart could be damning; every piece of evidence was crucial. Who would have thought this little gold heart necklace would be even more valuable as evidence? I was anxious to get Angus and end this nightmare. I wore the wire to become accustomed and used to it so it was more comfortable. We needed one good session. If he continued to be as bold and careless as he had been with both me and Jess, my part in this scenario should be a cakewalk. Confidence took the place of apprehension. Mr. Angus had met his match. And if, Heaven forbid, anything went wrong, Officer McShane and two other officers would come to my aid. My part was vital, and I had no other choice if we wanted him out of our lives and off the street.

The infinite night dragged as I counted down the hours with Thursday's dawning at last. I played the next day over and over picturing me, Angus and *the* wire. What I couldn't picture was a time when I would need Divine Intervention more. I dreaded today and yet I had never been more relieved to see the light of day. The plan called for Aunt Nona to be out of the house at Bible study, and Officer McShane would be inside the undercover van with the other officers and the recording equipment. I had been coached on phrases and words to use. If Angus lived up to his usual antics, he would spout off with little prompting from me. He liked to run the show, run his mouth, and brag about his sordid plans. He wore his depravity like a banner, perfected over a lifetime. No doubt he got off seeing how foul his impression intimidated me. To bolster my imaginary assurance, I suspected he had no hope of rehabilitation and by his behavior pleaded to be caught and put out of his misery.

I heard Aunt Nona crying as I entered her room. "Oh, Aunt Nona. Try not to worry. We'll be fine and finally put an end to this nightmare. It's all coming together with just this final detail and Officer McShane is the best. There'll be undercover officers outside, so please don't worry. Go be with your friends at the church, and remember we must do this for our safety and for others. It's not right to let this monster control our lives and hurt anyone else. He has caused the last heartache and anguish he'll ever cause us in his pitiful life. We have to stop him or he'll continue to hurt others. It'll all be over when you get back home."

Even though I understood her concern, one thing I did not need right now was distraction. I tried my best to reassure her. Life had taken an ugly turn for us, and now we had to fight back. It's rare to have guaranteed solutions without risk, and this was not one of those times. I had a handle on my guilt until now but seeing her anguish proved more than I could manage. Useless and worthless as 'if only' is, the worn-out phrase continued to pulsate in my brain. The phrase endured with one redeeming quality, a hollow and futile reminder of yet another one of my mistakes. From small child to adult, I retreated to 'if only' too many times to count. There could be nothing positive wishing we weren't in this dilemma. I knew only too well living in fantasyland offers no escape or remedy from problems.

She got up out of her chair and hugged me tightly. "Please, Valentine, be careful. Are you sure you're up to doing this?"

"I've never been more positive of anything in my entire life. Now stop worrying. I'm ready to get this ugly, evil man put away and get our lives back!"

She managed a faint smile and then slowly got into the Caddy and backed down the driveway. I spied the undercover van across the street. At eight o'clock, she backed the Caddy out and started down the street. The undercover van marked A-Z Air Conditioning and Heating parked across the street. The recorder and microphone had been tested and so far, so good. Angus customarily did another neighbor's yard several streets away and then ours. He should be here at 10:00 or even 10:30. Officer McShane and I took advantage of the time to go over our plan step by step and to test the equipment. Everything was ready.

I heard Angus' truck at 10:15. I waited until he unloaded the mower and some of his tools. Then I saw the newspaper still on the sidewalk as intended. I walked out about to bend over as he started up the sidewalk to approach me--our first stroke of good luck. I did not have to go to him. Minimizing risks was a priority and making an advance toward him would be unnatural and suspicious. I tried to be my usual sassy self, prepared for his suggestive remarks. I was nervous and felt myself noticeably shaking. Would he see or suspect the wire? Did I look or act different? I didn't want to be conspicuous and arouse Angus' suspicion. He wasn't stupid. My choice of blouses had been major with the wrong selection disastrous. I decided on slightly suggestive but one that safely concealed the wire. Too late but I doubted I had made the smartest choice.

"Well, aren't you supposed to be at work, Miss Tight Ass?" His brown smile and crinkly eyes narrowed to a brown slit had already taken inventory of my turquoise pedal pushers. "I saw your aunt's car leave a while ago and right on schedule. Set my watch by her comings and goings. Good old Bible study again today. Too bad won't do her any good. She'll need more than Bible verses to help her when I get through with her. She's not long for the world, old and weak like she is. She's got a bad heart, eh? Good chance it's her time especially since she's old and in the way. I should give more consideration to getting rid of her. She's probably got some money, but right now I need to get you and soon."

He watches our every move! Realizing we were microbes under his microscope made my skin crawl. Terrified but intent on what had to be done, I struggled to keep my composure. What I needed to do was claw his eyes out. My nails dug into my hands. What nerve! I cautioned myself. *"Keep your cool, missy. Let him torment to his heart's content."*

"I'm going in at noon today. I'm so disappointed. You don't you have my schedule memorized by now?"

"Don't get smart. I've been saving up for you and nothing's going to stop me. If you're smart, you'll keep your mouth shut. The harder you fight, the harder it gets. Right after I get those damn pricks off my ass. That friend of yours thinks she's so clever; she could be next on my list. Trust me. But you, little girl, I'm just about to get you where I want you. You'll beg me, one way or the other." He paused. "And I know you know what I mean. You're couldn't be that dumb."

"I guess I made a big mistake. If I had listened to you, I would still have my favorite heart necklace. Do you still have it? Do you think I can get it back?"

He reached in his pocket and pulled out the gold prize. "You mean this little trinket? I'd like to see you beg. We'll see how I feel and how convincing you are." He gazed closely down at my unbuttoned blouse and the wire that had popped out. I tried to back out of his reach but too late. I had to keep my wits about me now. Everyone depended on me; lives were on the line.

"So you're playing that game! And I thought you were smarter than that, missy." He jerked me toward him and I could feel his hardness. He fumbled in his back pocket and rammed a small gun in my back. I felt nauseous and faint as my knees gave way. Limp and weak, I gave in. He grabbed me around the neck, dragging and choking me. I faded into waves of blackness struggling for air and losing my vision. I had to make my move; I was about to pass out. Somehow I had to hold on. Keep breathing. Stay strong. Valentine, you can outlast him. I detached from the action. I was watching a slideshow as a blur and nonstop, split second, then in slow motion.

"I'll pull this trigger bitch. I have nothing to lose. Just try me."

He opened the door to his truck and tried to push me in and shoved the gun sharply into my ribs. In an instant, I spied the undercover officer across the street. I timed and aimed my kick perfectly and violently. I was not going anywhere with this psycho. He bent over, distracted, dazed and hurting. At the moment of perfect opportunity, Officer McShane in one motion burst out of the van directly in back of Angus' truck using it for cover. As he yelled for Angus to put down the gun, Angus turned and fired. It was too late. Officer McShane had shot him dead center. Angus' gun hit the curb as it fired the one errant shot. The undercover officer came around the front of the truck gun drawn. I lay crumpled in a heap on the sidewalk just as Aunt Nona's car appeared up the street.

The onslaught began. Sirens and flashing lights of screeching squad cars sped onto our street, and a blanket of blue uniformed police officers covered the yard. Doors opened and neighbors flooded into their yards and onto the sidewalks. Two ambulances roared to a stop and attendants loaded Angus' limp, lifeless body. I helped Aunt Nona into the house. Officers outside began their inquiries and investigation as they marked off the area with yellow tape. Aunt Nona and I sat in stunned silence. I kept my explanation short preferring to wait for Officer McShane and the investigators. The fewer times I had to recount these details the better. The hot water had scarcely hit the tea when the police appeared in the kitchen. They took my statement, asked their questions, and told me to come downtown to the police station. The officers left to canvass the neighborhood for witnesses and additional information. Officer McShane met the press answering their questions. His interview would appear on the local evening news.

The blur of the day gave way to hysteria and tremendous fatigue, verging on collapse. In contrast, Aunt Nona became quiet and composed and began comforting me. Disjointed images playing repeatedly stuck my brain on overload. Physically drained and full of regret, I felt barren, empty and used up. We sat in the comfort of the kitchen quietly trying to console each other. The less said now the better. The force and ugliness of the day stunned and subdued, too much for us to manage. The remnants of violence, death, and destruction left us in its wake. We sat silent in the eerie quiet staring into space. I suggested

Aunt Nona lie down and she agreed. She asked for one of her sleeping pills and some warm milk. Thank God it was over. What a waste. All this horror, destruction, and death for what? Good versus evil? I sensed Angus in his desperation and wantonness willed this day as the one for his demise. Perhaps I attempted to come up with a rational reason to make amends since he was dead; he had pursued us knowing he couldn't get away with it. Guilt didn't consume me, but relief didn't either. A human being had been killed. Who was I to pronounce judgment? We did what we had to do. My eyes closed, my body gave in to exhaustion.

∞

CHAPTER 23
AFTERSHOCK

My trip to the police station was uneventful except it was *my* trip to the police station. A police woman escorted me to a room and left me there to sit for what seemed hours. I carefully surveyed whether I was being watched as I waited. No nervous twitches or shifting in my chair. I had nothing to hide and much to tell. Then why did I feel guilty and self-conscious? The end to a nightmare had come, long overdue. Approximately fifteen minutes later, two officers entered the room for a full interview to complete their report. I explained my story with infinite detail starting with the day as a nine-year-old on my way home through an unfamiliar neighborhood. The grimy details never came easy, but I had no choice but to give a full accounting of that awful day. I continued to Angus' present-day threats, lewdness, and vulgar suggestions and his coarse behavior uninvited and terrifying. I explained he had hunted me down and watched me and my family and my friends. He stalked our every move, memorized our schedules, and knew our whereabouts. I described the gold locket with Mother's picture I had lost that day in the struggle and traced it back to the day my aunt had given it to me after Mother's death. I explained in detail how he had taken the necklace from his pocket and flashed it in front of my face along with his comments of what he might do to me with no guarantee he would return my necklace. I recounted the long weeks I lived in terror for my Aunt Nona's safety and mine and his haunting threats; he had no problem hurting or killing her if I called the police. I detailed his following Jessica and her return to my house petrified with fear.

On the way home, I vowed not to allow this tragedy to overshadow what time remained for my aunt and me. I recognized the heavy toll the past weeks had taken. I couldn't undo the past. As characteristic of our mistakes, my vision cleared to a perfect 20/20 about what I *should* have done. Come to an understanding, Valentine, of your weaknesses caused by your shortsightedness. Yes, I was a child but my instincts were clear. I chose to ignore the voice inside my head, my conscience, whatever you want to call it, and allowed fear to control me and make my decision. Primarily, I was concerned about me if I were blamed for the problem, not the unnecessary suffering of my aunt. And now look at the result-- her distress is a thousand times worse. I could not have predicted the outcome if I had blown the whistle on the old man, but it would have been preferable to where we were today. That said, the way out was to forge ahead. Somehow I must cope with my guilt. I believed in my aunt's strength and sheer fortitude and in my resilience and tenacity. I had grappled with suffocating dark roots of evil believing I would rise above its force. Abusers are the same no matter the face or the name, good-looking and physically appealing or dirty and revolting. They're all gutless bullies who thrive on controlling, intimidating and keeping us in the ditch with them. However difficult and uncomfortable, evil both disguised and apparent, whether stranger, friend, or family begs to be revealed and stopped.

Aunt Nona was waiting and wondering. "How did it all go, Valentine? I've never prayed harder in my life with you having to go through all this over and over. I just hope since it's over, you can put this ugliness out of your mind. I'm so sorry you've had to carry this load for so many years."

"Please don't worry, Aunt Nona. Everything necessary to be done is over and I'm relieved. He has made our lives a living Hell. But now we get to close the chapter. It's hard to let go of the images but they'll fade with time. I've been wrong to keep this secret from you. Look at what I've caused. I'm so sorry. Can you forgive me?"

"There's nothing to forgive, my sweetness. You carried the weight because you cared about me and didn't want to cause me concern. I want you to think about it this way, the way I do. You were selfless and loving in your decision and you were a child. How could you have known how evil works? I love you for being unselfish and trying to be grown and take care of me. You wanted to protect me so don't you give it one more thought. We need time but we'll recover. Your old auntie is a tough bird and you're no pushover either. Notice I didn't say 'pansy' because pansies are tough in their way. What other flower blooms in the dead of winter?" She was consoling me as always. She put her arm around my shoulder and gave me a squeeze of reassurance. Her gentleness soothed a ravaged spirit.

"Jessica called while you were at the police station. She was checking in, worried about you. Bless her; she's such a good friend. I'm thankful we have her and Officer McShane in our lives."

"We're so lucky to have them and I can't be without her. She's come to my rescue so often it's scary like she's on call 24-7. You and Jess are Godsends, Aunt Nona. Kind of pitiful to require all these keepers."

"And you mine. We are all together in this life and need our loved ones to get through it. Can I get you anything? Are you hungry? I have leftover roast beef."

"Thanks, but what I honestly need is rest. If you don't mind, I think I'll turn in. You should get to bed, too."

I kissed her on the cheek. "Good night, sweetie." She smoothed my hair. "We are blessed. God has watched over us through another dark day."

I heard a thud in the middle of the night and awoke with a start. Aunt Nona. I rushed into her room. She lay on the floor gasping. I called 911 and then called her doctor to meet us at the hospital. The ambulance and EMTs arrived in twelve minutes and started resuscitation. The oxygen was flowing, and the IV hooked up to her arm. I searched her face now gray as stone for the slightest tinge of familiar rose pink or any sign she would be okay. As the ambulance sped along the dark streets in the middle of the early dawn, I tried to be encouraged despite the ominous. The trip to the hospital took fifteen minutes but seemed more like an eternity. As they checked her in through Emergency, I tried to explain her heart condition and frantically searched my brain for names of her medications. Why didn't I have the presence of mind to bring them? The glare of the posted rules for ICU surely didn't apply to me. Family members were directed to wait in the waiting room and visit at scheduled times for fifteen minutes. She was in triage. I looked at the giant black clock which glared back, 3:30.

At four o'clock, I returned to the desk to inquire and was told there was no change. At four-thirty, still no change. At five o'clock, an emergency room physician emerged and called my name. He came and sat down beside me. My aunt had suffered a myocardial infarction or heart attack. She was heavily medicated and on a breathing machine, but I could go in for a few minutes to see her. I could make no sense of any of it and asked how severe the attack was. Dr. Collins said her heart could not support her breathing, and she would be moved to intensive care.

I was directed to take the elevator to the third floor and robotically followed the signs. I stopped at a visitor registration desk and was taken into ICU. There were white curtains on both sides of the room separating the beds of patients with the nurse's station in the center. The nurse pulled back the curtain on the right side, fourth bed from the large double steel door. I tried to take a deep breath, but I couldn't fill my lungs. She was hooked to IV's and several machines including a ventilator. Tears ran hot down my cheeks and my heart pounded. "Can she hear me?"

The nurse motioned for me to come to her bedside. I spoke softly and gently touched her left hand. "Aunt Nona, I'm right here. You're in the hospital and they're taking good care of you. Do you need anything?" I knew she couldn't answer, but I stood there stunned and speechless grasping for what to say. I was not in control of *anything* now. I was helpless. But I had done this to her. Precisely what I envisioned happening was happening. My safe, predictable world of brightness and hope had collapsed once more. What was the point of building a life destined to have it fall in? *Humans with our overblown self-importance are tiny, deluded creatures scampering about without a clue.*

Her eyelids moved, and the nurse motioned for me to sit in the small black straight chair next to the bed. I tried to take inventory of what was happening. Beyond my capability, I decided to focus on my aunt. She seemed invisible--a small background of a figure in a blanket of white on a cold gray metal hospital bed. Black and gray wires and clear plastic hoses and medical paraphernalia took over the room. The smell of antiseptic overpowered. I tried to concentrate on comforting her but was she even aware? How sad my preoccupation with guilt seemed my overpowering emotion in the midst of crisis. I couldn't resolve the image of damage I had caused: how could someone who loves another have the capacity to do such terrible destruction? Crushed by the weight of guilt beyond my capacity to endure, I felt suicidal. *Dangerous, life-threatening character flaw had reared its ugly head again.* Faced with a situation beyond my control, I refused to call for help. Now the perilous consequences exposed my lack of trust in others and my arrogance.

The nurse motioned for me to come into the outer area. "I know you want to be with her and it will be good for her. The posted schedule outside ICU is for visitors. We limit the visits to about fifteen minutes every few hours until she is stronger, but you can be with her as much as you like. And even when you are not here, you can phone and check on her. We understand you want to be with her as much as you can."

"How long will she be on the ventilator? Is she conscious?"

"The doctor will go over her condition and the tests that need to be done. It's important to keep her comfortable, so she's medicated. She will be monitored and her condition upgraded as appropriate."

"Thank you. I'm so worried about her and I'm not sure what to do. I guess all I can do is wait and pray." The nurse put her arm around me and encouraged me to call someone close to be with me.

I didn't know who to call except for Jessica. We were a family of two with no one to call. We were not connected to our extended family. I should wait to call Jess. After our ordeal, it was too early. Hopefully, if I waited, I would have an update on Aunt Nona. Then I remembered Jessica was leaving for New York in a couple of days. She'll insist on postponing her trip but I won't have it. The timing might not be the best, but this could be her only opportunity to get her modeling career off the ground.

I spied the waiting room and poured myself a cup of coffee. It tasted good and warmed me. I found an empty chair and saw countless family members waiting for news of their loved ones. Pillows and blankets, half-empty coffee cups, soda cans, snack crackers, and candy wrappers littered the area. Some slept on the sofas or in chairs. Others, bleary-eyed from worry and lost sleep and traumatized, still attempted, if somewhat robotically, to function. Others tried to comfort each other whether family or stranger. The waiting room served as an emergency camping ground for those longing to be as close as possible to their loved one. Strangers in strange surroundings bonded by distress. *Life and death*. ICU could be the last stopover. The survival of our loved one balanced in healing hands while we functioned in disbelief and helplessness and faced the agony of the unknown.

∞

Chapter 24
Purgatory

Her voice startled me. I tried to gather my thoughts. I had fallen asleep and struggled against the fuzziness of my confusion. "Oh, Val, I'm sorry to awaken you."

I had never been more relieved and grateful to see anyone. "Thank you for coming, Jess. I hated to call this early, but I wanted to catch you before you left for work."

"Is there any change? Have you talked to the doctor again?"

"The nurse said I should get an update later this morning. She seems the same; I've been in to see her several times. Of course, I'm going by how she looks. She's hooked to so many machines I can't tell much. But she hasn't responded."

"I bet you haven't had a bite to eat. What if I go downstairs and get you something? I passed the cafeteria on the way here. What can I do? Please eat something."

"I don't have much appetite, and I can't go anywhere right now."

"I'll go get you anything you want. What do you think you might like?"

"Oh, Jess, I don't know. How thoughtful of you. Whatever you bring will be fine. Thanks."

In a few minutes, she returned with a sandwich and milk. I stuffed down a few bites to be polite. We sat in silence. "Val, I've got to leave but if there is anything you need, just call. Promise me. If I can, I'll drop by tonight."

She hugged me teary-eyed and sad. There was nothing she could do. She hurt for me. "Remember, we love you, Val. You're not alone."

The doctor came to the waiting room about an hour later and led me into a small conference room. He was somber and matter of fact. The heart attack had done severe damage. She was on life support. The prognosis was not favorable, but he insisted more tests were needed to assess the damage. "The next forty-eight hours are critical. We don't have a lot of answers at this point so we'll wait and see how she responds to treatment. I'm sorry I don't have better news, but we need to give her time to respond."

The waiting room of ICU was home for five days. I did return to Morningstar to clean up and get fresh clothes and to check on things. I saw Jess and her dad briefly when they stopped by on their way to New York. They would be gone a week. Jess argued they could postpone, but I knew that was not an option. If she canceled her interviews with the modeling agency, the likelihood she could get another interview, nil. I insisted she go; she had waited a long time for this opportunity, and I wouldn't risk her missing out on a career chance of a lifetime. The pastor and several ladies from the church came by to give their support and offer their help. Aunt Nona occasionally opened her eyes not in recognition but rather with a glazed over, wild-eyed terrifying stare. I could not see any improvement; she appeared to me the same as the night of her attack. The doctor had not committed to a prognosis. I guessed at why.

The cruelty of this situation is no control and being forced to accept the helplessness of you and your loved one. Others in the waiting room familiar with my predicament offered their encouragement having gone through the waiting and not knowing. There were fleeting moments when I allowed myself to be mildly optimistic. The long days and nights took their toll as her condition remained unchanged. Hopeless, empty, and alone, Aunt Nona was all I had. No matter how I tried to rationalize the past few weeks, the wildfire of guilt and regret raged. The rippling effects of my decision to keep the dark secret continued to be crippling and catastrophic. Cruel but apparent, the medical probability persisted. Odds were against her coming out of this.

The tenth day, the doctor told me what I suspected. The tests showed no brain activity, and medical probabilities of recovery were against her. Before going home, I spoke to her softly and gently to tell her I was by her side, how much I loved her, and prayed for the day she felt better so I could take her home. I touched her loving hand that had cared for me and loved me all these years. These were beautiful, working hands that never stopped doing good things and helping others. As I bent down to kiss her open space of cheek not covered by the plastic of the machine that breathed for her, the harshness of the sterile and the clinical greeted me. No matter how intensely I longed and prayed for the familiar, there was no warmth, no emotion, no reaction, or response. *All taken for granted without a thought until now, too late.* Ominous signs pointed to more crushing bleakness. I stood in the shadow of life and death. The clinical description separating the two blurred--both complicated and catastrophic. Decisions had to be made, and no one to make them but me. Death watch did not come close to describing this prolonged agony.

I spent another sleepless night but at least I had the comfort of my bed. I concentrated on thinking clearly and weighing the consequences of my options. I was scheduled to meet with the doctors this morning and get a full report and their recommendations. I dressed in comfortable clothing fitting for the day ahead. My Aunt Nona wouldn't have objected. She taught me to be practical and comfortable. I fell into the nearest chair with head spinning. I started to cry on the verge of hysteria; I had no desire to control my sadness. I tried desperately to let go, but when chained to restraint, release wasn't an option. Keeping my wits and making clear-headed decisions remained my role and mine alone. Traumatized and exhausted, I closed my eyes to pray. I was not a stranger to heartache, but in my 20 odd years, losing my Aunt Nona headed the list as inconceivably heart-breaking.

I had closed the door to her bedroom several days ago to ease the pain but now it looked formidable, a barricade. I opened the door, and the light from her windows poured in through the delicate white Priscilla tieback curtains she loved. I opened the windows, and the breeze pushed the fresh air through the screens like a powerful fan. There is something ethereal about fresh air and sunshine showering the room with clean brightness. I sat on the edge of her bed thinking of all the times she had comforted me, encouraged me, supported me, scolded me and allowed me to make mistakes. She was the whole package of what I needed whenever I needed it whether a pat on the back or a gentle subliminal kick in the rear end. Her instincts of whatever was required were right on. I had always credited her teaching experience for much of her expertise in taking care of me, but now I realize it was much more. She had an innate quality of allowing the individual to blossom and grow with gentle direction and persuasion. Her patience allowed me time to grow up and develop my value system. She had been my guide through the times of my life, good and not so good. When I lost my mother, I did not foresee my life would amount to much or account for much. I knew back then my Aunt Nona was a good person. I did not see my life beyond mediocrity and didn't see any way I could follow in her footsteps. Never in my wildest dreams did I envision the complex and intricate nature of a relationship this strong and sustaining. She nurtured and loved me, comforted and supported me, instilled confidence and belief, and provided the environment for me to blossom and prepare me to take on the world. I remember her blushing as she described 'coping ammo' aka strength and resilience of character. In her grand style of excellence or bust, she held up her end of the bargain with flying colors. Now it was my turn.

The telephone rang insistent and irritating. I ran to the phone to stop the noise, but I held my breath it might be the hospital. Relieved, I heard Jess' voice.

"Hi, Val. How are you? I just had to call; I'm concerned about you and wondering if Aunt Nona is any better?"

"Oh, Jess. I planned to call you so thanks for checking in. I'm getting ready to leave for the hospital. The news is not great this morning. I talked to the doctor last night. He confirmed what I suspected. The medical tests and opinion of the doctors is that she will not regain consciousness. The brain scan showed no activity. I haven't been given any positive reason she can recover." I strangled on the words. "There's no hope, Jess."

Silence except for Jess softly sobbing on the other end of the line. "I should be there with you. It's wrong for me to be in New York now. What can I do?"

"I'm sorry to say, Jess, there's nothing any of us can do. I came home last night to get rest. I have some decisions to make, about Aunt Nona."

"Val, we're coming home. I've already had a couple of interviews so whatever will be, will be. My place is with you and Dad agrees. We've already changed our flight. We'll be back tonight."

I cried out loud with relief and couldn't speak. I had to compose myself. She's a thousand miles away, and nothing could be gained by focusing that she couldn't comfort me in person. Shape up, Valentine. Save your hysteria for private moments to fall apart. Think about someone besides yourself.

"Thank you so much, Jess. I won't do anything until you and your dad get here. There is no hurry to do anything now. Have a safe trip and I love you, Jess."

"I love you, too, Val, and we'll be home soon. Hold tight, sweetie. You're not alone."

I drove to the hospital on autopilot. The turns, stop and go of the other cars, streets, houses and buildings blurred past me in a daze. I could visualize Aunt Nona sitting beside me smiling and pointing to various points of interest along our way or even flowers she could name without hesitation. She'd explain the origin, scientific name, and a myriad of details I might or might not understand. She knew the history of our town intimately and could tell you what house or building stood before the newest addition and what family lived where when. She could name names--the founders, the mayors, the respected citizens who carved out this place and kept it flourishing. She laughed that she had outlasted most of the historic buildings and could be on the National Register herself.

The parking garage appeared out of nowhere. I stopped as the attendant gave me a ticket and inched along in the dark cavern packed with parked cars. I made a beeline seeing tail lights as I spied a car backing out. This trip to the hospital could be my last. I sat frozen in place. She loved our outings in the old Caddy even more now since I could chauffeur her. So many happy years we shared. I dabbed the unending flow of tears and dumped all the damp tissues onto the floorboard. What an insult to litter this old car, but forgivable today. I'd attend to the tissues later, no disrespect intended, Aunt Nona. Everything I seemed to do or think now reflected back to her and her guiding hand.

I rode the elevator to the third floor and pushed the button to enter through the giant steel doors to make my way to Aunt Nona's bed in ICU. I stopped at the nurses' station to check in; there had been no change. She looked peaceful. I took her hand in mine and smoothed her shining silver hair as she had done to mine all those times in consolation. Our roles had reversed in an abrupt and alarming way. I had expected the process as a natural and gradual one as I matured and as she became older and more fragile. I did not foresee the shock of sudden agonizing heartbreak then watching her linger with my hand on the plug as executioner. What a horrific thought! I sat silently praying for her and for the strength and wisdom to continue life's journey without her. Her nurse came in. Her doctors were waiting. Each time I had to leave her became more and more difficult as I began to foresee her as a *memory*. I arose from the same black chair and took inventory of the finality of this room. Why? I wanted to forget the details of Aunt Nona's final days here, and yet I hoped by locking in the present sometime later I could understand these dark days.

The conference table felt too large and imposing for this discussion or consultation. I'm not certain what to call it. I had in hand auntie's legal documents--Living Will, medical, and legal power of attorney. I hoped to have this conversation in a small, intimate setting but then I wasn't in charge. I took my appointed seat at the side of the mahogany table in the midst of white jackets. The doctor in charge of her case sat at the head of the table. I spied the box of tissues at hand and within easy reach. I hoped I could stay calm and composed. This has to be the most horrifying and cruel decision a human has to make in our modern society. The medical miracles and technology are without question saving lives and extending lifetimes but not without downsides and this is the grand prize winner. The doctors agreed. The MRI and other brain tests showed no activity. Her heart and its arteries were severely damaged and not capable of functioning on its own. Her high blood pressure and the probability she could suffer a stroke at any time added to her problems. The only good news, medication kept her comfortable. Again, the doctors agreed she was not aware and not in pain. Although it's folly not to accept their assessment, I can't help but question how they know.

The decision facing me has to be based on medical opinion and probability. She could remain on life support, but my Aunt Nona cannot recover. The other school of thought is, not even the doctors can say for certain and there have been cases where patients have recovered. Her condition would continue to deteriorate. Dr. Collins assured me my decision does not have to be made right away; whenever I am ready. I asked my lingering questions whether any other treatment was possible. Then I made sure to express my appreciation to those who cared for her. Without question, she had received state-of-the-art medical care but without a miracle cure, she would not recover. The nurses and doctors had my enduring gratitude. I had witnessed the highest dedication to their calling and to their patients. My heart went out to them. Their training prepares them for the care and treatment of patients, saving lives. But in cases like my Aunt Nona, even more is required of them to cope with being unable to heal or help a patient recover. Ill-prepared and merely called by default because I had the deepest love and commitment for Aunt Nona, I had to carry out this horrendous act. But then, I am not alone. Thousands of us face such a dark hour without warning, preparation, or relief.

I returned to ICU to speak to her nurses. Each time I asked, I was told there had been no change or sign of improvement. I could see the pain the caretakers feel when a patient is in Aunt Nona's condition. The doctors, the nurses, the aides--all medically trained to save lives and to do their utmost to ensure the patient recovers--must carry the failure and frustration. My heart was heavy for all of us. I hugged them and tried to express my feeble appreciation for their meticulous twenty-four-hour care each day. *Earth angels.*

∞

CHAPTER 25
GOING HOME

I telephoned Pastor Leland to update him on Aunt Nona. It was important he know I was waiting for Jessica and her dad to arrive from New York so they could join me at the hospital the next day. I mentioned I had not made a final decision. I needed his guidance and asked him to meet me at the hospital. Aunt Nona loved and respected Leland. She valued the friendship of her church family, and she would have wanted them near. Many of the members called and came to the hospital offering their prayers and support. They sustained and comforted me I wasn't alone. There is no stronger connection to your loved one than those who loved and cared for them. Over and over, I heard the sweet refrain of how loved my Aunt Nona was along with stories of her kindness and generosity. I was honored and humbled to be her family and would forever be reminded to make her proud.

The youngest pastor in the history of the First Baptist Church was also the most loved. My aunt adored him. He spoke softly and gently with the demeanor of someone you could believe and believe in. He shared his challenges and pitfalls; his admissions affirmed he was one of us. You knew he cared about your wellbeing as well as saving your soul. Raised by his grandmother in Louisiana to be well-versed in the scriptures and from a lifetime of study, his sermons were riveting and without restraint. He took pride in making the congregation uncomfortable, remorseful, and openly accountable. He did not speak from an elevated stature even at the pulpit; there were no doubts he walked with us as a sinner. These were not feel-good messages designed to make you reflect on how well you were doing. Rejoicing was reserved for being thankful for a loving Heavenly Father who always forgives us. As he prayed with me, I felt the calm. Her life had been one of preparation for this time and the Final Judgment. She was going Home to be with her Lord. I prayed for peace with my decision.

I met with hospice and Chaplain Chamberlain at the hospital several times to guide me through the process of letting go. Now I needed and demanded solace. The medical experts and the people who loved Aunt Nona had given me counsel. No one was in my position and no one carried the weight of my decision. My aunt made her wishes clear. I counted on my heart to tell me the time. No one could save me from this oppressive decision or take over or share the responsibility. I would carry the decision and its consequences for the rest of my days.

Jess and her dad arrived late in the afternoon. They had left New York after midnight and got into town in the wee hours, so they had been up all night and rested very little this morning. They both wanted to see Aunt Nona one final time. They understood my need for solitude with the decision weighing heavy, so I'd decided to go to my sanctuary on Morningstar tonight. They were my family now, and I'd share my decision when I'd made it. I could tell Jessica was uneasy, and I wondered why.

"Jess, I can tell something is bothering you. What is it?"

Her blue eyes sparkled through her tears. "Oh,Val. I'm not sure what to do about this, but there's something I have to tell you. It's hard for me to bother you, but I don't think it's right to ignore his request and pretend it's not worth considering. Rowan--"

"Stop there, Jess. I understand you're trying to do a good deed. But there's no need, okay? He can take care of himself, whatever the problem."

Jessica continued undaunted. "Anyway, as I was saying, Rowan is home this summer for a week or so and called me this morning. He's concerned about you. He asked if he could come by the hospital. Before you say no, please think about it. He's worried and concerned and wants to be with you. He cares about you."

I wondered what he could be thinking. And Jess, too. As far as I was concerned, I expected him to bring me more of what I did not need. Stress. Some good news in this, I suppose, he had a conscience after all. Jessica looked at me with pleading eyes. She wanted me to say yes. Sometimes I chose to ignore her good sense when it was against my inclinations. She had a point. I honestly didn't need the distraction and felt he would be an imposition. Rowan had shown his true colors about my Aunt Nona; I could not forget his selfishness. But to appease Jess and to have one less dark cloud hanging over me, I would consider her plea. Saying no to Jess could be difficult, no impossible.

"Thanks, Jessica. I appreciate what you're trying to do. But I'm not sure Rowan and I have any unfinished business. I'll sleep on it."

She and her dad hugged and kissed me good-by. "We all make mistakes, Val. Give him the benefit of the doubt. It's tearing him apart that he can't shoulder some of your sadness." Jessica blew me a kiss and disappeared down the hall.

The thought lingered I had the upper hand--pride without substance. In control of what? We weren't in a relationship and here I was beating my chest--he was at my mercy. Do my actions show the person I am or strive to be? I'm taking baby steps in this process but I need to send the true message. I should take the high road. It all seemed trivial and petty. In the midst of hell, I had to deal with baby Rowan.

Maybe I wanted to hear his voice, but for certain I would not call him. If he wanted to talk to me, he had my number. He could have called me if he wanted to see me, but he called Jess instead. But then again, so did I. She was definitely our mediator. When I called her, I told her the same thing; if he wanted to talk to me, he knew my number and should call me, not Jess.

He called later that day. I surprised myself with my indifference, but being cut to the bone has that effect. "Hi Val. I have a lot to say to you, and my timing is way off, as usual. I hoped we could get together but realize it may not happen. I'm so sorry about your Aunt Nona. Is there anything I can do? I feel so bad about what you're going through. It's hard to talk about; I've been such a rat fink."

I tried to be accepting of his condolence, although questioning his sincerity and ignored his attempt at self-deprecation. "Thanks, Rowan, I appreciate your concern. It's been hard, trust me. How are you?"

"Oh, good, everything's good. School and baseball, going according to plan. I'll be on the baseball field much of the summer and taking some classes. Keeping up my grades best I can. Wish things were good between us."

"Rowan, listen. There's no need to be sorry. Our priorities were different, and we've gone our separate ways which happens. I'm glad you're doing well. I wondered if you liked Stanford."

What a lie; I could have cared less and never gave a thought to him and Stanford. I had more important matters to think about way off his radar, but maybe he appreciated I could make brainless conversation. What else did I expect? The harshness of dealing with life or death and loss made me bitter and cynical. The outside world continued to turn without as much as a hiccup--a stinging slap in the face. Life doesn't stop or even slow its turning. *Reassuring.* Our abject insignificance didn't change even though dealing with terminal illness and death.

Rowan ignored or more likely failed to notice my detachment and continued with his update. "Oh, Val, you'd love it. Stanford is a top-notch school, and I love the Bay area. There's so much to see and do and the weather is great. Not sure I can come back to Texas. Will have to see what happens. Wish you'd consider coming out here."

The conversation drifted becoming mundane and effortless. I'm making it way too easy for him to get back into my good graces. He should have to work for my forgiveness. He had stabbed me through the heart and left me in the coldness of the dark night while he licked his tiny, imaginary wounds and ran home to mommy. What makes him think I'm the least bit interested in coming to San Francisco? What world is he in?

"Listen, Rowan, it's been good catching up but I've got to get going. I need to get to the hospital. I hope you enjoy your time in town."

"Val, don't cut me off. Can't we get together some time in the next day or two for coffee or a bite to eat? I need to see you."

I was tired, and he made me even more weary trying to figure out what he wanted from me and why he found it necessary to stir up the waters. He might have been distraught, but he hid it well. I faced a decision of horror which would haunt me until my dying breath, while he extolled the virtues of the City by the Bay. Didn't that sum up our relationship?

"I could come by the hospital. Don't they have a cafeteria or coffee shop where we can get a bite?"

"Yes, Rowan, they do. Tell you what; meet me there in an hour. If I'm not in the cafeteria when you get there, I'll be down as soon as I can." *Fat chance he'll show.* But at least I won't be inconvenienced. My place is at the hospital with or without him.

"Thanks, Val. See you there."

I changed clothes. I had to look my best, not bedraggled and pitiful in case he showed. I washed my hair that morning, and my skin and eyes glowed considering what I had been through in the past few weeks. I doubted he even knew about Angus.

No matter how many times I entered, I always took a deep breath when faced with those massive double doors of ICU leading to the taciturn world of terminal illness. I wanted to turn and run. Aunt Nona lay there in repose with her lifeblood no longer her own; hooked to machines keeping her *alive*. I held her precious hand in mine and spoke to her softly and gently in my usual manner. I hoped I reassured and comforted her. I pretended she could hear me. I had to. How else to keep up this nightmarish masquerade? I looked at my watch. It had been nearly two hours since I spoke to Rowan. He'd had ample time to get here, and the cafeteria closed soon. I should go downstairs or I could stand him up. Not a productive way to begin our meeting. I could have cared less. All I wanted was to be with Aunt Nona in quiet peace, to remember and reflect on her goodness, and to keep her with me for a few more precious hours. I could hear her voice. Valentine, at least have a positive attitude.

The ride in the elevator was too short. I was unsure how to approach Rowan. I peered into the entrance of the cafeteria scanning the tables. Did I want to see him or prefer not to see him there? Then I saw him get up and come over to me.

"Hi Val. It's so good to see you. I've missed you." He took me by the waist to his table. "Not sure what you wanted, but I got you coffee. Do you want anything to eat?"

"No, I'm not really hungry." He looked wonderful, just as I remembered.

"I can't stay long, Rowan. I'm losing Aunt Nona. What is it you wanted to say?"

He sat in stunned silence at my abruptness. He didn't like being on the spot but too bad. Let's get on with it. Hearing what he had to say took most of my benevolence. I had no patience or time for anything but Aunt Nona. He was keeping me from my last moments with her. For the first time, I allowed my hurt feelings to surface. His cruel dismissal and rejection because he didn't get his way had left a deep scar. I questioned his motives and passion for me and wondered what he expected.

"I'm sorry, Val, for all the pain I've caused you and for the hurt and for being selfish. I ruined everything. I can't explain my reaction except when you hurt me, and all I could think of was to hurt you back. All I can say, no excuses. Can you forgive me?"

I looked in his eyes, now dark gray, for my answer. He seemed full of remorse but who can tell? Selfish people like to get their way. They're good actors. If he had an ulterior motive, then he might not be sorry. I questioned if I could wipe the slate clean. What a monstrous undertaking! I doubted he understood the enormity of what he asked of me. Didn't he realize the giant leap of faith for me to trust him?

"Rowan, I tried to understand why you lashed out. I didn't want us to be over. But months have gone by, and I haven't heard one word from you. If you were truly sorry, why haven't you told me?"

"Pride. Couldn't face it. Thought I'd get over you, didn't need you. I didn't count on the power."

"What power? I have no idea what you mean. Please don't talk in riddles. I'm tired and don't have the time, and I'm not interested in playing games."

"The power of us, you. The idea of you and me has been a part of me for so long I didn't come to grips with how hard it would be to let go of it all. I can hardly say it, it's so final, *no future for us*. I tried to forget you but it didn't happen. It's too much for me." Tears welled up, and he brushed away the wetness from his cheek.

I reached across the table and took his hand before I could restrain. Soft-hearted me, just like Aunt Nona. Now I found it necessary to comfort someone who had let me stew in my self-pity for months. Not to mention I was in agony losing my beloved aunt. What can I be thinking? He should be consoling me. Upside down, inside out craziness because he's tearing me apart. I might still turn out to be the bad guy.

"Rowan, please look at me. I understand. We all make mistakes but we shouldn't lay blame, okay? Maybe we need to accept our relationship didn't withstand the storm and go on. So don't blame yourself. It takes two, right?"

We sat in silence for a few minutes. I took a sip of my coffee. I needed to go to Aunt Nona. I hoped he and I had a clearer understanding. He shouldn't shoulder all the blame for our downfall. Our rocky relationship lacked a firm foundation from the beginning. And we were young and headstrong. The maturity and commitment wasn't there, and neither was the timing. Chemistry makes for exciting fireworks but then poof all dark. I wanted and deserved more and so did he.

"Rowan, Aunt Nona is on life support. The doctors hold no hope, so I have to make the decision of when. I need to be alone and have a clear mind with no more distractions. You can understand, but as far as you and I are concerned, I can't say what will happen. I need some time. That's about all I can say. I still have feelings for you but with reservation. For me, the trust is gone, a giant hurdle. May not be fixable. So can we leave it this way? I'm not trying to be mean or unfeeling but emotionally I'm used up. Surely you can understand how hard losing Aunt Nona is on me. She's my everything."

He kissed me on the cheek, and I wanted to believe we were back together. "Okay, Val. Thank you for seeing me and listening. Is there something I could do? Do you want me to stay with you?"

"No, I'll be fine. I appreciate your offer but it's something I have to do. It must have been hard for you coming here and your time is short in town. So thanks for coming by."

"Okay. Well, I'll let you get back to Aunt Nona. So sorry about her and that you have to go through this. I'll be in touch, Val." He kissed me briefly and held me. Our faces brushed and I could smell his freshness and the musky hue of his after shave. I felt myself surrender, so I drew away and turned to leave. He followed me through the cafeteria door and then we parted.

I returned to ICU and spent the night in the hospital chapel. When the early morning light warmed and flickered in the stained glass, I phoned Leland and returned to the black straight chair next to Aunt Nona. I spoke with the nurses to advise the doctors. With Leland by my side, I held her in my arms. Aunt Nona was disconnected at 9:22 a.m.

∞

CHAPTER 26
IN MEMORIAM

The First Baptist Church overflowed with folks from the church and town, relatives from East Texas and Louisiana, teachers, and past students. Aunt Nona had left detailed instructions for her service not because she obsessed about her funeral but precisely the opposite--to take the load off me. I had few decisions. I chose the orchid casket, her soft violet dress and the spray of her favorite pink peonies. The music and mood of the service was respectful and traditional, but I knew Aunt Nona would have objected as outlandish hoo-hah and bother. She would have preferred no service but knew that would not happen. The choir sung her two favorite songs *I Come to the Garden Alone* and *The Old Rugged Cross*. Pastor Leland's poignant message invited lost souls as his and Aunt Nona's fitting conspiracy for this final tribute. Jessica and Michael McShane sat on the pew beside me. After the service, Aunt Nona was buried beside my mother in the city cemetery. I churned on the inside but outwardly I conducted myself in rhythm and respectful as any true southern lady. It's frowned upon to lose control, so I kept a grip on my emotions. Time would come later for my return trip to the cemetery, but today I was host to a beloved congregation attesting to the legacy of Nona Emmaline Monroe.

The church served lunch after the burial. The day began with the 10:00 service, the burial, and the meal served to over one hundred guests--a long and exhausting day. I greeted and grieved, hugged and cried, shook countless hands and met strange faces with strange names as I listened to personal stories about my aunt and answered personal questions about her last days. I spoke kindly and thoughtfully to each one and thanked them all. Emotionally depleted, I remembered my upbringing and reminded myself to put my grieving on hold. This day was for all the other folks who loved my Aunt Nona, not about me, and to show my appreciation to those who supported me and loved Aunt Nona. Despite my efforts, I subconsciously searched for a sign of Rowan, hoping he would appear. He did not. I continued to be disappointed. What a show of faith if he truly wanted a relationship with me. He's seen how important Aunt Nona is; no need for this annoying echo. He didn't get it for whatever reason. His standards and mine apparently cannot be bridged. We seem beyond rehabilitation. *I need more than he is willing to give.*

I pulled the Caddy into the garage at 4:30. I sat in the car listening to the radio playing a favorite tune. I dreaded going into the house. How many times would I have to go in there before I was oblivious? Content, I sat in the comfort of the plush leather seats and bawled my eyes out. *Empty and hollow.* In surrender, I abandoned the cozy shelter of the car and the garage. On my way through the living room, I opened the door to grab the mail. On the front porch, a tall white vase reflected in glorious splendor. Its expected contents astonishingly contained no customary fillers, thrillers and spillers. There were no obligatory red dozen roses with ivy and baby's breath. Orchids in lavender and brilliant white, dazzling tropicals in yellow, orange and bright pink, and exotic greenery saturated the alcove with breathtaking color. I fumbled opening the card trying to guess who would send such an extravagant arrangement. Tears clouded the handwriting as I read the note: **Thinking of you my beautiful Valentine with my love and sympathy in remembrance of Aunt Nona. Rowan**

I struggled to lift the tall vase of flowers onto the coffee table. The entire house came alive with their beauty and fragrance. I lay on the sofa trying to breathe in the magnificent blossoms of kindness and thoughtfulness from the one person I had branded as selfish and incapable of such sentiments. I gazed longingly into the smallest detail of this amazing showpiece dissecting each tiny leaf and petal of the Cymbidium orchids and Stargazer lilies. My eyelids were heavier than my will. I awoke in the middle of the night and dragged the weight of it all--rumpled funeral clothes, used-up body and an overload of mental baggage to the bed.

I awoke with a start thinking I heard a noise from Aunt Nona's room. I rushed into the hall before I came to my senses. But I had to go into her room to ease my mind. I assured myself. I would hear and even think I see her for a time as I adjust to her being gone. Why can't I live in the moment? Projecting what may or may not happen is more than a waste of time, it's foolhardy. I put on the coffee and spied the disarray, not acceptable. The contents of auntie's safe deposit box covered the kitchen table. I poured my coffee and ambled over to the table sifting through the documents. I was not in the mood. Wasn't procrastination called for in this case? But realistically, when would a suitable time be? I had an appointment with her lawyer tomorrow morning in preparation for his filing my aunt's Will in the Probate Court so it would be helpful to be somewhat prepared. I made a list: two life insurance policies in the amount of $50,000 each, a copy of her Last Will and Testament, a key (presumably to another safe deposit box), Deed to 4112 Morningstar and another Deed to land in East Texas along with an oil and gas lease. Then there were the personal documents: my birth certificate, my adoption papers and an envelope addressed to me. The other large envelope was labeled Family Documents. I decided to wait to open the last envelope which for some reason screamed personal and confidential and in all likelihood pertained to relatives I had never met or heard of. The lawyer had the original Will and said he had already contacted the life insurance companies to make a claim for the church and for me as beneficiaries. Her generosity seemed boundless. I felt guilty to inherit anything from Aunt Nona. How could anyone so deeply in debt willingly accept more? The morning sun's rays highlighted the shimmering gold initials on the ecru paper. I touched the back of her empty chair as I felt her calm presence at the table. The warmth of her smile and strong reassurance continued to radiate in this house. Aunt Nona's spirit would forever surround me as would the images of her, her voice and laughter. No need to read the note. I knew her so well; its message would be one of encouragement. I unfolded the handwritten letter and could hear the steady resonance of her tone and diction.

NME
April 20, 1962

My dear Valentine,

No last-minute instructions or wishes, my sweet. I have left what little worldly goods I have to you and my Church. I gently remind you the well can go dry so use your resources wisely. I have no doubts that you will. You are a grown young woman now and fully competent to make your own decisions. My hope and prayer is for you to continue to flourish with the talents God has given you with a renewed commitment to inspire others. I have been blessed by our time together because you have added fulfillment to my life. Forgive me please if I have unintentionally failed you. I treasure our overpowering love, affection, and respect for each other. I hope you will remember how much I love you. Thank you for sharing your gift of spirit that has brought me sheer joy and for being the earthly light of my life.

With all my love,
Aunt Nona

∞

Chapter 27
Wrapping up the Rap Sheet

Michael McShane called the following week to say he needed to stop by on his way home from the police station. I saw his squad car out front and met him at the door.

"Valentine, sorry to load you down with more unpleasantness but figured the time was as good as any so we don't have to dig all this up later. Then you don't have to be reminded."

"No problem, come on in. I just got home from school. I've missed more classes than I can count so I've been making the rounds to my teachers to schedule makeups for all my absences and incompletes when Aunt Nona was in the hospital. Should we go into the kitchen? We can use the kitchen table."

"First thing, I want to return your necklace. You must be glad to get it back. We've got all the case information on Angus so the case is closed. I wasn't sure how much you wanted to hear but it's an eye-opener. At one time, he seemed to be a respectable citizen or everyone thought so. He taught high school history and his last name was Neely."

"Are you serious? The thought is outrageous--straight out of Ripley's Believe or Not--and scary." If there was a human I couldn't visualize as respectable, Angus would be the one. He worked too hard at being despicable.

"His troubles began in the late 1940s when he got kicked out by the school board. He attacked a student in the gymnasium after hours and the school tried to cover the whole thing up and said she lied. He destroyed her reputation (and credibility) when he paid some high school boys to lie to say she was a sleep around. It took a while to complete the investigation, but eventually the facts came out. Other high school girls came forward about their experiences with Neely and his advances. The school went through a slow and painstaking process but eventually got rid of him. She and her family hired a lawyer and kept digging for evidence until the school had no choice and agreed to fire him. The family settled the case out of court, and no charges were filed against him. Back when this happened, taking the word of a student over a respected teacher was practically unheard of. He could never get another teaching job and took a nose dive from respected to outcast and started a landscape business to make a living. He changed his name and moved over to the red brick house on Blanchard. He'd never been married but during his teaching career he stayed busy chasing high school girls. It's unthinkable he got away with what he did for as long as he did. His secret seemed safe. Kids didn't have a chance against an authority figure and were afraid to get into trouble, so they resigned themselves to putting up with his shenanigans or worse. Who would take their side? He could make trouble and life difficult for them, so the girls kept what they knew between them. He did make a name for himself all right. The girls called him 'touchy feely Neely.' They didn't have a clue how dangerous he might be. He lost everything--his teaching job, the community's respect--and got a belly full of hate for the whole deal. He stayed under the radar for a while but then got convicted for assaulting a twelve-year-old girl shortly after your incident and served several years in the penitentiary. He was a bad hombre full of anger and hate and beyond rehabilitation. You were lucky."

"I know it. I'm trying my best to forget. I remind myself when I'm down it could have turned out much worse. But my biggest regrets and the ones hardest to live with revolve around my Aunt Nona. The one person I sought to protect had to suffer the brunt of this tragedy, and I'll never forgive him. Somehow, someway I have to figure out how to live with everything or it will eat away at me. I'm focusing on school and trying to graduate in three years so I can start my teaching. In fact, I got a part-time job at the new high school. Jillian needed someone she could count on for more hours than I could give her. She's been more than patient during Aunt Nona's illness so she understood, but she had to be relieved to see me go. It's hard to run a retail business when your assistant manager is habitually absent."

"You've had a lot to deal with. You and your aunt were traumatized and victimized, Valentine. There's no need to sugar coat the situation. Listen to me. It's okay to ask for help. We all have times when we need support. So don't hesitate to contact us if you need anything. We're a phone call away, anytime."

"You've been my guardian angel, first with my mother and now this mess with Angus. I can't tell you how much I appreciate all you've done for me and Aunt Nona. I've used up more than my share of your coming to my rescue. Who would have thought all this would be on your shoulders? Again, I thank God for you and your kindness to our family and for being there for my mother. No one understands what the thin blue line means until you or someone you care about is in danger. Thank you again, Michael." Words failed to describe my feelings but sometimes it's the best you have. Michael McShane hadn't magically appeared in our lives by chance. *Destiny.*

He gathered up his paperwork and gave me a big hug. "You are so welcome, and I'm glad it worked out I was on duty. Our families and our lives are connected for the rest of our days. That's the way it should be. Call me if you need anything, Val."

"I will, Michael. Thanks for coming by."

"Oh there is one more thing. I guess you heard. Caroline Rossi has asked Jessica to help her with the modeling event for the big charity ball in October. Then she wants to take her to San Francisco and introduce her to some people in the modeling business. I appreciate her trying to help Jessica but things are moving in a direction I'm not sure I agree with. Anyway, she will tell you what's up. I'm just her old man usually the last one to know and limited to how much she wants me to know, huh? I might be slow, but at least I've learned something."

"You're her rock. She counts on you and your advice to keep her straight. She's growing up and thinks she wants to be in charge. I know the feeling. But she'll always come to you for confirmation. She looks up to you. You're her hero."

"Okay. Thanks. I appreciate the vote of confidence. I've got to get going. I'm here if you need anything. Oh, by the way, I'm not bragging but I made Captain. It's been in the works for months but my promotion finally came through."

"Congratulations. You certainly deserve it." I watched him drive away in awe how Aunt Nona and I were so fortunate in the midst of tragedy. He kept us out of harm's way during our ordeal and extended his hand in a bond of lifetime friendship. We never doubted he would always be there for us. I had wondered how he felt about Caroline's influence and her taking a major role in his daughter's life. Captain McShane didn't strike me as requiring the aid of Caroline Rossi, but apparently his daughter felt otherwise.

I gathered up the battle-scarred gold heart necklace with its knotted, broken chain and dented, dull, and scratched heart, looking much like it had been run over by a tractor-trailer rig. I decided against my first inclination to toss it in the trash and be done with it. Instead, I hid it away in the bottom of my jewelry box. My attachment to the necklace and all it signified were not the same. He tore away my childish delight and innocence. Before Angus, I was all smiles filled with happy memories to wear it as a reminder of the goodness it meant. Now repulsed when looking at the necklace, the thought of wearing it made me sick to my stomach. Venomous dark memories defied me and my hopefulness. Angus would be another debilitating reminder of my past as long as I permitted his intrusion. There had to be an end to my self-destruction.

∞

CHAPTER 28
STARGAZERS

I wanted to see Rowan. I planned to call and thank him for the flowers but the thought had come and gone days ago. My distractions were well-founded, numerous and varied but unforgiveable and rude in this case. I hated calling him at home for fear Caroline Rossi would answer. I put on my brave face, took a deep breath, and dialed the number. Rowan answered.

"Rowan, hey you. How are you? I'm surprised to hear your voice. I thought you had gone back to California."

"Hi Val. Yeah, I'm here for a few more days. How are you? Been thinking about you."

"Me, too. I mean, I got the flowers you sent, and they were so beautiful, really breathtaking. Thank you. Thoughtful and I have to say, unexpected."

"I'm glad you liked them. I wanted you to know I was thinking of you, but it was Jess's idea. I'm just a thick-headed guy. Beyond my paygrade."

"Come on, Rowan. You're capable when you want to be. At least you remembered *my* flower of choice." Jessica knew my favorites, but I searched for a sign the flowers had some deeper meaning. I wanted to hope *we* had some deeper meaning.

"I've been intending to call, but it's been one thing after another around here with so many details to take care of." I tried to hide my disappointment. I wanted the flower arrangement to be his way of telling me he cared. Maybe I hoped for too much; best to make this call short.

"I can imagine. Lots of loose ends and you're the one left to do it. You've got all those decisions and taking care of everything your aunt did. It must be hard without her."

"One thing's for sure, I have to mature whether I'm ready or not." When I tried to reach out to Rowan about my relationship with Aunt Nona, I hit a wall. He could not get the crushing sadness of having no one.

"I say you need a break and a night out. How about you and I grab some dinner tonight? We need to get reacquainted. I'm heading back to school day after tomorrow. Where would you like to go?"

I had no idea. I did want to go, only if someone else made the plans. "I'm not up on where to go, Rowan. It would be a relief just to have you pick me up and surprise me."

"I can handle it. Let's say seven o'clock so we'll have plenty of time together and still make it an early evening. Can you be ready by then?"

"Sure. That sounds great."

I tingled with excitement and wanted to let myself be encouraged and getting ready for a date could be a way to feel better. I soaked in a long bubble bath and curled my hair. I took extra care doing my makeup and picking out my dress--bright blue and yellow sundress and ballerina flats. The evenings were hot and sticky, and I wanted to be comfortable with one less thing to worry about. For once, I didn't fret about how I looked. The mirror reflected a well-put-together me. Although how I looked would not be an overriding or determining factor in this relationship. He knew my physical attributes and weaknesses as well as I, so no surprises. I made little effort to put on a show, but I did want him to like what he saw. I did my best to look my best.

He appeared at the door wearing dark pants and a white and navy striped button-down shirt. He looked tanned and divine. He gave me a kiss on the cheek and whispered, "You look beautiful, Val. I love the scarf. Going nautical, hey?" He touched my neck and my mother's red, navy, and green silk scarf. "Might come in handy later." His familiar swagger had not faded.

We had dinner at his family's favorite Italian restaurant with sparkling mirrors and chandeliers. Our reflection shimmered perfection in the candlelight. Dark hair, olive skin, tall and slender. From the beginning, I noticed we were similar physically, and our likeness shone in the mirror. I felt at ease and secure with him. Could we make our dream come true? We engaged in polite dinner conversation, mimicking adults. He asked me about auntie's estate matters and whether I liked her attorney and if he or his dad could help since the firm handled probate matters. I assured him there were no problems. I wanted to keep the conversation on a light note. I tried to ask about how he was doing in baseball but lost track somewhere in his explanation between being drafted by the minors and getting MLB lucky. He mentioned Angus understandably concerned but hesitated to ask specific questions. I assured him but added that recovering would be slow. I tried to conceal the toll of the recent traumas, but I would never be over losing Aunt Nona, and preferred not to talk about Angus. Someday I might want to tell him but not tonight. Once I got started, toxins would shoot out like a geyser. And one thing we didn't need was a mood destroyer.

"I've got an idea. Let's ride out to the marina. The boat's docked and we could take her out for a spin. Supposed to be a starry one just for us. What say?"

I was ready with my usual objections--it's too late, too windy, too dark, too hot, too dangerous--when I caught myself. "Okay. I'd enjoy some night air, sounds fun."

We rode in the darkness with starry crown overhead and city lights all around us. "Mom usually leaves a sweater in the bin over there if you're cool or you could come over here and keep me company. I'm lonesome." I took the scarf from around my neck and tied it around my hair and retrieved the navy sweater.

"Here let me." He pulled me close as he wrapped the sweater around my shoulders and brushed his lips against my cheek.

I spent the rest of the evening snuggled up next to him in the captain's chair. The music was playing, the moon shining, and all seemed well with Rowan and Valentine for the first time since our first time. He stopped the boat in the middle of the lake and pulled me close. "This is the happiest night of my life, Val. You and I are back where we should be, together." I gave in. He kissed me like I'd never dreamed of being kissed. His warm, full lips were on mine and our young warm bodies were aching to be one. I started to cry.

"What's wrong, Val? Have I done something?"

"No, No. It's not you. I'm so messed up, Rowan. I'm not sure I'll ever be what you deserve." Typical Valentine mood spoiler in spite of herself. I could not for the life of me picture me as good enough for Rowan Rossi. The real problem, I couldn't keep my inferiority to myself. Somehow if I confessed, did I expect he would spend our time together exalting my virtues? Pitiful wallflower plucked out of her element pleading for compliments and praise. Your job, Rowan, is to make me believe I am worthy when I feel inferior and not up to your standards. I should grow up.

"I'll tell you how, my love. Because you *already* are everything I ever wanted and whatever it takes and for however long it takes, I will be waiting for you. There's no hurry. We'll take our time. You've been through enough hell in your lifetime for ten people. All I ask is you don't shut me out. Promise me." He wiped my tears and held onto me. Then he clasped his hands softly around my face.

"We're still young, Val. But you're the one for me and I hope you feel the same. I want your toothbrush hanging next to mine. Can you say corny?" He knew how to dry my tears and ease my fears. He looked longingly into my eyes. I couldn't look away from his questioning.

"Yes Rowan. You're all I have ever wished for. I promise I won't be so quick to slam the door on us; I just don't want to be hurt again. Deep in my heart, I feel we're meant to be together and I like the idea of our toothbrushes snuggling."

"It won't be easy with me in California. But trust me it can happen. We have to commit to each other. If we can ride out the rough periods with an eye to tomorrow, then we won't throw away the best thing either of us can ever hope to have." Serious and intent, I knew I felt the same and wanted to tell him but I could not. I was testing the waters.

"My goal is to begin teaching in three years so it's summer school every year and full semester hours or more. And you have your baseball career; who can say what will happen there. It won't be easy but I'm willing to do all I can." My heart overflowed again after months of empty, unfulfilled promise. I felt alive. The memory of us together blazed through me as if it were only yesterday.

"We better get back. It'll be midnight when I've finished getting the boat in the slip and everything stowed and anchored. Come here, Val." I snuggled close again. "You smell so good and your hair is sweet and soft against my face. I don't deserve to be this lucky, so I'll just say 'Yee Haw'!"

I laughed at his attempt to be down home hokey cowboy Texan. He held me close and kissed me again. He whispered in my ear, "I love you Valentine Monroe. Don't ever leave me. You're the one meant to be next to me." I searched his face for my answer. I wanted to say it back to him but the words wouldn't come so I kissed him. *Exhilaration of two young lovers sharing their once-in-a-lifetime adventure.*

∞

CHAPTER 29
CAROLINE ROSSI

Rowan called the next morning still excited about us. He wanted me to come to San Francisco in the fall. "Mom and Jessica are coming out so she can hook Jessica up with a big modeling agency honcho. She's planning for Jess to scoop a contract with some name designer. Anyway, you should come, even for a long weekend."

"Rowan, I have classes just like you do and it simply won't work with our crazy schedules."

"Well, you can at least think about it. It would give us a chance to be together even if it's for a few hours. Otherwise it'll be Christmas break before I get back."

"Okay. I'll try but I'm not making any promises. Besides, your schedule is packed, how will you find the time for me?"

"Val, I'll make time. I've been thinking about you, sure miss you already. Didn't we have fun last night? Listen to me, there are many, many more of those nights ahead. You're my girl."

"I hope so. I'll miss you."

"Maybe we can get a quick burger before I leave. No ice cream though. I'm in training and I don't intend to let you indulge while I watch. Catch you later."

Life slowly began to take on a routine and schedule offering promise and encouragement with morning classes and afternoon at the school, working in the office. The teachers opened their world to me and I grabbed the chance to be hands on grading papers, learning to make lesson plans and designing classroom teaching aids. I always liked staying busy which meant my mind didn't have time to wander and wonder. I didn't hear from Rowan for almost three weeks. I refused to call him. Then when least expected, he called to tell me how busy he was and asked again if I was coming to California. I said I would think about it. He reminded me I had to make a quick decision. His mother and Jessica were coming out the following week. What he said next floored me.

"Val, I hope you don't take this wrong. But I've been thinking (dangerous, I know), I wish you would seriously consider coming out here to school. There's nothing holding you there now. With you here in California, we could get rid of a big hurdle. It's tricky enough without this distance thing."

My end responded silent. What could he be thinking? I'm supposed to follow him around the country like a puppy dog? What happens if he changes his mind and returns home? What about this baseball thing? I've heard tales of how unstable trying for a career in baseball can be. He thinks he will get signed by a west coast team but that's dream weaver stuff. He could get injured or have a change of heart or wake up in a new world. Who can say what will happen? I'll predict one thing. He'll be upset when I say no. Past is preview of what's to come. I should use a diplomatic tactic for a change instead of my direct in-your-face abrasive approach. A tiny black speck appeared on my radar. Why didn't he respect my career goals as meaningful and substantial rather than an annoying complication to be changed, re-arranged and moved? He seemed quick to dismiss my plans.

"You have an interesting idea, Rowan. I hadn't thought of changing schools. I guess it would work as long as you stay the course and don't switcheroo on me." Now he seemed short of words, so I continued with my speech.

"Let's see how things go for the rest of the year since we're both so focused on our goals. Right now, it's best for me to stay here. And as far as coming out for the weekend, your schedule is full and so is mine. Let's not add to our loads, okay?"

"Okay, Val. Whatever you say. But promise me you'll at least think about it. Listen, got to run. I'll talk to you again soon, I promise. Love ya. Take care."

Caroline Rossi called on a Monday evening to say she and Jessica were leaving Thursday afternoon for San Francisco and asked if I would accompany them. I thanked her politely and assured her I had all I could handle carrying fifteen semester hours of college courses and working five afternoons a week at the high school. "Oh, I forgot. Rowan mentioned something about you were studying to be--is it teaching?"

"Yes, I would like to teach English. I'm planning to graduate in three years."

"Wow, aren't you the ambitious one. Well, okay, Rowan will be disappointed, but it's for the best. He barely can take a deep breath with his schedule. I can't imagine how he thought he would have time for guests. All I've gotten so far is he'll meet Jessica and me for a quick dinner."

"I appreciate your asking. You and Jessica seem to have a full week so maybe later would be better. I would love to see San Francisco."

"It's a glorious city and in a league of its own." She laughed. "Sorry, my baseball son is rubbing off on me. One of the great things about graduating from Stanford and one of the long-term benefits of a prestigious university, I made several lifelong connections. Of course, a local state college is beneficial in its way, the good old boys mentality. One reason I offered to introduce Jessica is because of people I know in the business. Plus, how could I not be under her spell? She has all the elements to be a top model; she's extraordinary. I could go on and on but I don't have to tell you how special she is."

"You're so right. I tried to encourage her but she wouldn't listen. She shrugged me off and called it flattery, building up her ego. But she's listening now. Guess you have influence since you have contacts in the business."

"She'll be great once she gets her foot in the right door. Oh, listen to me. I'm her biggest fan. I have to admit initially I thought she and Rowan would make a divine couple but she's loyal. She set me straight immediately, feisty and in-your-face. Your friend is one in a million. She's practically flawless with her beauty and talent and good heart. Oh, listen to me go on and on. She's the perfect package. But I don't have to tell you how great she is. You two have been friends since you were munchkins. Okay, I'll let you go for real this time. I have to run. Take care and I'll give Rowan your best."

I hung up and called Jess. "Can you come over for a few minutes before you take off for California?" She was taking the afternoon off tomorrow to get ready for the trip and would stop by. I shouldn't interfere, but concern about my best friend was my business. Caroline Rossi took an unusual interest in Jess and in manipulating her future. How Jess felt continued to trouble me. She could be intimidated and riding a wave. I knew Jessica. She had no misgivings about telling me how she feels even if telling me to butt out. But would she be as direct to Caroline Rossi?

Jess came early in the afternoon hoping we could go out for lunch to a new place she wanted to try with an outdoor patio. "Val, let's go. It's too beautiful a day to be cooped up inside."

"Okay. But could we talk for a few minutes here? Restaurants are crowded and noisy and not an ideal place to catch up. We haven't sat and schmoozed for ages. I miss our conflabs. How long will you and Caroline be in San Francisco?"

"Just a week. I hope we can complete the checklist. She has every day booked with appointments, so I've got high hopes; I might come home with a contract. And you thought I was just another tall bony hanger for high-priced duds!"

"Oh, Jess. Hope the best for you. You've had your heart set on a modeling career since our early days with Monique. Caroline makes sounds like she has a shortcut to bypass the detours."

"As they say, it's not what you know, but who you know. And Caroline's people can help kick start my career. She's made it clear there won't be any funny business either which is reassuring. Modeling offers its share of casting couch perverts."

"I'm glad you mentioned Caroline. Are you okay with her taking the lead like she is? I suppose she means well, but it's kind of unusual.

I'd say pushy. Rowan mentioned she latched onto you like the daughter she never had."

"I don't usually let someone take over. But I consider her my agent. She would like our relationship to be more if that is what you're getting at. At first, I knew she wanted me to hook up with Rowan, so I had to quash her plans early on and set her straight. She can be controlling so I let her down in a nice but firm way I had no romantic interest in Rowan. As the months passed, she eased up on her matchmaking and took more of a personal interest in me. She saw someone who didn't have a ghost of a chance and knew she could help and stepped up. We've gone over this too many times to count. She understands and even appreciates my position."

Jess never ceased to amaze me. Insight could be her middle name and don't forget perception. "Okay. I was curious if you were okay with her taking such a large part. She can be overly assertive or so it seems to me, anyway."

"Glad you mentioned the Rossi's and their issues. You and Rowan. He's crazy about you. But he's confided you're constantly pulling away and pushing against him. I'm not taking sides here but think about how he feels. I wouldn't say this to him. But we both wonder whether you're committed to this relationship."

"Why would he think I'm uncommitted? Just because I balk at moving 1500 miles to change schools at his whim? What he needs is a pet, not a girlfriend. Honestly, Jess, I don't get it. It's foolhardy to put all my eggs in one basket. What if he changes his mind about me or his priorities? Pardon me, if I'm booted and spurred, it's to protect myself. Remember our history."

"No guarantees, Val. People who love each other make compromises, whether they're 19 or 90. I understand your position and the viewpoint if you two have the will and substance, your relationship will stand the test of time and distance. Then there's the possibility no matter how strong the relationship, communication breaks down for a third party to take over. Just sayin'. I can't advise you but I do know Rowan is exceptional and crazy about you. Take it for whatever it's worth. It's a once-in-a-lifetime thing, the beautiful music between you two."

"Maybe. He could have long-term plans even for us. But until he gets his billboard outside this town saying 'Home of Rowan Rossi,' he won't be satisfied so I have to be cautious. I don't want to put myself in the lurch, be at his mercy. I won't be satisfied unless I stand as his equal. I have career goals of my own. Besides, I've never wanted to live anywhere but here and I'd certainly be content in this same house. I must sound humdrum to someone who can't wait to spread her wings, but it's what I want."

"You're right. You and I are different. I do want to go and see and be. But there is absolutely nothing wrong with what you want, Val. And someday I will want to come home. I want the best for you, whatever you decide, and hope you and Rowan can be happy together. But as far as Caroline, don't worry. Dad and I agree. He wants me to take my best shot at modeling so he can quit hearing about it! Now, let's go get some food. I'm starving and soon, I'll be on a permanent diet of green and every variety of rabbit food. Caroline wants me to drop five pounds. Ugh."

"Yeah, okay. Just one more thing. I want to show you what I found in Aunt Nona's treasure chest. Stay here; I'll go and get it. Then we can go."

I carefully placed the cherished items on the coffee table. These few treasures told a brief but poignant history in memorabilia. Yearbooks from the local high school for 1910; WWII ration book with stamps; Navy I. D. tag of Nona's father; faded photograph of Aunt Nona and Andrew Rowan; dance card for the Senior Fancy Dress Ball filled with signature 'Andrew Rowan'; her gold class pin inlaid with seed pearls; gold heart necklace with initials NME on one side and JRA on the other and a photo of her parents with her and her sister who would be my grandmother. There were several newspaper clippings and articles about family weddings and deaths in Mississippi; funeral notices; and commencement pamphlets. Two photos of Aunt Nona with her 4th grade students––the first class she taught and the last class when she retired. A ribbon-bound pamphlet of ivory paper yellowed with age entitled *Sweet Uses of Adversity* in handwritten calligraphy, its black ink faintly decipherable. Now yellow and faded, a forgotten newspaper clipping stalwartly remained to serve its purpose as an announcement of an upcoming social event of the season--the wedding of James Andrew Rowan and Felicia Caroline Farroqua.

I turned to the pages of Class Favorites for senior year--James Andrew Rowan and Nona Emmaline Monroe. "Do you know who that is?" I pointed to the picture.

"Oh my gosh, Val. Do I know? As if there was zero resemblance. You'd have to be blind not to see--"

"Yes, Rowan's grandfather on his mother's side. Isn't this unbelievable? And to think I never knew. And this dance card is taken up with Andrew Rowan for every dance. Aunt Nona mentioned him when I said Rowan's name. But I had no idea. I guess we both considered it a mere coincidence and didn't connect since one was a first name and the other a surname. She did say they dated in high school and then he went away to college and law school. Curious, I didn't pursue because I didn't want to embarrass her. She didn't bring up her past." For someone I adored, I thought how much more there had to be about Aunt Nona.

"Val, there's a giant puzzle piece missing with your aunt and James Andrew Rowan. Look at this wedding announcement. Just the fact that your aunt kept it for all these years says volumes. Maybe, just maybe, their relationship meant more than anyone other than those two ever knew. I'm weaving a fairy tale, but it could have been *the* love for Aunt Nona. Didn't you wonder why she never married?" As Jess overreached into territory I preferred not to explore, we could only guess and fabricate their storybook romance.

I chose to ignore her summation. "I understand what you're saying, Jess, but they were young. Probably just puppy love. It's such a small world. I wonder if Rowan knows."

Jess picked up the little gold heart. "Look at this. How utterly romantic! There's one bittersweet untold story here."

"I think so, too. I'm embarrassed and ashamed. I'm sorry I didn't find out more about Aunt Nona's past. I was too busy with *me*. I never even thought to ask her, to be interested in, you know, her past. It's like when you're young, you can't imagine the old folks being like us, having fun and romance, heartache, excitement. It's like you don't see your elders any other way other than how you see them now. We miss so much of our history and what makes our loved ones who they are. How can we understand who we are if we don't know who they were and where we come from?"

I felt proud I could share my discovery with Jess; Rowan and I shared another connection. It begged the prayer we didn't end up in the discarded memory pile. I took away a powerful lesson going through Aunt Nona's keepsakes. She seemed content keeping her past in the past and not sharing many memories. But seeing her memorabilia before me opened my mind to another side of her. Precious items she kept for all these years were much more than trinkets and faded memories. Remembrances paint a picture of the person and their family and become a part of family history. It's our connection which would otherwise be lost forever. *Artifacts never lie.*

∞

Chapter 30
Healing Heart

My life changed dramatically after Aunt Nona's death but I kept busy and productive--her number one rule to cope with sadness and to ward off self-indulgence. I followed my customary modus operandi; if not a daily priority, then bury the unresolved. A structured schedule of classes in the morning and work at the school in the afternoon kept my goal of teaching alive and real; soon I would realize my dream. Remembering Aunt Nona's joy I would be a teacher kept me going on the days when the future seemed fuzzy and faraway. Occasional weekend trips to San Francisco to see Rowan and Jess offered me diversion and fun, but there should be more. Pastor Leland recognized turmoil and encouraged me more than once to give counseling a chance. I did feel drawn to him as someone I could confide in. I had made up my mind. The enormous energy and focus required to function in pretense and cover-up demanded too much to live with for the rest of my life and with fewer returns than I deserved. Simply stated, I failed miserably at fixing myself. Leland became my demon slayer.

It was not an overnight feat, but in large part, because of his patience and understanding, our relationship developed slowly, and he became one of the few people I allowed myself to trust. There again, another sign of my dysfunction and a root cause of my relationship problems with Rowan, insurmountable *trust*. For the first three months, I appeared at Leland's office three evenings a week and did little else. Oh, for sure, I did participate in the sessions; I'm all about saving face. I freely recited my sad tale, so Leland became acutely familiar with the grisly details of my childhood and the offenses suffered. Not as forthcoming about the latent effects to my psyche, I preferred to pretend and minimize the damage and scourge to my soul. I did not question his abilities but was skeptical about my willingness to openly and candidly reflect. I spent the majority of my life conniving and hiding from ghosts, so it takes practice and effort to defy and push them out for public viewing--not easy to reflect as a walking, talking anger puppet. Pull my strings the wrong way and I'll erupt. I had carried an unmanageable load for a lifetime and continuing down the same old path, I ticked away, a walking time bomb. Living in trepidation and anxiety--ruled by fear to step out and step forward--took on a debilitating permanence. Terrified of rejection and therefore commitment, I hoped *my desire for individuality would be stronger than my fear of rejection* so I would no longer need a mask. My relationships suffered as superficial or non-existent as well as opportunity at the slightest hint of rejection, commitment, uncertainty or risk. Trust and optimism were rare gems awarded to the worthy, not to someone like me. Carve away my disguise and my empty reflection.

A simple example is my name as the mother lode. Before I claimed my *rightful* birthright, I loathed being called and having to answer to *Valentine*. People were attracted to me because of my name which defined me. The vision of a stream of red and pink sweetness of love, flowers, pink hearts and romance, adoration, and perfection repulsed me. What a fraud. Vacant eyes attached to a montage of scattered pieces of a person were neither sweet nor pretty. Irrational though it may seem, my name remained a constant reminder I felt ugly and unworthy. Ultimately, I grew into the name given me by my mother out of love and affection for her precious gift, and I grew to treasure her unwavering belief in her daughter's worthiness.

I took pride in my evasive tactics and answers I thought Leland wanted to hear to get me off the hot seat. *Roadblocks and detours to progress.* I measured and preened my words to portray my presentable self and, if left to my creative devices, I refused to regurgitate the ugly truth and to empty a heart filled with vicious hate. Leland refused to be deterred by my mixed messages. He slashed through my veil with razor precision. My tricks were old hat; his firsthand experience prepared him well. Clever and difficult to deceive, he outlasted my futile attempts and made mincemeat of my challenges. No excuses or camouflage allowed. I poured the toxins. The predominant leader fear followed closely by guilt and anger. Planted and cultivated early, the seed of arrogance developed my higher sense of aloofness. I longed to belong but instead detached and hovered as if a spectator.

Conveniently wedged between my ego and my invisible barrier of fear, I cried for acceptance. "No, no, I'm not the way you think. Why can't you see me?" I used an armor of superiority as protection against anyone who looked down on me. Being a victim became synonymous with being pitied and being pitiful. Ashamed, I clung to my pride. I devised my defense and developed a skewed point of view. From the age of five, I knew suffering firsthand. I saw hurtful people as superficial, self-absorbed and oblivious--energized by distraction and disconnected from the crucial--scampering fools tending to their frivolous activities as if world-shattering. My disillusion warped my view. Survival to them was a foreign concept seen in jungle and war movies. The biggest challenge their children faced on Christmas morning had little to do with suffering disappointment when having only eight out of ten gifts checked off their Santa list. An example of my looking down on Emily Larson showed my sneaky arrogance. As a person of substance and good moral values, I would not allow myself to go around hurting people like Emily just because she had bags of money. She was beneath me and pathetic. My staying aloof meant staying out of the mud pit with the rest of the world.

Eaten away by relentless and insidious anger over my mother being taken away, I saw myself as double-punched without a parent. Thanks to Aunt Nona who didn't tolerate self-pity, I opened my eyes and came to grips with how life works--no warranty and no guarantees. I looked around and saw children with no one and felt ashamed. I made a conscious effort to let go of the anger and replaced it with positive power beginning with love and gratitude for Aunt Nona. *But the anger of having my innocence destroyed permeated every cell and surfaced unpredictably and viciously.*

Leland was nonjudgmental and undaunted by my confidences. The more I divulged, the more compelled to continue my healing because I trusted him. He inspired me by his example. He had overcome so the pain of his past did not control him. The guilt I had indirectly caused Aunt Nona's death consumed me. Even though I was a child when Angus attempted his abduction, I irrationally blamed myself. I connected my memories of Will with the Angus incident and concluded--I must be bad. Some element in me invited inappropriate behavior. *Evil equipped with radar to pick me.* In retrospect and with maturity, I clearly needed to use better judgment and make wiser choices but even then, no guarantees. My rational side knew loved ones could not be protected from every threat and stressor. Even careful and cautious, we are human and vulnerable. Aunt Nona was frail and her health deteriorating--a condition she could not tolerate long-term. Her delicate constitution could not tolerate a vigorous approach to life, and she refused to watch from the sidelines. The light of truth began to force its way into my subconscious shining the light into the sorcery of Angus. His hold on me would not continue after pure purge and reflection with no space in my mind, body, or soul for his evil to reside. The lack of physical presence doesn't mean absence. I had years of practice permitting the effects of evil treatment and its poison to brew within. Once Angus entered my life, he took refuge to rob me of the chance to experience life to its fullest. The evil prodding was a constant reminder I was unworthy of any positive emotion and therefore unable to contemplate wholeness whether it be love, happiness, fulfillment, acceptance, achievement, or success. Destined to be empty, incomplete and undesirable for all of my days, nothing within my power could change my fate. A powerless victim of others who are stronger, smarter, and more fortunate became my crutch extraordinaire to carry my mandatory load of crap. There's a self-destruct book in here somewhere. How to stunt development and growth with a clear conscience; it's not my fault. I silenced the voices of evil temporarily when I made small efforts to change but they reappeared without warning. I coped the best way I knew how, by pretense. Pastor Leland and I laid it all out bare to the bone without restraint. How would one accomplish such a task of renewal and where would one go for assistance?

From years of personal experience and failure, I conceded redemption was not within my power. I began a search for healing and experienced the cumulative effects of counseling, meditation and prayer seeing life in a new light. My mission reflected as a relationship with God. I humbly sought guidance in every aspect of daily life. My heart softened with thankfulness. The jagged ugliness, anger, and hopelessness were honed away.

I felt encouraged about myself and about life and made a close friend in Pastor Leland. I called on him anytime without hesitation or questioning my motives and timing. He would not be replaced. I grew to depend upon him more and more; he did not let me down. His counseling on my relationship with Rowan enlightened me I had to give it my all or give it all up in fairness to us both. My lingering questions about the relationship centered on our immaturity, different values, and lack of common goals and priorities. The skiing vacation incident continued to trouble me as a red flag; we were mismatched because of our value systems. There would be other instances of our getting crosswise if our values were incompatible. Things have a way of falling into place or exploding despite best efforts. I wanted simple but in this complicated world, simple likely wouldn't be the case. We must test our relationship. I needed to find out whether our relationship was *substance or sham*. Willing to compromise and change *to a point*, I had misgivings. Leland didn't hesitate to call me down. How can you love and be loved when your heart is filled with resentment?

We talked frankly about my relationship with Rowan. He encouraged me against restraint in my commitment if I believed in our love for each other. "Valentine, do you want to look back and wonder if you and Rowan would have made it? Only you can answer the question, but I don't think so. You have to find out if your relationship is as strong as you think and whether you both are bound by the same ideals. There is no other way. I would caution you to compromise but not when it comes to your values. If your values are inconsistent, no amount of compromise will remedy your problems. Happiness and fulfillment in marriage is a delicate balance like a three-legged stool--

spiritual, emotional, and physical wellbeing. You two haven't had the opportunity to be together and need to experience the influences of family, friends, outsiders, events. You will not live in a vacuum after your marriage and need to experience the synergy and interaction as part of your preparation for a lifetime together. I've seen couples who find out what they've signed up for and who they've signed up with have fewer surprises and are more successful as a couple. You don't have to be alike but you'll have a better chance of happiness if you have the same outlook and goals. I say, if you love each other, then why leave it to chance? See if you're compatible and on the same path."

The catalyst for me to change appeared in an unassuming little pamphlet from my Aunt Nona's treasure chest. Adversity is given a bad rap. Deep provoking thoughts of the author almost one hundred years ago inspired my first serious exposure to an upstart idea--adversity as the sweeping positive regenerative power! The seed had been planted to use my experiences as precious energy to fuel my change. The message of the commencement speaker in Hazlehurst, Mississippi to a group of aspiring graduates beginning their life's journey in 1890 is as relevant today:

Sweet are the Uses of Adversity

When we speak of prosperity, we think of the sweetness of life; when we speak of adversity, we think of its bitterness.

My subject tonight invites us to consider adversity has its uses and that its uses are sweet. The great dramatic poet does not stand alone in this declaration. Many others have been testimony to the same general fact. Horace says "Adversity has the effect of eliciting talents which in prosperous circumstances would have lain dormant." Rogers says, "The good are better made by ill, as odors crushed are sweeter still."

Do you ask me to show you how it is true that "the uses of adversity are sweet"? As most of us are more familiar with adversity than with prosperity, it will be well for us to learn its uses.

Nothing can so well teach us knowledge of ourselves as adversity. When the cable lies coiled on the deck, in the calm and peaceful days of voyage, we do not know how strong it is or how weak it is. But when the storm comes, when the ship is imperiled and the wild waves are beating fiercely against it, the cable is put to the test. It is only when men are brought to the test that they can tell what their real nature is or how strong their instincts and passions are. A house built on the sand in fair weather is just as good as if built on a rock. A cobweb is as good as the mightiest chain cable when there is no strain on it. It is trial that proves one thing strong and another weak.

Adversity shows other people what we are. Sorrow often reveals and develops our noble qualities. What prosperity had concealed, adversity brings to light. Nobleness that we had never suspected with powers that would have remained uncultured and unfruitful are manifested. They are like some grand mansions surrounded and hidden in summer by large, leafy trees. Those who pass by cannot see the fine proportions and ornamental sculpture that make it "a thing of beauty"; but when winter tears away with ruthless hand every leaf until the limbs stand clear and bare, then behold the magnificent handiwork appears in all its glory and splendor. The best natures show best when most tried and they are lovelier in poverty than in wealth.

Adversity has a sweet use in the development and perfecting of noble character. Woods may grow up rapidly. They are rank, ugly and worthless. But the finest woods are those which have withstood the storms of many winters. The precious mahogany grows with veneering knots and quirks and contortions of grain. That is the best timber of the forest which has the most knots. When the knots have been sawn and polished, how beautiful they are! The gem cannot be polished without friction nor man perfected without adversity.

The adage, "Prosperity gains us friends, and adversity proves them." There are some birds which stay with us during the summer but fly away at the first frost. They sing their cheerful notes when we least need them. In the winter, they don't give us a single note. I care nothing for such birds as these. Give me the bird which will sing in winter and seek to my window in hardest frost.

There is no testing of friendship but adversity. He who is not ashamed of me when I am in prison, when I am trampled on, when I am poor, when I am despised and forsaken--he is my true friend. I'd rather have one ounce of that man's love than a world full of fawning and flattery in the days of prosperity.

Author Unknown

Hazlehurst, Mississippi
June 18th, 1890

∞

Chapter 31
Non-Negotiables

R owan and I started our New Year with a resolution to make a better us. I agreed to make time for weekend and holiday trips to San Francisco (as my classes permitted) and stay with Jessica to give our relationship the best chance. I also requested we go to couple's counseling with Pastor Leland once he graduated law school and moved back home. Counseling had opened new doors not only for me but for us as a couple. But I had a long way to go. Rowan had been more than patient; most other guys would have long ago taken a hike. The light of possibility dawned; he and I were substantial and lasting. I adored him but stopped short in my analysis, of all the choices he had, I was the one. The faintest negative signal I took as personal which would send me scurrying. Rejection by Rowan and end of the relationship.

"Val, there is one thing big enough for me to mention because it's a killer habit. It's come close to destroying us, so I hate to think about it much less say it."

I cringed and knew before he said it. I'd gotten my toes stepped on often enough to admit my bad habits.

"Don't kill the music in us." He continued to amaze me with the depth of his feelings. I had no inkling I was guilty of yet another such unintentional and hurtful deed. Habits are hard to break particularly if one is unaware. When I asked him to explain, he hesitated and dug in his heels. He hesitated to hurt me or to start an argument. Who likes to be criticized? I did my best to reassure him, as part of my counseling with Pastor Leland, I had become less sensitive.

"I'm not yet tough-skinned so I might cry." We both tried to laugh. It couldn't have been easy for him to call out my faults, in the heat of anger and hurt, but not in good times. We were getting along smooth as silk, and he didn't want to rock the boat.

"I love you and want us to be together all our lives. There is this one thing you do I can't stand. I call it the 'Val way or the highway.' You have a way of slamming up a wall. I don't know how else to explain what happens when you disagree or refuse to discuss something. Maybe I do it, too. I don't know. There has to be a better way for us to discuss something when we disagree. The first time was when I asked you to go skiing. It happened again when I asked you to consider coming to San Francisco to school. It's like you're not open for any discussion, case closed, how stupid. I shouldn't have asked you to leave Aunt Nona, but the reason I got unreasonable and angry was your attitude of, 'Why are you so infantile and unfeeling, Rowan?' Val, why can't you open up to me? You know, we lawyers love to argue and persuade since we're always right. I use bad judgment and yes I like to get my way, but I want our relationship to grow stronger, not fester and erupt when we're older. You've seen those couples; they look sad and detached because they are. I'll be alone before I'll be that."

I nodded. Didn't he just admit a major part of our problem? I would have sworn "we know we're right" just came out of his mouth. Hmm. A bobble head yes doll could be in his future but absolutely not in mine. Don't you have enough problems when you're old without another old person to drag you down? I held the thought but knew too well what he meant. Those failed relationships are everywhere and you don't have to be old. It's another challenge of being older because your options have run out. What are the chances of a match made in heaven when your goal for the day is to survive? I'm sure couples who stay together miserable have their reason, being a couple is preferable to being alone. *Not a slogan I wanted on my kitchen wall.*

"When two people meet and the sparks fly, there's a connection and chemical reaction. And as they get to know each other, they move to the rhythm of their special music. I want ours to last as long as we do. Guess I'm just a hopeless romantic. I want the excitement I see in couples who've been together for eons but act like young lovers." His eyes glowed with renewed confidence.

"Who is that Rowan? I mean, the couple you describe is rare if ever and primarily seen on the big screen. Relationships like people mellow with age, don't they? It doesn't mean they aren't happy, but the relationship does change. We're not rabbits." Rowan's naiveté annoyed. Could he be serious? I loved romance as much as anyone but didn't kid myself. The flame flickers as the fairy dust evaporates.

"Val, do you mean change or grow stale or just plain die? The couple I have in mind is my mom and dad. You have to admit they're still going strong after all these years."

I agreed they were well-matched but stopped short of saying it. Not to mention, Rowan's dad let his mother run wild and free. No bridle and bit for her. She had free rein. He had captured the essence of my know-it-all-attitude which rears its ugly head out of frustration, usually when I feel trapped without options, and painted into a corner, what I felt on both past occasions he mentioned. He knew how to hurt me like no one else. I lashed out or slammed up the wall when he disappointed me because I cared so deeply about him. The resolution to our problems emerged as larger and more complicated than either of us knew how to handle or simply stated, we were not meant to be. I harbored major doubts.

"Val, I don't have to tell you. You have an old and dark side. I don't know how else to describe it--always casting shadows. I just want you to let go. Be free. I've seen you when you do and you come alive being loose and not wound as tight as a coil spring trying to control everyone and every situation. We're only young once. I guess we kind of need to dial it in somewhere in the middle between my way off-the-chart romantic, and you, Miss Practicality, down-to-earth keep-us-on-track schoolmarm."

"You better grin when you say that, Buster. The picture you paint of me is not inviting considering I'm not even twenty-five years old."

"I'm grinning, I'm grinning. But you know what I mean. You have to admit you are the practical one in the group. Even Jess agrees with me."

"Okay, okay. I get it but I still want the same for us as you do. We have different ideas of how to get there. You blur the lines; I do not. I'm on a new path. Not to say the two-headed monster won't rear its ugly head but I'm more aware and I'll do my best not to be hurtful. I have a vision of better together than we are apart--a formidable couple of one. Thank you for loving me enough to be patient. I know I'm not the easiest person to get along with; but then, who is? Even a rose has its thorns."

He kissed me and held me close. I had never dreamed someone would love me with such passion, patience, and forgiveness. It would be so easy to give in now. I took his fabulous face in my hands and brought him close, "Just because I only let you undress me with your eyes doesn't mean I don't want you, slugger."

"I know. It's a constant battle but it'll be worth it. I can tell it's not easy for you either or maybe my ego's talking. You want me; I'm your heartthrob. Too bad, little lady, you have to wait. Let's see if our love at first sight turns out to be love to the last light."

∞

CHAPTER 32
STORMY SKIES

G ood Afternoon, Ladies and Gentlemen. We're at twenty thousand feet and climbing to our sustained altitude of 32,000 feet. Weather looks clear all the way to the beautiful City by the Bay. Our trip today will take us over the Grand Canyon and other points of interest I'll point out in our short three-hour flight. Now sit back and take in the view."

"Jess, what in the world do you have on your feet?" Christmas break and we were on our way to spend New Year's in San Francisco with Rowan. We had the last-minute rush to make our flight, and this was the first chance I'd had to catch my breath, much less check out her wardrobe. Her modeling contract unleashed her fashion wild side. I never knew what to expect to see her wearing.

"Shoes. Those are shoes, Val. Y'all did get those in Texas didn't you?"

"Ha. Ha. Clever. I can see they're shoes. But you have to admit, they're different. And wouldn't you have been disappointed if I didn't ask about them? Come on, Jess. Exactly what are they made of, some sort of plastic? And do I see unidentified floating objects in the heels?" Clear wedges with the floating animal in the heels might be a first, but somehow I knew it wouldn't be her last fashion enigma.

"Peasant girl, these are the latest trend, not your everyday plastic, not for my shoes, acrylic. And yes, those tiny teddy bears are suspended in the heels. Aren't they just the cutest?"

"Okay. I'll give you cute, unique and even one of a kind but like how large is the market for those or are you a walking prototype for a launch you and Caroline have in the works?"

"Val, you're hopeless. Don't you ever have the urge to jump out of the rut of safe and boring? As often as you've come out West, you know we aim to trend set, one of California's standout virtues. We thrive on original and first. It's against code to be like everyone else."

"Different for sure but too far out for me. You eat and breathe fashion and look fabulous in everything or nothing. I wear clothes so I won't get arrested; plus in California they are touchy about visual pollution. I have to say, your shoes are adorable. Also, I see the agency is letting you grow out your hair, a good thing. What a bizarre look when you came home after the *stylists* got through with you! Have modeling contract and flaming red cropped hair, will travel to next call for Raggedy Ann. I almost went into mourning over the loss of your magnificent blonde ponytail."

"Now you're being just plain mean! It's part of the job. You have to be willing to stay ahead of the curve. How many girls have you ever seen with *that* hair? Ha! Thought so, ME. It's a small price to pay to get $1000 an hour. Speaking of shoes, did I tell you where I got this shoe fetish?"

She didn't wait for me to answer. "I started reading this series of books about a top-notch assistant district attorney who worked as an undercover detective and had an affinity for crazy shoes but had to wear black pumps to the office with no more than a three-inch heel. So on Fridays after work, the attorneys would go out to the bar for a few drinks and afterward she shopped for new shoes. She bought the craziest shoes she could find decorated to the hilt. Flats, wedges and heels were merely the foundation for the creation. She adored spike heels and kept her collection on a special glassed-in shelf in her closet. She had a pair of red leather with big bows on the back with little Santa faces; heels that lit up; black leather with tiny chains and charms hanging down the back and sides; wedges with her initials in rhinestones carved in the heels; and a pair of acrylic with a tiny shark suspended in the heel. A patriotic pair of sneakers decorated like an American flag flashed Fourth of July. All bought through mail order. I latched onto the idea and searched and searched until I found these."

"Intriguing. Are the books any good or is it all about the shoes?"

"Oh, the stories are dynamite. She gets the tough cases and is a smart cookie. The writer has to glamorize being one of a dozen attorneys hopelessly lost in a big city D.A.'s office. The shoe thing takes the edge off the gruesome cases although her spike heels came in handy working vice. Can you imagine the stories those heels could tell?" She rolled her eyes. Then reluctantly but intent on her plans, she returned to her world.

"I'm socking away the dough. I want to start a line of accessories. Modeling is purely temporary. I'm reminded every day when I look in the mirror and don't see the fresh-faced sixteen-year-old the agency wants to sign. I don't plan to be a--"

"I know. Your dad told me and he can't wait. We both want you to come home but you've got to complete your plan."

"--plastic surgery junkie. I'm thinking another two years tops for modeling. I hardly spend any money except for rent which is out of sight. Can't you see it? Shoes, handbags, belts, scarves--you name it-- all with my label? And there is more to tell. Caroline will back my venture. She wants me to finish my contract so there are no legal issues. We need all the good will we can get; it's cutthroat, any advantage we'll take. Oh, I have to tell you. She and I will go to Italy this summer to look at factories. She wants to look at the costs and the differences in quality so we won't be blindsided. Be prepared is her mantra. She's hiring some numbers people who are experienced in this kind of startup manufacturing. One guy with ten stores found factories for major New York labels. Of course, any leather manufacturing in Italy will be the best. It's their specialty. I'm telling you, girl, the sky's the limit. I'm excited out of my mind. I love modeling but having my designer line JMAC would be stratosphere good."

"You don't have to convince me. You've got everything it takes. You're smarter and have more fashion savvy than 90% of the labels out there. I can't wait for you to get going so I can wear all your fabulous goodies, at a discount of course. Jillian will want to be your first retail outlet. I always knew you would find a way to do it. You're edgy, fashion forward and we can't forget another power asset in your arsenal––Caroline Rossi in your corner."

"Well, Jillian's is an option. But what we're aiming for are the top stores like Sak's, Neiman-Marcus, Bloomingdale's and Nordstrom's, where the big money is. The little mom and pop places would be fine for smaller cities but my line will be designer and too expensive for most of the stores. We want the big names."

She saw me staring out the window intent on the landscape below.

"What do you see down there so fascinating? You have to have the landscape memorized by now."

"It's such a big world out there. I never get tired of this scenery and how tranquil the world seems from up here. Look down there at the maze that is New Mexico in perfect squares and rectangles. *Peaceful*. Makes you think all is right with the chaotic old world. This trip has become like going home. It's uncanny I have become attached to this craziness. But then, San Francisco is unlike any other. Who isn't captivated by this mystic city?"

"I know. Did you ever think when we were kids we'd be in the thick of the big, exciting spinning world instead of on the outside looking in? I thrive on it. I love going home and seeing my dad, but there has to be more or it'd be curtains. I have too much energy and ambition. I'm curious and like to push myself to the edge. I'm not the one to stay in the same town in the same dreary dead-end job––we're talking a life sentence."

"How rude! Did you just call me a dead-end kid aka boring spectator? I have to agree to a point. But I like my surroundings to be familiar and the people I love near. I find it comforting and comfortable. No need to be supercharged every minute like you and Rowan."

"You just get your happy in a quieter, more sustained way, don't you agree? For your and Rowan's sake, it's a good thing I moved out here. Rowan and I laugh about it. He says if it weren't for me moving to San Francisco, he likely would have never seen you except when he came home. He thinks I have more influence on you than he does, and if he wants you to do something, he just tells me so I can work on you. You know, I might be Matchmaker of the Century. I'm not just your ordinary fifth wheel; I make love happen. All this magical power is going to my head."

"Ah-ha! What I've always suspected about you two. *Conspiracy.* But for sure with you both here, I've become a jet setter or at least in a new category, frequent flyer. Do you have any idea how many miles I've accumulated in the last five years?"

"I know. Me, too, but close to 100,000 I'd say. With Rowan finishing law school, you won't be coming out to see me so often, huh? I guess I'll have to hog tie you to get you out here."

"Not by a long shot, Sister. You and Rowan have created a monster. I can't get enough of this place. Just because he's coming home doesn't mean a thing. We're both addicted to San Francisco so we'll have our getaways. Besides, I can't live without my Jess. I'm harder to get rid of than bubble gum on your $500 shoe." I shuddered to think of life without Jessica McShane.

"Did I tell you I want to donate the Tudor to the church as a parsonage? They need a house and I've been thinking about this for some time. It might be premature, depends on the future with Rowan and me. It would make Aunt Nona proud." Sad but I had little to contribute about my plans. Rowan and I were on a high wire. I'd been waiting on *us* but my impatience was taking over. How long can I stand by? I was one-half of an important plan that needed to come together.

"So great and generous. I wondered what you would do with Morningstar. It's all coming true for both of us, huh Val? And we're still young so we can have it all--success, money, marriage, family. Wow, I'm impressed with us! What a way to ring in the New Year. Speaking of ring--"

"I know. Don't ask." I held up my left hand selectively moving my ring finger. "Doesn't this bare finger say it all? I thought the time could be right since Rowan is finishing law school, but I'm trying to keep the attitude it'll happen when it happens."

I looked out the window of the 727 and thought about the blur of the past five years and the inevitable changes. I taught English at the community college. Rowan was finishing law school and joining his dad's practice. His dad planned to retire so he and Caroline could move to their lake house. Rowan had recovered from two shoulder injuries accompanied by a sharp realization his baseball career remained dreamland and farfetched at best. Baseball came in second. His affection for his dad and his place in the law practice were too precious to be trifled with. His priorities and decisions had a narrow window; otherwise his dad would hire an attorney from the outside. I remembered last Christmas when Rowan drove me home after dinner with his parents. He seemed so excited to talk about his future, but he didn't seem as anxious to plan *our* future. We were stuck.

"Val, I can't throw away my chance to practice law with my dad for a few years. I've had this dream since I was a kid. He'd take me to breakfast on Saturday mornings and then to his office while he'd catch up on paperwork and explain in simple terms what he did each day. I felt grown up and important. I saw a gleam in his eye that came from his passion and dedication and belief in what he did. The image stayed with me all these years. It's a long shot at best for major league baseball, and I've been around the diamond enough to know my chances are slim. Besides when I'm old and gray, I want to remember my dad and me in the courtroom together, preferably on the same side. He would kick my butt." He laughed. Then his gorgeous green eyes flickered. I knew the look he had when he said something fun and when he couldn't wait to say more. Togetherness can prepare you for what to expect. But what I wished for was the unexpected. *We* never seemed to be the priority. What didn't occur to me was I should initiate the conversation. Content to stew in my juices, I used it as an excuse for laying blame so I would be free and clear. He could have changed his mind about us marrying and was delaying the inevitable. Rejection loomed.

"Aren't you proud of me? I'm finally growing up. Thanks, Val, for believing in me and for believing in us. All those trips back and forth sure helped. It's brought us closer and more connected, right? We certainly have gotten to be together more. It hasn't been easy for you, but it's been a life saver so I didn't have to travel as much." Rowan had been through his challenges of giving up baseball and finishing law school so we were familiar with stress. Too bad miles are not the lone culprit as a kiss of death in a relationship; its companion *distance* joins in there somewhere.

The screech of the intercom and the deep, bass voice of the captain brought me back. Note to self: red flag alert. *Stalled Val and Rowan, faulty connection.*

"Okay, Ladies and Gentlemen, fasten your seatbelts and put your tray tables in their upright and locked position. We're on final approach and will be landing in approximately 25 minutes. Again, thanks for flying with us today and enjoy your stay."

∞

CHAPTER 33
FAMILY COLLUSION

Rowan met us at the airport with a big smile and an even bigger surprise. His parents were flying in to California tomorrow morning for a long weekend. They had a big announcement for our family dinner at *Nikko's* tomorrow night.

"I can't imagine what's going on. They certainly have kept it under wraps from me. Mom usually can't wait to blab but now she's Miss Tight Lips. I don't think it's about my joining the law firm (old news), but who knows what they've got in mind. Those two seem to always be brewing the pot. Just be prepared, girls, for anything. Maybe they're buying us a condo in Sausalito. We should go pick one out just in case while we're over there for lunch." He grinned the grin of an only child of doting parents, a somewhat farfetched idea but not absolute fantasy either.

We raised our glasses of wine to Rowan as he made his toast. "Here's to no substitutes."

"What do you mean, Rowan?" Obvious and oblivious, I wondered what I had missed.

"Just what I said. Here's to the real thing--health, happiness, family, friends, and true love. What else matters if you don't have those?"

He did amaze me at the most impromptu moments with his out-of-character remarks. I didn't think he was incapable of subsurface thoughts, but those occasions were few and far between. The shadow had been cast, and I felt helpless to stop it as I slipped into darkness. I should be light of heart but instead unhappiness weighed heavy. I felt taken for granted and invisible.

"What's your big drink-to-words-of-wisdom since you're scoping my toast putting me on the hot seat?"

Jessica jumped in to save the day. "Here's to back stabbing, throat slitting, power, greed, and corrupt deals. Another day at the office." Devilish and funny. Who else better to tie the real world up into such a crisp, succinct little package?

"Way to go, Jess. Impossible to top. You win toast of the day. Sick but true." I took a big gulp of wine. I tried to banish the recurring thought of getting plastered out of my small mind.

Jess and Rowan were laughing, talking, and joking around about inside stuff. They spent time together without me, so I understood their memories of last month or last year or last week. Lost in thoughts of myself, I didn't keep up. The subject turned to Jess' new business venture and going to Italy in the summer. Rowan commented Italy would be a fun trip for everyone. Suddenly I felt uncomfortable and left out. Jess and Rowan have always shared a strong bond, no news flash there. Their personalities click and they have fun, so what? Maybe there's more or not. No wonder I'm like the invisible outsider. I need to try harder to contribute to the conversation. Bring something to the table. I was suppressed. Why? Rare sunny day in seaside Sausalito, 8 x 10 glossy, accented by seagulls, sailboats, Bay breezes, ferries and all the abalone I can eat. Three young up-and-comers sitting in the open air of one of the premier spots in the world. Two of us spark vitality stimulated by each other's company. The third appears markedly out of place with her lifeblood sucked clean leaving her sullen and lifeless. I could not come up with a rational reason for my behavior. *Put me out of my misery and be quick about it. I yearned for the refuge of Morningstar Lane.*

"What say you, Val? You're awfully quiet all of a sudden. Jonathan Livingston Seagull got your tongue?" Rowan teased. He touched my arm. "You seem so far away. Are you okay?"

"I listen if it's about me." More truth than fiction to my snide comment. "Music to my ears and all." My shutdown of his sincere inquiry was obvious and mean-spirited but he took it well. My emptiness overwhelmed.

"Aren't you the comedian, in a well, dark way?" His green eyes lingered then turned downward as he twirled his glass.

"Just taking it all in. Too bad we can't store up the sea air and bottle it. I want to live here. Well, not Sausalito, way too many tourists. But over there in fantasy land––Tiburon or Belvedere calls my name. We should rent bikes and go for a ride along the Bay one afternoon. I would never imagine saying this but our landlocked part of Texas is losing its mystique."

"Geez, it's taken you long enough. No place sweeter as far as I can tell. I'll take a clue and predict I'll never leave." Jessica looked fabulous in her big name aviator sunglasses and designer scarf, jeans, and sweater. No mistake, she's a local for sure.

We spent the afternoon browsing in the shops and then took a break before dinner. Rowan went to the hotel, and Jess and I hailed a cab to the Mission district to her apartment on the second floor. The light poured in the large contemporary windows onto the hardwood floors. The two-bedroom one bath unit was small but beautifully decorated.

"Jess, I love the condo. This place looks like a magazine layout. Every trip here, I see something new on the wall or a new chair or rug. Decorator has been busy, I see. It's too perfect!"

"Isn't it fabulous? Thanks to Caroline. She helps keep me focused. Now she won't let me buy anything or put anything in this place without her approval. My taste offends her sense of interior design and sends her into anaphylactic shock. I swear she breaks out in hives by my choices. *Allergic to ugly and gauche.* So if I want to keep the peace and have a great place, I abide by her wishes. I do save a lot of trips back to the store; she has cut into my reverse shopping."

"What are we doing tonight? I vote to stay in but I know you and Rowan have different ideas."

"You bet we do. We thought North Beach. It's been too long, and it's always such a hoot. You never know what you'll see down there. I like off-the-chart cool and crazy and more. We'll make it an early evening; wind it up about midnight or so."

I wanted to pass. Nothing about the strange scenario sounded the least bit appealing. I was in a funk. The image of trudging along in a crowd of strangers on a street entrenched in a never-ending row of strip clubs and bars didn't improve my attitude. *Too much strangeness.*

"Jess, I better stay in. I might be taking a cold or something, I'm dragging. I'm sure y'all won't miss ball-and-chain tag along."

"Oh, Val. Come on and give it a try. You'll have fun. It'll do you good to get out."

"I've done North Beach, remember? Not interested, really."

Rowan called and said he'd come with a cab at eight o'clock to pick us up. I gave him my sorry tale. He sounded annoyed so rather than cajole and pretend he wanted me along, he said he hoped I felt better. Then suddenly invigorated, he said Jess needed to be ready when he got there at eight o'clock, no waiting.

They made an early evening of it all right--early in the A.M. The last I checked the bedside clock I saw 2:00. But she was in and asleep when I put the coffee on the next morning. I heard the shower upstairs a couple of hours later, and then she appeared fresh-faced and stunning as ever. All-nighter, no problem, no telltale signs. Just another rosy day with no droops, no bags, no dark circles, no red eyes. Blessed with looks that never disappoint.

"What's going on this morning, Miss Val?"

"Rowan called. He'll pick up his parents later at the airport and take them to the hotel. They'll spend the day together so we have a free day. We're supposed to meet them tonight at eight o'clock for cocktails and then our reservation is for nine at *Nikko's*."

"Oh, good. I need some time to get it together. We kind of overdid it last night. I kept waiting for Rowan to call it a night which became the problem. You wouldn't believe we closed down North Beach."

"Oh sure I would. Glad it was you and not me. The first time was an eye-opener but the same old weird, same old wacky gets monotonous. I swore the last trek would be my last, and I aim to make good on that promise. They don't need me; plenty of crowds on parade inside and outside."

"I agree. But some of us get a kick out of odd hullabaloo, so call me crazy. You know Rowan and me. We're so competitive we won't give in or give up. No matter how exhausted we were, neither one of us would call it a night. So guess what--we didn't!"

"Oh, well, you're young once and if you do it right, once is enough."

"Let's stay in and do our toes and nails. I'll do yours if you'll do mine. How does that sound? I like it. For sure, it sounds more fun than going out to some crowded salon. We'll have our down home spa day. I have two new shades of polish so pick out your color as they say."

We spent a relaxing afternoon together getting our nails, toes, and hair ready for our big evening. Neither one of us had ever been to *Nikko's*, so this was a big deal. Dinner for five with wine easily cost four figures. Short on discriminating taste, I questioned how dinner at a fancy restaurant could be worth the price tag. But then, I wasn't paying the bill. I shouldn't be concerned, but the Rossi extravagance was almost as troubling as the thought of spending the evening with Caroline Rossi. I liked Rowan's dad. Personable, funny, and easy to be around, he did not put on airs as my Aunt Nona liked to say. Down to earth and interesting, he enjoyed telling stories about happenings in the courtroom or in the judge's chambers; and, of course, we were sworn to secrecy with no breach of confidentiality. Caroline occasionally appeared willing to make the long trip down to our level. She craved attention and had a knack. She enjoyed seeing others as small and insignificant and had mastered the art of intimidation, manipulation, and superiority. If you crossed her in any way, you came out looking stupid or at the very least like the bad guy. I kept my mouth shut when, if truth be told, I would have preferred to set her straight. What was I getting myself into? How and why did I live in a state of delusion? No matter how you deceive yourself, you marry the family. Caroline was in charge of this family, make no mistake, and she made her choice crystal clear, it was not me. I smiled. Too bad Jess didn't agree with her matchmaking. I had no qualms about Jessica and me. Friends may come and go but Jess and Val are tried and true blue. Our relationship continued to prove everlasting and impenetrable despite Caroline Rossi.

I had visions of how contentious Caroline could make my life and Rowan's. Up to now, I managed to take her in small doses. But who was I kidding? An occasional two-hour dinner is a world apart from constant contact and involvement. I wanted to confide in Jess but why be a downer and ruin her trip. With the right opportunity, she would understand. She already knew Caroline Rossi did not qualify as my choice for mother-in-law of the year. We looked elegant in our little black dresses as we alit from the cab at the hotel and made our way to the bar. Rowan greeted us and escorted us to a large round polished walnut table with five caramel leather swivel chairs. His parents joined us in a few minutes and made a pre-congratulatory toast to Rowan for graduating law school in the spring. Caroline raised her glass.

"I would like to make a toast to Jessica and Valentine. How lucky can we get; we have two beautiful girls on the road to success."

"Thank you Caroline. You're too sweet." Jess leaned over and gave her a cheek. I merely blew a kiss. Her announcement did not live up to the hype but at least it did materialize. Sadly, my hoped-for announcement appeared destined to languish as fantasy.

"I would also like to say Alan and I have a special surprise for everyone. No surprise, Jess is embarking on yet another amazing aspect of her career in the fashion industry. She has already taken the modeling world by storm in case you haven't seen the latest issue of *Trendsetter*. This summer she and I will visit several Italian factories. We're all set to prepare for the first phase of manufacturing prototypes of our accessories."

"Okay, Mom. We see you've created your personal fashion monster. But what does all this have to do with the rest of us?" Rowan was curious but impatient for his mother to make her point. Anxious for her to get on with it, his fascination waned, so I grew hopeful his impatience meant he had an announcement. He would graduate from law school in a few months and return home to practice law. The timing for our engagement seemed perfect to me. Rowan liked surprises. Stranger things happen. I waited.

Caroline did not waver and continued to enjoy her limelight. "Patience, my child. I'm getting to it. Alan and I thought this would be an ideal opportunity for a family trip. We're inviting all of you to join us in Italy for two weeks, all expenses paid, and we want Captain McShane to join us if his schedule permits. You've all been working hard with school and work, and we want to share our good fortune with the people we love. Alan wants to explore this beautiful country and locate his relatives in the northern part of the boot. It'll be the trip of a lifetime."

Everyone cheered, toasting and hugging each other. The false bravado made me ill. I needed to get out of this fiasco. Focused on my absence from the family trip said it all. I needed to make other permanent arrangements. *Valentine moment of truth.* Because I wanted Rowan and I to make it so badly, I'd closed my eyes to all going on around me--blinders to block out things not meant to be. Rowan and I apparently fell into the fateful category. No one was to blame, but I shouldn't postpone or prolong the aching part of my awakening. He would be hurt but not as hurt as if we continued. He and I were as mismatched as any two people could be and it was folly to think otherwise. *His mother had always known best.* Dinner delightful, the restaurant undeniably elegant, and the conversation and company stimulating, but this had to be my finale. I had no intentions of denying and delaying the inevitable. I had to extricate myself from my self-imposed snare. I had made the best of the evening and these last five years; now my grand exit called. I told Rowan I needed to talk with him.

"What's wrong, Val? Have I done something? I can't understand why you're so upset. We can fix this. I'll make you mad when I say this, but you looked like you had your mind made up to be unhappy this entire trip. What's going on?"

I assured him there was nothing to fix; my decision had been brewing for months. I didn't want to hurt him; I just wanted out. He hung on my every word, searching my face for answers. Then he withdrew. I saw a flicker of relief and then he seemed distracted. At least I would not be the one to cause him further grief with his mother. We would not be the *miserable* old couple on a park bench. Since I was the one dissatisfied, he took the opportunity to say he had his doubts about us, too. These last few years had settled a few questions but had also brought up some new ones. We had not made substantial progress. Whatever the pretext, Rowan and Valentine did not make the mark. And who wants to settle?

"You're right, Val. You and me, it's just too much work. Relationships shouldn't have to be forced; they should happen. I know what you're going to say. You and I are too different. We're better apart than together. Anyway, thanks for being the brave one. The decision wasn't easy. I want to argue and beg you that we belong together, but I'm kind of tired. There's something not right about my always trying to convince you how much I love you. I've tried to make you and make us happy, but it doesn't seem to last. One thing is for sure. You'll always have a special place in my heart. Whatever problems we have can be solved, but I can't do it alone. I'm done." He looked beaten.

"And you in mine, Rowan. I opened my eyes and my heart and looked around me. I wanted us to be together so badly I guess I pretended we'd find a way and it would naturally happen. Somehow, someway, we would be okay. But I have no regrets. We gave it our best shot. So it's not like we didn't try and make a go of it."

I kissed him good-by. He hailed me a cab and paused as he helped me into the back seat. I thought I saw a tear trickle from the corner of his eye. Waving away my wishful thinking, I gave him the go-ahead to go. I rode to the airport in silence bleary-eyed and a bit sad but still reeling from my boldness. The lights blurred by mist and fog, how appropriate. But then, it's misty and foggy here 90% of the time, no special occasion. I hoped to be lighter, brighter and more hopeful than I'd been in months. *I wanted to feel free.* Living in pretense requires being bogged down in make believe and takes a lot of energy to project false fulfillment from delusion. I needed to feel secure and wanted to get home to my little Tudor surrounded by its warmth and comfort. I called Pastor Leland from San Francisco International. There were no questions, no explaining. He would be at the gate to meet me and take me home.

∞

Chapter 34
Fight or Flight

I sat in the coffee shop waiting for my flight to be called but instead heard my name echoing through the terminal. I located the bank of telephones across the concourse. Curious who was calling, I also dreaded answering a phone call. There wasn't anyone I felt compelled to talk to and felt entitled to my emptiness and not being interrupted by an outside voice. Selfish and immersed in the aftermath, I wanted to be left alone. I had just declared the quietus on the love of my life creating a swath of damage akin to a Texas tornado. If Rowan was calling, what would I say to him? I discarded the thought as so improbable as to be ridiculous. The fact I even considered such an absurd notion said a lot about my mental state.

"Valentine Monroe."

"Val? What in the world is going on? I'm so relieved. I was worried I wouldn't be able to reach you. Everyone is concerned about you."

"Hi, Jess. I'm fine. There's no need to be worried; Rowan and I decided to make a decision about our future. Nothing more, nothing less. We don't bring out the best in each other. It's been coming for quite a while. My timing might have been better, but we agreed we're better off apart and no more dragging it out and dragging us down."

I heard Jessica crying. "Oh, Jess. Please don't be sad. It's for the best. We gave it our best shot but--"

"Oh, Val, is there anything I can do? You left so sudden; I was crazy with worry."

"I'm sorry. It began as one of my spur-of-the-moment things and grew out of control. Probably not the most logical but I just needed to *be* home. I hope you'll understand. Please forgive me. I don't want you to worry. I'm actually feeling better about myself than I have in months. I'm so tired of pretending it's what I live for to put my life on hold waiting for Rowan."

"I understand you're upset, and it's hard for you to talk about it. But please, if I can do anything or if you need me before I get back home, call me. It's so good to hear your voice. There's got to be more to all this than you're letting on. Call me soon when you get home. Okay? I only wish I'd known you were so unhappy."

"I know, Jess. It's hard to share what you're feeling when you're not even sure yourself. Thank you so much for calling. Love you." I hung up quickly before I cried. She knew I was hurting, agonizing, and even second-guessing my decision. These emotions should be expected when you still care, Valentine, I reassured myself. Stay strong and steady, true to the course. There's no backing down unless you have a magic potion or wizard handy to conjure up magic.

If ever I needed a constant stabilizing force, it was now. Thank you, Jessica, my precious friend, for being at my side no matter what--*even if it's crazy to be on my side*. We were as different as any two friends could be but bound by our common denominator--trust. We gained strength from each other during trying times like a wellspring.

The dark clouds of disappointment were gathering overhead. Distraught, I fought against the thundering questioning. *Why now?* Valentine didn't get what she wanted, so she gathered up her toys and left. Look deep inside at what you're trying to hide, girl. I wanted--no I *expected*--an announcement of our engagement. We should have spent our honeymoon in Italy. Okay, I took to heart fairy tales as if reality. It's irrational to expect someone you adore and want to share your life with to have your same vision on the same schedule. In Rowan's case, it's illogical, irrational and supernatural. Okay, he can't read my mind, but he should know me well enough by now to know what I expect if he can't initiate things. But the real upside down story here is I held the picture of coming attractions as real. I fully expected Rowan to announce our engagement and upcoming marriage. For years, unmet expectation had turned into resentment and now I had hit bottom. The risk with setting yourself up, someone is waiting to knock you down. I waited for him to say what I thought everyone expected. He never stood up calling for everyone's attention. He never gently clinked a crystal glass smiling and beaming. He never turned toward me with a devilish grin anticipating his earth-shattering news. He never held my eyes in his. He sat glued to his chair. How could someone who professes to love you be this oblivious or blatantly cruel? We had been on hold for five years while he finished his checklist--college, baseball, law school, and heaven knows what else--why not say what I felt? "Buster, it's past time for us to go to the next step or let go." I answered my own question. *Disappointment tinged with fear.* Suspecting he was through with me, I saved him the trouble. Take that, Rowan Rossi. How juvenile! What are we, emotionally trapped in the sixth grade?

I grappled with feelings held under wrap for months or longer. I was disappointed, dejected and duped. Since the beginning, the idea of marrying his family was distasteful because of his mother. See her now doing a happy dance. Hallelujah! Her son had come to his senses. If I hadn't cratered, would Rowan have continued our fiasco? Was he man or mouse? Ah-ha! Another weakness and another reason to despise him. Love might be blind but only if convenient. Caroline Rossi would forever be my nemesis.

My plane landed with a thud and brought me to my senses. My constant force waited unwavering. Leland was my Godsend. His wise understanding and enlightenment far exceeded any explanation. What else needed to be said? He met me at the gate and welcomed me home with open arms. Somewhat anti-climactic and unsolicited, I offered my immediate summation of the situation, "My relationship with Rowan is over. It's mutual. We understand there's nothing left to be gained by continuing to pretend we're a couple. Now we can begin our lives apart."

Leland kept his eyes on the road ahead. "Valentine, you have put your heart and soul into this relationship with Rowan. Whatever your feelings you can't pretend they don't exist. Trust me, you have wounds.

I'm not sure you fully understand what has happened this weekend. I hope you will come to face your fears and your dreams."

"I'm numb and reeling. Surprise is an understatement. I can't say what came over me. I was suffocating and desperate."

Pastor Leland Shepherd had been called to our church, but there was no doubt in my mind he had also been called to me. I recognized the magnitude of our paths crossing as life changing and so did he--the damned child and the leader of the flock. We continued our counseling sessions despite my continuing objections and my frequent assurances. I didn't need further therapy. He once again suggested joint counseling and wanted me to call Rowan. I admitted my admirable progress with therapy, but I didn't have the slightest inclination how someone, especially me, would go about making the phone call. I refused to consider calling Rowan as out of the question.

Our twice weekly discussions were soul-wrenching; it would be easier to get on with my pretend life. Intense light into the infected recesses were not conducive to exposure. When I withdrew into my shell and preferred my dark secure place, he was patient. At times, I resented him and his intrusion. I felt delicate and shattered; then I emerged to lick my wounds, became revitalized and prepared to heal. Each step of progress had meaning. There was no turning back. There were occasions when I had to experience the reality of stagnation. A retreat to my old ways meant a return to darkness. The old questioning returned between physical, material life, and eternal life. What was the big whoop about change if no Hereafter? Girl, if there was ever anyone who needed help, it's you! Whatever evil beset me and others along my journey was a job for the Supreme Being. I opened my hidden spaces--however dark and blasphemous. Leland continued as neither offended nor repulsed. The more I spewed, the more cleansed I felt. The weeks and months marked my progress and the strength of our relationship. We built a foundation of affection and respect based on our beliefs. As I sorted my feelings about Rowan and his family, Leland steadied as my rock, although resolution persisted as elusive. I loved Rowan but faced the reality of difficulties requiring solutions which would not mystically appear. Leland made one last plea.

"Valentine, offer to go to counseling with Rowan. At some point, you meet the devil head on. You are brave and realize fear is your enemy causing destruction, and inhibition keeps you from life's opportunities. Our backgrounds cannot be changed. It makes no difference the objections which cloak our fear, there is no rational prejudice. Whether we believe our bias or prejudice has a basis or not is the devil's tool. Prejudice is fear-driven and destructive until we face it head on. You fear Rowan will think you're unworthy. Now you must overcome fear or it will continue to eat away like a cancer and control you and your life and take away your joy. To change, at some point you have to let go of being the cursed child."

"You're right, Leland, as usual. It's curious, isn't it; we don't accept each other at face value. Maybe I don't have to tell him. It nags at me and it's the root cause of thinking I'm inferior and used."

"Let's keep it real, Valentine. I'd hardly refer to prejudice in any form as 'curious.' But I'm mincing words. It's hard to accept but you have no reason to be ashamed. You had nothing to do with causing or initiating. Bad things happen even when so-called adults are in charge. But we've talked about this. Openness and forgiveness is our hope to heal. And remember you may be underestimating Rowan."

In my heart, I accepted the possibility Rowan might consider someone with my past unacceptable. I could not divulge openly to him, too ugly and menacing. Intelligent, educated and tolerant, I understood not to allow such a malignancy to distort my thinking. Such belief and behavior was reserved for the delusional who denied any accountability or responsibility. I admitted my phobias and to being disillusioned, angry and fearful. But deep secrets no one had a right to see betrayed. I rationalized all of us share some type of irrational fear but that doesn't make us bad people. I understood acceptance of a dark blot such as mine might be too much. I would not confess the evil trespass against me to Rowan. It would destroy the perceived Valentine he loves. My disfigurement would be permanent; I was used goods. Not everyone has the foresight and wisdom of Leland who can see past imperfections. Not to mention Caroline Rossi.

I preferred to focus on my goals to accomplish. My teaching career gave my life meaning and direction. I understood the continuity and significance of my career. I had known from the beginning I had selected teaching because Aunt Nona was a teacher. I admired and wanted to emulate her and yes I wanted to make her proud I had chosen her profession. I wanted to please her, and by choosing to teach, I hoped she would be impressed. I was obligated to Aunt Nona, but my love for her deeper and amounted to much more than obligation. She had in her way given me life through her love and goodness and generosity. She neither demanded nor expected anything in return. Thankful she had lived long enough to know I would become a teacher, I knew now this was the destined path. I had wanted her blessing more than anything. She encouraged growth and did not shy away from challenge; I felt her spirit with me. In my third year teaching English at the community college, I decided on getting my doctorate and eventually a professorship at the university. I was blessed to have teaching enrich my life as stimulating and rewarding, and it provided me a way to make a difference. Teaching gave me something to hold on to that gave me something back.

Leland inspired me to grow and challenge myself in my career and not be content with the status quo. He expanded his counseling services and along with his church ministry, he kept the education building at the church open five days a week and hired a full time assistant. His premarital counseling services were in high demand; he had appointments booked for three months and more. Couples headed down the aisle sought his guidance and were drawn to his no-nonsense, cut-to-the-core sessions. He educated couples who wanted to be aware when they were headed toward a minefield littered with compatibility problems. He continued to advance his education in theology, psychology and counseling. Other than a counseling session, we rarely saw each other during the week. He continued to preach, counsel, and take care of his congregation as if he would be here the rest of his days.

He never expressed dissatisfaction with our little church congregation or expressed his desire to seek out a larger church with more opportunity for growth. He seemed content with us. Occasionally I cooked a simple meal for us, but our day to come together was Sunday. After services, we savored our quiet contemplation and discussions whether trivial or troubling. From the beginning, his ministry was his priority. But his religious devotion and commitment did not diminish his impact and the effect of our friendship. The Valentine-Leland era was coming to an end. Leland had been called to pastor a church in Louisiana. He was returning home.

∞

CHAPTER 35
INTERVENTION

I was as dejected as Leland was ecstatic. I attempted to hide my selfishness and celebrate his assignment. He would be here another three months as a transition period for his parishioners before he relocated, and so that the new parsonage could be completed in Louisiana. For the first time since he was called as a minister, he would live in a home of his own. He never complained about the small one bedroom studio he occupied here for five years, but he must welcome moving into a larger and brand new house. I was trying to share his optimistic outlook. I needed him here with me and the church needed him. Who wants to break in a new minister who knows nothing about us? The fact we would know nothing about him either wasn't such a pressing concern.

Here we go again with a recurring theme--another adjustment requiring more of me than I wanted to give. Just once, it would be refreshing if I welcomed spontaneous change. I should try a new approach instead of my unending questioning and protesting short-sighted self. I should move to Louisiana. Such desperate thoughts were smoke screens; diving into life full force was the remedy. The idea of life without Leland was not only bleak but terrifying. I depended on him without reservation. He was my counselor, my friend, my family--my spiritual leader--all rolled into one and likely never to happen again. Painful but true; I was losing my Dalai Lama.

There was a bright spot. Jessica was back from California. She and I were having dinner at our favorite Thai restaurant. Spicy food and lots of it seemed the perfect anecdote. We hadn't been together since my split up with Rowan in San Francisco although the instantaneous connection of our phone lines kept us close and current. Distance didn't separate or interfere with us. In the back of my mind, I knew she would have news about Rowan. I was curious but restrained, since there was no therapy in hearing about him. The tender spot remained. As intense as I was to remove him, the more he lingered. Even though he had hurt me deeply, and I was determined to protect myself, I thought and dreamed about him and held on to a tiny ray of hope. It would require effort and self-control, but I was determined to make the adjustment of life without Rowan.

I pulled the Caddy into the parking lot and decided to use valet since it was getting dark. I didn't see Jessica's car, but I was a few minutes early. I checked in with the hostess, and she remarked she had reservations for a table for three and would seat me. Jessica didn't mention bringing anyone, which was not like her. I was instantly unnerved and sensed an eclipse over my prospects for the evening. Why did she spring this on me? I resented the third party intrusion; I had counted on tonight as our much-needed Val and Jess catch up. Then I saw Jess come in the door with Caroline Rossi, and all my good intentions flew out before the door shut. Now here's Caroline Rossi interjecting herself in our téte-à-téte. It was hard keeping up with Jess; she boggled the mind. What was she thinking? Whoa Valentine, just go with it. *Calm yourself.*

Jess, you have some explaining! What is happening here? I fought the urge to hide in the ladies room, head out the door and into my car. *Get yourself together.* I arose from the table to greet Jess and Caroline. Jess and I hugged and then kissed each other on the cheek as was our custom. It didn't matter if we saw each other every day or whether we were apart for weeks or months. We were familiar with the unpredictability of life early on; it didn't take much effort, and it wasn't worth the risk not to greet and part without our affectionate gesture.

"It's been too long, girl. We have to find a way to cut this distance." Jess looked amazing even for Jess. Her short boyish cut was growing out reflecting a softer auburn. I never saw anyone who looked beautiful no matter what you did to her--no matter the hair color, cut, or style, makeup or not, clothing casual or fancy. Rather than annoyed, I reveled in her beauty because as a person she was as beautiful as they come. Not to mention her *moxie*. I should take lessons from my best friend, but no matter how aware and admiring, her charm didn't seem to rub off on me.

"Ain't it the truth. I missed you so much I've even considered getting on an airplane and you know I'm desperate." Flying might be fast, convenient and necessary but no longer an adventure.

"Well, what a pleasant surprise. How are you, Caroline?" I gave her my most enthusiastic pretend hug.

"Hello, Valentine. I hope you forgive my intrusion. I realize you and Jessica haven't seen each other for a while; she was kind enough to invite me with a little prodding." In one easy motion, her hand slipped the $2000 handbag off her shoulder and slung the gold chain on the back of her chair. She was a woman on a mission. I was outmatched and not in the mood for confrontation. All I wanted was rare, quality *private* time with my best friend and the best Thai food in town. Seems simple but here we have cluttered, complicated and intrusive.

"Oh, I'm glad you joined us. I'm the one who needs to apologize for my rude exit in San Francisco. I hope you understand. Rowan and I were going through a rough patch and home was all I wanted. There's no rational explanation for my behavior. It happens when I allow frustration to take over. Let's hope I overcome my immaturity; I've given up on outgrowing it." I had some other creative reasons (or excuses as my Aunt Nona would say) but there was no point in continuing the drama.

Caroline and Jess laughed uncomfortably to be polite. Jess expertly switched the conversation. "Val and I have a way of connecting after all these years. No problem and no one seems big enough to get in our way. We bounce back, together."

They broke the mold after Jess. She always has my back and control of the situation. I trusted Jess and knew there was a story behind Caroline Rossi being here. It might not be apparent tonight but I was patient.

We made small talk as we looked over the menu and made our selections. "Shall we order a bottle of wine; can we possibly agree red or white?" Jess was a pro at anticipating my every need and a spot on diffuser for the evening.

"Sounds like a good plan. Spicy food demands red." Caroline was quick to jump on the idea and take control.

"I like red or white or blush." I smiled. My feeble attempt to be funny manifested as trying too hard. "Miss Sommelier, you're in charge and we'll do our part. We promise to enjoy every drop of your selection."

"No problem, Miss Val, you know my secrets. Red is the winner. I've been wine tasting in Napa and Sonoma so often as part of my unofficial tourist guide duties, I'm officially a connoisseur or a wine-o depending on your point of view." Jessica was speaking some truth here.

So far, the evening was uneventful just the way I hoped. The wine and food, delicious, the conversation lively and relaxed, but I reasoned it was too much to ask for the pleasantness to last. Then Caroline's big bang moment arrived, and my hopes dashed she was here to enjoy our Thai dinner.

"It's obvious I invited myself, so you have to be wondering why I'm here." Caroline took off her glasses and accidentally banged her two chunky gold bracelets against the wine glass.

"Oops, guess I'm a little nervous. Break it and buy it. Don't need any more wine glasses or wine, apparently." She winked at me. Uncomfortable and dreading the speech she came here to give, I felt compassion for her. Time to savor the occasion--Caroline Rossi not in charge and her subsequent confession--but I had not developed the hardened heart to take pleasure in someone else's distress however minor and however detached I tried to be.

"Maybe I can help." Jessica wore her serious face.

"Well, you two have me in suspense for sure. Whether it's good or bad, no more stalling. I can handle it. I'm a big girl. What's going on?" I knew Jessica was the automatic and likely reluctant go-between but what a risky business. I wished she had prepared me for this A-bomb. At first, I guessed Caroline had undergone a miraculous change of heart. Then I switched to the notion she had additional payload designed to get rid of Valentine Monroe for permanent.

"I know you and Rowan haven't spoken for several months. He wanted to call you but was sure you didn't want to hear from him. He didn't know what to do. Once the events of the San Francisco weekend settled, he was distraught. He hoped you were going through a temporary thing and didn't understand what happened or what he'd done to make you upset."

Jessica reached for my hand. The transformation happened before my eyes but was difficult for me to grasp. Caroline's capacity to control the situation seemed exceeded only by her audacity. She was no longer running interference but directing intervention for her son's relationship. I felt like a cornered animal struggling not to pounce and to hold my tongue which promised to be a piece of raw meat by the end of the evening.

Caroline cleared her throat. "Valentine, I'm at a loss how to say this any other way, so I'll just be blunt. Are you in love with Rowan?"

What nerve to ask the question Rowan should have asked. What was I supposed to say? Why was she here with her surprise meeting and questioning me about *our* business--mine and Rowan's? We didn't manage our relationship as well as we should have, but I resented the intrusion. I didn't recall asking for her assistance, and I doubted if Rowan did either.

I ignored the question. "You're right. I haven't spoken to Rowan. I've been busy with teaching and my priorities. We left each other on good terms, so he could have called me if he cared enough. It's no secret we have unresolved issues, but I'm open to discuss and work through."

"My son loves you and he doesn't know what he did wrong. It's breaking my heart to see him so unhappy. He's had to cope with giving up his baseball dream after his injury and then the shock of your breakup with him. Valentine, I don't think you realize the intense weight on his shoulders. His life is spiraling and he doesn't know where to turn. I've never seen my son so dejected and hopeless. I can't continue to stand by and watch him struggle. There must be something I can do to make up for the hurt I've caused."

"I'm sorry to hear Rowan is unhappy but there's nothing I can do. It's time for him to step up. The best I can do, if he wants to talk to me, I'll talk. It's up to you and Rowan to work out the rest." Guess the Rossi's didn't consider my trauma major enough to be a culprit for unpredictable behavior. Umm.I took my purse off the back of the chair calling an end to the evening while everyone was still civil and still speaking--a perfect time for my exit.

"For what it's worth, Valentine, I'm sorry you and I haven't been close, but I want you to know anyone my son loves as much as he loves you is number one in my book. I sincerely would count it an honor to have you as part of our family. I was wrong to be judgmental and manipulative. I've learned the hard way not to run my son's life and hope you won't misunderstand my intentions here tonight. My hope is to help bring you two together so you and Rowan can work out your differences."

"Thank you, Caroline. I appreciate your kind words. Your invitation to join the family is premature, but I'd like to think there is hope." Not so long ago her words would have sent me reeling. Her approval had lost its charm along with the faded fantasy romance. Convinced his mother had a prominent place in our problems, no matter how much I loved Rowan, we had to resolve Caroline Rossi. This evening had not changed but reinforced my opinion.

"The main reason I came tonight is that I accept you and Rowan are meant to be together. He's a different person when you are in his life. A mother would be foolish to protect her pride and downright cruel to ignore the authentic joy of her son." She sounded and looked as if she meant what she said; maybe because she had lost the battle and didn't want to lose her son.

I hugged her briefly and said goodnight as I made a quick exit. Upset, confused, and blindsided, I needed to sort out tonight. Caroline Rossi was accustomed to getting her way much like her son. I had no doubts she was a good mother and loved her son passionately. Otherwise, she would never stoop so low as to confess and apologize. I wanted to give her the benefit of the doubt she was genuine in her concern. Interference or intervention, as well-meaning as she may be, tonight's surprise verging on shock was not the ideal way to reach the best me.

∞

CHAPTER 36
BROKEN HEART
CONNECTION

The tale of the mystery dinner continued to unfold. My key was in the lock when I heard the incessant ringing. I smiled hurrying to the phone. I knew Jess was calling. "I hope you're still speaking to me although I'd understand if you weren't. Is it okay if I come by for a few minutes?" I heard a rare hesitancy in Jessica's voice.

"Sure, come on, with your tail between your legs, begging for forgiveness. I'm hopeful, too. You should have a good story of what tonight was all about. What *were* you thinking?" Jess ignored the obvious and continued, "I'll come in through the garage; I'll make a giant leap of a guess we'll hold conflab in the kitchen. See you in a few."

A few minutes later, I heard her car in the driveway and opened the kitchen door. "Come in and bring your sad tale and it better be good, Miss Jess. Let's sit here at the kitchen table aka official conference in session and kick butt area. I'll put on tea." Aunt Nona's way was fine with me.

"Oh, Valentine, I hope you can forgive me. This whole thing just mushroomed out of control. Caroline is beside herself about Rowan and about to go ballistic because she can't fix it. She knows how close he and

I are; and, of course, my relationship with you, so what chance did I have? I'm in up to my eyeballs. I agreed to her joining us tonight for dinner. We all know she's vital to your and Rowan's relationship. But there is much more."

"Okay, you've got my full attention. Come clean. You and I don't mince words. She was trying to apologize and make amends. But where is Rowan in all this? Now he's got his mother doing his PR and promo?"

Jess played with her tea bag, dunking, dunking, splattering tea all over. "Not sure where to start, so I guess the beginning is as good as any. Caroline hasn't been a big fan of yours and she's got a grudge. When her father passed away a few years ago, going through his personal papers, she found a letter still sealed in its envelope. She intended to tell you tonight about the letter but chickened out and asked me to tell you. It's something you and I have circled around but had no way of being for sure, a *Dear Nona* letter." She handed me a worn blue linen envelope addressed to Miss Nona Emmaline Monroe. I saw the blue ink return address from James Andrew Rowan.

23 April 1920

Dearest Nona,

I take the coward's way. I expect you must have seen the newspaper wedding announcement. I cannot face you now that our time together is over. I can barely think such a thing much less say it. There is no future for us. Surely no more horrible words have been spoken. I must marry Felicia for reasons that cannot be changed and I shall not burden you with my troubles. Her family and mine are close and our backgrounds well-matched. Selfish I know, but I wish I loved her then all would be well in my world. Sadly, this is not the case. So we must be content with two worlds in shambles, yours and mine. I have consecrated my thoughts and energy to you and me my love and cannot forge ahead with a solution to make our dream a reality. For whatever consolation, if any, I will love you with my dying breath. My empty soul is comforted by memories of your sweet goodness and loving tenderness. I pray in my sorrow you remember me as the one who loved you endlessly despite my

*human foibles. We know each other's hearts and right or wrong
our souls are united forever.*
Your forever love,

Andrew

I couldn't look at Jessica. I was lost in the swirling memory of two separated young lovers whose paths crossed for a lightning moment and then vanished as mere memory, destined to be strangers. Wasted tears bubbled up, and I didn't have the strength or desire to stop them. Their flow burned my eyes but could they cleanse my soul? Aunt Nona, my heart is breaking for you. If only I had known, but what could I have said or done? It's the idea I didn't inspire her trust and confidence. Why? Focus on Valentine, her needs, her wants, her problems, her past, present and future. The fact she had agonies and struggles never crossed my small mind. I devoted my energy to my troubles. After all, didn't I have a monopoly on being the injured party? Aunt Nona hid her pain, but I was also unmindful.

Jessica put her arms around me. "I know you're hurting to think Aunt Nona endured such pain. There is one other thing. The letter either never reached Aunt Nona, or she returned the letter unopened. When Caroline found the letter in her father's papers, it was sealed. Nona apparently never received it or certainly never read it."

"I'm not sure if that makes an iota of difference. But several things are explained, such as why Aunt Nona never married and her curious mention of Andrew Rowan when she was in the hospital. We don't know what other people--even people we think we're close to---have gone through. She never showed any bitterness or resentment she had been wronged. Even when she mentioned Andrew Rowan in the hospital, she never let on. I love her even more than I thought possible. She didn't so much as intimate her shattered dream. She didn't want to burden me with her sadness." Characteristic confirmation of Aunt Nona's unselfish and compassionate nature.

"It's not easy to explain away, Val, the connection now with you and Rowan." Jessica was intent on a link.

"What I wonder is why Caroline took it upon herself to make sure I knew about this letter. I'm confused about how I fit into this." I preferred to continue to ignore any attachment.

"It was a shock for her to find out about her father and Nona in a letter saying he married her mother Felicia although he loved Nona. Can you imagine how the letter turned her world on its axis, a bitter dose. She saw Nona as a stranger who continued to be a threat and where her resentment of you came into play. *Outsiders in the family inner sanctum.*"

"What? What did I have to do with anything? Just because I was Aunt Nona's niece? How ridiculous and unreasonable to think I had a part or even a remote connection. Classic Caroline though." I would hold on to my negative feelings for now; I was not giving Caroline Rossi the benefit of the doubt.

"You have to imagine being in her place, Val. I'm not taking her side, but this letter either reinforced her father was never happy with her mother or he might have hidden his feelings. I don't know. She didn't share such information. But for sure learning your father loved another woman so deeply he was miserable sent Caroline into a dive. And the other woman happened to be your great aunt. Come on, Val, you aren't insensitive. Imagine yourself in her place. Her world turned upside down in a heartbeat."

I was spinning from seeing facts in print. But didn't I suppose Aunt Nona had someone in her past even though I didn't question her or allow myself to fantasize? The fact Rowan's grandfather was the someone disturbed me, but I couldn't say why.

Jess persisted with the revealing. "Come on, Val. No more playing coy and detached. Caroline doesn't want the same thing to happen to you and Rowan. She's admitting she was wrong to be against you and wants to do whatever she can to make up for not supporting you two. She realizes how deeply he loves you. She and I have had several conversations (and slightly heated discussions), but she wouldn't listen. Her agenda didn't include you, and she acknowledges she tried to sabotage the relationship. She's been the guiding force behind the Jessica-Rowan twosome that never was and never will be. I love Rowan and would do anything for him. We've been like brother and sister from the beginning, and it's never changed. We've become closer friends through the years but not remotely connected romantically, no thanks to his mother. She's tried her best, there's no doubt. I have to be honest here."

"I appreciate your frankness, Jess. Rowan and I have unresolved problems, and I'm not sure how any of this scenario relates. Granted, his mother has been a roadblock but I have to be fair. Our relationship has a long list. Rowan needs to step up and be a big boy if he wants us to make it."

"Val, you can tell me to butt out but why did you pick the weekend in San Francisco to call it quits with Rowan? My rational side says you have a reason you're not sharing. My emotional side says I'm not sure you know. Sometimes you shoot from the hip and analyze later."

"Okay, I deserve your zinger, but trust me on this one. I've put up with a lot trying to love Rowan. The crazy weekend was the topper and not the cherry on top."

"Okay. But what caused the breakup? If you talk about it--"

"Listen, Jess. Nothing will magically appear going over and over the same tired territory. Rowan and I have a different set of priorities and always have. Our values have faced off several times, and I doubt either of us will back down. The inherent is not easily changed or even compromised. When we give in and give up on our standards, aren't we settling? I still have to face the one in the mirror." I sounded stubborn and lofty, but I liked my values and had spent a lot of my time and energy forming my Valentine foolproof guide to survival.

The quiet was deafening. I verged on letting loose with tears flooding and emotions spilling. I needed Jess to know; I wanted her stamp of approval. But I knew Jess. Empathetic and sympathetic when called for, she would not be reluctant to tell me I was being unreasonable, unrealistic and difficult. My lack of foresight was likely the culprit. No stranger to heartache, she coped with her demons. She knew the drill, and I could count on her. She refused to be my yes man, and I relied on her honesty.

"Okay, Val. None of us is perfect. But yes, you're right. Two people should be together on the big things to be a successful couple. It's painful to watch you two split apart because you can be amazing together. In fact, you two are so physically matched, it's scary. All this from an outsider. You and Rowan have to make the call."

"I don't react well when bombs are dropped on my dreams." I harbored my hurt deviant and deep. I had perfected my strong suit from years of practice.

"Who in their right mind does? But what does make a difference is, was it deliberate and purposeful or was it a byproduct of lack of communication?"

"I can't say. When the big announcement was made at the family dinner that night, it was not what I expected. The trip to Italy was generous and an exciting surprise adventure. But in my mind, a more pressing concern loomed overhead."

"Let me guess; your and Rowan's engagement."

"You win, no contest! You can't imagine how invisible I felt; I was as insignificant as if Rowan had picked me up on Beach Street. Timing could not have been better. He was set to practice law with his dad, and I was teaching. All those airline miles, planned weekends, and holidays to be together suddenly amounted to zero. I felt used and taken for granted. 'Oh, good old Valentine, she's okay with however I want to treat her, no commitment needed here. There's no reason to give her a ring or make our plans official. She's reliable and will always be there. *Rowan's girl.* Family is #1; she doesn't fit in our family; she's below my pay grade. I'll face her later.' You talk about devastated; you have no clue."

"You're right, I don't. But what matters here, did Rowan know how you felt and what you expected? Did you two make plans? Communication is part of what's missing with most of us. And I have to say, you're being unfair. Rowan never thinks of you as beneath him and neither should you. No self-defeating tactics allowed. We all have enough to deal with dodging arrows from the outside."

"Okay. I get carried away and my imagination takes over. But why do I have to tell him? He should know. We love each other and have been in full transport mode in this relationship for years back and forth. What's so difficult? Besides, he should want to set the engagement and wedding as much as I do. The big problem, I shouldn't have to beg him or instruct him on what's next."

"Not necessarily true. We assume a lot. Maybe he wasn't thinking. He might have been in man mode, just enjoying the occasion being happy we were all together for the night, he might have been lost in the hoopla. I can't say. But one thing's for sure, he's crazy about you and lost without you. Whatever you want to do, if anything, is up to you. I've said more than I probably should have. It breaks my heart to see you two hurting because I love you both. I don't want your love for each other to be scrapped because of pride or because it's difficult to compromise and work out your differences not to mention talking, and the way we find the way."

"Okay, Jess. You're right and make some good points. I want to make us work but there is so much going on in our heads blocking our way. I've got to think this through." Now I was more troubled by the continuing emotional reveal of Aunt Nona and Andrew Rowan. A convenient distraction or something more? I tried to shift my thinking to concentrate on Rowan and me and resolving our problems.

Jessica knew how to encourage my rational side with a dash of hope and reason, and she knew speaking freely was encouraged rather than frowned upon. Definitions and boundaries weren't permitted in this friendship—no killer obstructions allowed. I relied upon her judgment. She knew me and she knew Rowan. *She was my rock.*

"I agree. A lot has happened. I hope I haven't exceeded my limits—like I have any. She grinned with white teeth flashing. "I'd do anything for you, precious Valentine. Love you. Just holler if you need anything." Her hug was warm and comforting; I knew her emotions for me ran deep. Our good-byes were meant to last and sustain, and something to hold on until we were together again. *A relationship of substance.* My friendship with Jessica and with Aunt Nona had taught me a great deal about relationships. These were the gold standard of relationships. Why didn't I let go and devote the same care to Rowan and me? *Trust.* Facts had emerged demanding inquiry and answers. There had to be an underlying reason and even inevitability for Rowan and me to fail. *Something was missing and terribly wrong.*

"Thank you, Jess, my precious friend, for your faithfulness." I struggled to keep from begging her not to leave me as I walked her to the door.

I waited and watched from the kitchen window as her car pulled away, and her lights faded out of sight.

∞

Chapter 37
Family Secrets

Pretending the news was ancient history and nothing that concerned me, the revealing of family connections proved too much for my inquisitive side. Knowing Aunt Nona and Andrew Rowan were more than a passing fling was too much for me to ignore or even willing to acknowledge to Jessica. Deep inside I started to suspect much more to this story at my fingertips. Reluctant, hesitant, and terrified and at the same time intent and unwavering, I suspected a missing puzzle piece but questioned if it was best left buried. Family papers can be an amazing cache of sweet memorabilia, factual documentation and precious collectibles. Caroline Rossi had done more than intervene; she had opened the fabled Pandora's Box. My inner voice grew louder and raged relentless. I had not given the proper respect and attention to Aunt Nona's cherished keepsakes, documents and perhaps essential information. Admittedly ignorant of her past, I doggedly contended she did have a right to her privacy. Could there be something I had overlooked relevant to the present? Maybe I made too much of the Nona-Andrew connection, letting my mind play tricks, therefore guilty of creating a troublesome scenario of complication which did not exist. I was haunted to the brink of obsession.

After Jessica left, I sat in silence processing. My brain and emotions kicked in on overload. I did not know what to do or whether there was anything to do. I had no choice. I must use the means necessary until satisfied there was nothing to discover. My logical side did belly laughs as my instinctive sixth sense at the same time whispered sweet nothings. I admit on occasion I give undue credence to feelings and intuition, but I also recognize there are times when it's absolutely foolish to ignore a nagging insistence. Torn between the comfort of delusion and the harshness of reality, I also had a suspicion what I didn't know and was about to find out would change my life and there wasn't a damn thing I could do about it. Sometimes what we don't know won't hurt us and may even be beneficial in our ignorance. Then again, being ignorant or unaware or uninformed can be disastrous. Was I willing to take the chance? I compared my mindset before Jessica's visit. Things were simple then. Just Rowan and me and our unresolved issues. Now an invisible third party hovered like a dark storm cloud threatening in deathly quiet.

I managed to get through the night in various stages of prayer and meditation until exhaustion gave way to a few hours of sleep. I awoke to dawn and knew my decision had been based on a logical and rational need to protect not only me but those I love. I had to consider the consequences of ignoring warning signs. I had only partially opened and not reviewed the contents of one other envelope in Aunt Nona's safe deposit box containing her personal papers. I assumed the documents didn't concern me, so it was unnecessary to pry and be intrusive. I was comforted for my inaction and guided by a sense of reverence about her and her possessions.

I put on the coffee and then sat at the kitchen table watching the sun rise and scatter its light through the window. Now was as good a time as any. Aunt Nona's room looked the same as if waiting for her to appear any minute. I opened the bottom drawer of her dresser. I had intended to put the envelope back into the safe deposit box but it was one of those out of sight, out of mind things to be conveniently forgotten because I didn't want to deal with it. The envelope glared at me from among the lost and forgotten--an old pair of Aunt Nona's gloves, her favorite scarf, and some handkerchiefs I had no idea what to do with but hesitated to get rid of. I reached down and retrieved the large envelope and took it to the kitchen table. I tore open the flap and turned over the envelope; pieces of every size and variety of paper imaginable scattered. I turned away and poured a cup of coffee and sat down to steady myself. I didn't really want to do this. Why was I compelled to enter her private world?

What captured my attention was the sheer number of cracked, faded photos now barely discernible. I recognized a few people in the pictures mainly Aunt Nona and her sister, my grandmother. I was captivated by a sudden striking resemblance--I'd never visualized my mother as a child. Blurry-eyed and overcome, I set the clearer photos of her as a baby and small child aside. I wanted to frame many of these photos and create a family gallery. But honestly there were so many photos I was overwhelmed. Pictures of Aunt Nona and my grandmother Estelle as babies, girls in school and then as young teenagers were almost eighty years old, so it was no wonder I had difficulty making out any details. I was amazed we had any family photos that had survived. But the majority of the photos were of my mother at every stage of development from baby to adult. I spied an envelope with Estelle's return address in Louisiana to Aunt Nona as thin as tissue paper and so very delicate I hesitated to pick it up for fear it might crumble and disintegrate. I used tweezers to slip the letter from its envelope and gently unfolded the yellowed paper.

August 20, 1920

Dearest Sister:

I hope this finds you well and at peace. I write with wonderful news of our baby Lila Jo who continues to flourish and grow into a beautiful child. She is healthy, happy and growing like a weed. We admit she is the center of attention and love for this family and will likely grow up to be more than slightly spoiled by love. She will be our only child since Dr. Ellis has firmly said I will not be able to carry a baby to full term. You know how blessed we are to have Lila Jo. She is exactly what this family needed. The relatives continue to swarm (some we haven't seen in months or years) to see the new baby and to congratulate and wish us the best. There is joy a baby adds to a family that is beyond words. Questioning so far has not been oppressive. Most are satisfied we adopted her as an infant through Dr. Ellis who has been a Godsend with getting the proper paperwork.

We splurged on a camera which we could not afford but had to have with a baby in the family. There is so much growth, development, and new things to treasure that must be captured in an irretrievable flash. So a camera was a must for every milestone and precious moments that would be lost except for a fleeting memory. You will be with us for her journey so be prepared for a steady stream of photos in your mailbox and letters detailing this loved child's every step.

My heart is full because of you, dear sister. We can't repay the debt of your kindness in entrusting us to the love and care and safekeeping of your most precious treasure. Tom and I will do all in our power with the Lord's guidance to raise Lila Jo with love, grace, kindness and in the spirit of the Lord's way.

I send our love and know you are anxious to begin teaching in the fall. Ever since we were kids, you have dreamed of being a teacher so it will be much more than a job. Teaching children is your passion. You are making an unimaginable sacrifice, but the joy you have shared is also unimaginable and would never have happened without your decision.

All is not perfect with our worlds but we are blessed we have a family who shares with love and hope life's challenges.

You and I are not only sisters but our souls intertwine so that Lila Jo flourishes with the gift of two mothers is our unwavering promise. We know the Lord's hand strengthens and guides us and will continue to bless our family.

We look forward to seeing you very soon at the family reunion in two weeks. Lila Jo sends you her love with a kiss and hug until you can get here.

In Christian Love and Thanksgiving Beloved Sister,

Estelle

I stared at the paper blurred by weeping eyes. Ensnared in a web of tangled history and events of over fifty years ago, nothing made sense and everything made sense. I grabbed a tissue and tried to re-read the letter in desperate hope to get a different result because I had missed or added my version. I looked at the few papers among the photographs most notable a copy of my mother's adoption papers showing father and mother as Anna Estelle Monroe Devereaux and Joseph Thomas Devereaux but no birth certificate. But even so, the net had been cast and the bounty brought in. My Aunt Nona had a child Lila Jo who was adopted and raised by her sister. On the verge of hysteria, I screamed in agony. I threw the contents of the envelope in every direction scattering old scraps of paper and photos over the floor and smashed everything within reach. I raged and cried and destroyed everything at my fingertips for almost an hour until I almost blacked out. I tore up pictures and paper and shattered glass and precious items until I was surrounded by garbage. My life was a lie. There was nothing precious or sacred in the human just dark, secret places to hide and pretend. We were all the same just in varying degrees of hopelessness--pathetic, floundering souls who don't know what to do, where to go or how to get there. Overcome by the staggering realization of interminable predicament I created over a lifetime, I had no one to blame but myself. I had woven such a magnificent tapestry of worthy people to look up to and emulate because of their wisdom and goodness, and my creation now suddenly and cruelly crashed in pieces around me, unable to be reconstructed. *Loved ones lost to me forever and consumed by meaningless misery and despair.* Everything and everyone of value had no meaning or substance. The vision of my beloved Aunt Nona as flawed and lost and holding dark secrets; how could I be expected to carry her with me as a lie?

My head whirled, my legs gave way; I was too weak to walk. Throughout life's assaults, my spirit never failed me. I arose fierce, stronger, hell bent. But now I was beaten. Nothing in me was worth saving-- a soul ravaged and empty. Did I even have a soul or a spirit? That likely was also a figment of hope and imagination to keep me from plunging into insanity.

∞

Chapter 38
Day of Reckoning

Today appeared and brighter than I expected. A lot of reconciling can happen in twenty-four hours. Some weight lifted because I was no longer agonizing about Rowan. I spent the night in my favorite chair in the study among my books where Aunt Nona and I spent most of our nights and weekends when I was a child. I felt comfortable and secure in this room and became quieter and at peace with myself and my family. I was in recovery, my tirade over. I had cleaned up my mess and threw the shattered pieces away with my shattered fantasies. I loved my Aunt Nona more than life itself and nothing had changed my mind. So she fell in love and had a baby without a husband. So what? She was human, with human emotions and desires and made the best of a situation which she could have let ruin lives. But in true Nona fashion, she made the best decision for the baby and in the final analysis for herself. I felt at peace with the discovery. I had enshrined my Aunt Nona. Then when her pedestal came crashing, I wallowed in a catastrophe of devastating disillusion I had created. What else could I expect? No one is designed and doesn't deserve to withstand such elevated status. It would take some time to think of her as my grandmother, but it really didn't matter whether she was my great aunt or my grandmother. I loved and cherished her. Her strength of character had not diminished in my eyes; if anything, her ability to cope with life was magnified. *She had experienced heartbreak.* At last, I came face-to-face with the recognition Aunt Nona was not some out-of-touch old maid who directed life lessons because she was inherently wise and aware as she sat back and watched other people make mistakes and wreck their lives. She lived life to the fullest and tried to instill the benefits of what she experienced and the mistakes she made. No wonder I always wanted to be like her. I was beginning to understand not only Aunt Nona but myself.

I stood there still considering my lack of foresight and my naïveté as I was burning the toast. I tossed the first piece in the trash and slammed the bread into the toaster for the second time. Why must I always burn the first piece? Panic mode set in as I saw the calendar on the refrigerator. Leland and I had scheduled an early lunch to go through his appointments to make phone calls, rescheduling and announcements about his transfer. I tossed the toast and made a beeline to get ready. My timing with Leland could not have been more perfect. This was one decision etched in stone. He would be the only one I would confide in.

I pulled the Caddy into the parking lot of the church and saw Leland wave as he came from the parsonage apartment. If coping is a pain now, wait until he is no longer at my beckoning call. Accustomed to him being here in an emergency or trouble or simply to touch base to see how he was or to ask his advice, the thought of him three hundred miles away was incomprehensible.

"Top of the day to you, Miss Valentine. How are you this beautiful day?"

"Wonderful, thank you and the rest of the day to you, Pastor. You seem extraordinarily chipper."

"Just peachy keen and hungry as a bear. Let's get to the restaurant before the pie is gone. Today's the day they count pie as a vegetable so they are notorious for running out. Seems like a lot of us substitute pie for the Brussels sprouts."

We still loved the comfortable surroundings and the home cooking at the BluePlate after all these years. This place continued to be an institution. I looked around at the blue checkered tablecloths and counter with red vinyl stools and doubted if much had changed since my mother worked here. The food and service were excellent, and the atmosphere friendly and welcoming. Leland and I ate here at least twice a month. I managed to heat a bowl of canned soup or cook an egg as the extent of my cooking, so we both indulged in the meat loaf, pot roast, pork chops, and chicken and dumplings and the pie. The BluePlate now satisfied our penchant for home cooking and comfort food. Our conversation was relaxed and upbeat. He and I reserved the serious topics for after we had a chance to digest our meal. No need to waste such a savored experience as lunch at the BluePlate on upsetting conversation.

"I wish you knew Mother. You would have loved her to pieces. She lit up a room like a roman candle. Just sitting in this booth looking around I can see her now refilling those coffee cups with her blazing smile spreading brightness for the day like a klieg light. I am closer to her here than any place I go. She loved working each day at the BluePlate because of the people. She said no strangers here but new friends. Ray still owns this place, and he gets the familiar twinkle in his eye when he mentions Lila Jo. His customers loved her and so did he. Goes to show it's not about how important you are or how long you're around, it's about the positive impact and connection."

"You're proud of her and rightfully so. Don't we all want to be hopeful for the day and to appreciate the day we're given? The joy we give means more than we realize especially when folks are going through trying times and, let's face it, we all are struggling with something." Pastor Leland *Shepherd* belonged with us and to us, and people loved him. His name said it all. He brought us together.

"Well, we should let someone else have our table so they can have lunch before the dinner hour. I'm buying. After you're gone, I'll be eating at the BluePlate and crying in my soup missing you. Did I put a guilt trip on you? Don't you feel bad because you're leaving me here to fend for myself?" I had difficulty hiding my frustration about his going. I already missed him and imagined my setbacks; I was a master at selfishness. More miraculous things had happened, and he could change his mind. I knew he loved his congregation and me. But I wondered if he was ready for the load I would transfer to his shoulders.

"No, sister. There's no guilt. I'm moving to Louisiana not to the other side of the world. I expect the old Caddy can take you that far, right? You should be planning not to forget me; besides, do you have the nerve to tell me our time together and my counseling had so little staying power? Don't kid me, kid. We both know you're capable of taking care of yourself."

As we drove along, Leland seemed far away. I guessed he, too, had something on his mind. "A penny for your thoughts, wise one, not because that's what they're worth but because I'm on a tight budget." Now with lunch over, his mood had easily converted to somber. I hoped he didn't have bad news. Despite my wanting him to stay, I didn't want anything to prevent him from going either. He deserved the transfer he had prepared for. Two of us with big loads to drop? Beyond unmanageable.

"Oh, you noticed. I'm plotting how to approach the rest of our day together. It's a sticky wicket." He looked at me with a serious inquiring look.

"Thanks for the warning. Shall I push you out at a slow speed and then burn rubber to avoid the 'sticky wicket'?"

"I hope not. There's a lot I have to do and you're suggesting such an ugly end. Don't get defensive on me. It's not a bad conversation just one we must have."

I couldn't fathom all this happening to me and said a silent prayer. Whatever he had to tell me had to come before my burdening him yet again.

We sat in silence the rest of the drive to the church. I parked in front of the education building at his office entrance and we started down the dark hall to the reflection of light. His office looked more disheveled than usual. Papers all over his desk, books on the table tops, dirty coffee cups, and old coffee in the pot. His Bible set high on the desk above it all with his notes close by. He was a scholar of the Word and never let a day pass without study.

"How do you find anything? It looks like a tornado barreled through here and not recently. How do you concentrate?"

"I prefer 'lived in' if you don't mind. Besides it's my office and I like it this way. I've tried organized and I can't find anything. If it's too neat,

I'm uncomfortable like I should sit up straight and look busy. You know the drill. Just clean off a spot on the lovely plastic chair and make yourself to home. I saved a chair just for you."

He busied himself with clearing a spot for himself on the surface of the desk. He held up his beautiful black leather Bible worn and softly supple with frequented pages sporting frayed edges. "Just for the record, I keep close tabs on this one, Miss Valentine. The Good Book is never far away and not out of my sight. I can't function without it. Let's start our afternoon with a prayer, don't you think?"

"Perfect. You read my mind."

"Thank you Lord, for this day and for my friendship with Valentine. We pray for your guidance and strength in our decisions and the choices we make in this physical life. May we always remember the way to eternal life is through your son Jesus Christ. There is no other way. We pray our lives bear witness to all goodness as granted by you as our Heavenly Father. Bless us in our discussions remembering respect and the grace to hear each other. We pray humbly for wisdom and tranquil understanding made possible by your sovereignty and benevolence. In Jesus Christ we pray. Amen."

"Amen. Bless you, Leland, and your new flock." Valentine had never been more conscious of someone's impact on lives.

"I had a surprise visitor yesterday."

"Let me guess. Caroline Rossi. She's been busy lately making the rounds."

"Nope. You're close, though. It was her son Rowan Rossi."

Valentine melted into her chair speechless. She wanted to run out the door.

Leland knew her well and smiled. "I see you eyeing the door. No, you're not locked in here but I suggest you stay put. I was impressed with the young man. I've wanted to meet him, but you wouldn't bring him around. I'm kidding, sort of. Anyway, it's on me for not making the effort to get to know him. Thanks to his initiative, we're on our way to removing one obstacle."

"I'm sure he was charming. It's his long suit." Despite my recent discovery, I persisted in a view of Rowan that came up short. He was special to me, but his faults hadn't magically disappeared.

"Charm armed with honesty. He came to me in desperation. He asked for my assistance and is willing to do whatever is necessary to have a faith-based relationship with you. He professes a genuine desire and has asked my counseling for the next few months before I leave. I'd go so far as to say his love for you is a driving force behind his willingness to make this turnaround."

"Sounds like confluence between you two but in a good way. Never in a million years would I have predicted Rowan would come to see you."

I was dumbfounded. Not by Rowan's behavior but by my well-honed ability to short change other people. My arrogance that he failed to meet my expectations covered us like a lead blanket preventing us from making even a baby step of progress. A deep sadness came over me of how little substance I had shown in this relationship. How far was I willing to bend and how much was I willing to give? Now I had an example set by the man I had loved of no mountain too high. My assessment of my smallness could not be quieted, as if it mattered now. My tiny voice whispered, "Valentine, you set a mighty low bar for yourself but not for others." Rather than obsess as I did about what decision to make, Rowan took action--action striking at the core of our stagnation and our impasse. My heart overflowed. It had to have been difficult and awkward for him to make the connection with Leland. I admired and respected Rowan for taking the first step. My conscience weighed heavy with shame.

"Oh, Leland. I deliberately wanted Rowan and me to fail. Much of our difficulty is on me. What makes someone take the way out instead of working it out? But it really doesn't matter now."

Leland shook his head knowingly. "Valentine, remember we're all in the same boat here. It's our human failing to run away. For our flawed reasoning, it seems easier to flee the problem than to face it particularly when we see our weaknesses coming to light. I have no doubts about you and Rowan. You have the foundation for a happy marriage and one of substance. You know how I approach premarital counseling. I don't pretend to be able to fix all. I can counsel you on possible problem areas and how to avoid destructive behavior. It's a process of discovery. Once revealed, the bumpy road of marriage can be daunting and lose some of its appeal. Marriage is risky with no guarantees but then what in life worth our while isn't? You and Rowan will make the call; it's not up to me to decide. I encourage you to go to him with open arms and an open heart. He's making some giant steps and needs your support. I'd like to schedule counseling sessions for twice a week for the next sixty days and then make an assessment of additional sessions. I'm in no hurry to get to Louisiana permanently. I'll go occasionally to make the transition and to check on my house which should be completed in about three months. I'm beyond grateful to have this opportunity. There's nothing more important to me now than your and Rowan's future."

Leland came over and put his arm around me. I was overcome with the strength of his dedication to me and Rowan. I was so blessed to have his friendship and his devotion. I had so many people in my life loving and supporting me. Humbled and grateful, there was hope my poisonous river of doubt and distrust might run clear and nourishing to my soul. But Rowan's good faith wasn't enough. This wasn't the backwoods, and certain morés were absolute and specific as to whether socially acceptable. I would not marry my first cousin.

"I am forever indebted to you, Leland. It's frightening to imagine my life without you and your wisdom. You'll have to flee Louisiana to escape me and now Rowan. You have no hiding place." I attempted to lighten the enormous weight of what I had to tell him. Now I felt guilty. Leland had just made what I had to tell him so much harder.

Leland threw back his head and laughed. "Valentine, I love so many things about you but mainly because you make me smile. And remember, we all need other people. You're every bit as important to me. I just happen to be a minister and counselor. But my flock keeps me stepping to the music. You make me feel loved and appreciated and a reason to get up in the morning. Now get going on your way. You have important business that won't wait."

"I would love to, but I can't, Leland. I hardly know how to begin, but I know you'll be patient with me. This is one of the hardest conversations you and I have ever had and we've had some doozies." My desperate search for an escape hatch proved futile; his hopefulness was bound to be a casualty.

"Valentine, whatever has happened, we can talk about it. There's nothing you can't share with me."

The silence was soothing and therapeutic. Too bad I had to interrupt the solace. "Leland, Caroline Rossi came to dinner with Jess and me the other night to plead her case. She's had a change of heart and wants Rowan and me together since all of her meddling in our affairs backfired, shocking but only the beginning. After her father passed away while she was going through his papers, she found an unopened letter he'd written to Aunt Nona. Rather than show it to me, she passed the chore to Jess. It was a love letter saying no matter how deeply he loved Nona he was marrying another woman. The romance between my aunt and Andrew Rowan was much more than I ever realized." Leland took his hand and placed it over mine. He was beginning to understand my apprehension.

"At first, I was curious but convinced Aunt Nona's romance had nothing to do with me. The more I thought about the magnitude of Andrew's letter and by the time I got home, the more distraught I became. My suspicions centered on an envelope of Aunt Nona's marked Family Documents that I hadn't gone through. I felt I was prying, so I had put it away to deal with later. I couldn't explain my haunting but the envelope lurked, threatening as a dark debacle."

"It was with her estate documents?"

"Yes. I was so overwhelmed with details, I didn't want to take the time to go through all her personal papers. I was simply not ready. Anyway, it was obvious I couldn't put off opening the envelope any longer. What I found was more than I was equipped to manage. Please forgive me, I'm trying to accept and understand my family." I started to cry. My sadness overwhelmed my hopeful spirit not just for me but for my family.

"Take your time, Valentine. We'll get through this however long it takes." His caring hand on mine and his kind, soothing voice made my journey so much more bearable and understandable.

"Pictures, Leland, hundreds of old photos of my mother Lila Jo as a baby and child at every stage of growth and development. But then the explanation of everything was in a letter from Nona's sister Estelle."

We sat together as I cried not holding back, shaking and sobbing.

He held me in consolation. "I understand, Valentine. Don't hold back. Your feelings are natural and nothing to be ashamed of."

We sat together for several minutes until I was ready to begin again. "Aunt Nona had a baby girl, my mother Lila Jo, and gave her to Estelle to raise as her child."

I broke down. I was shattered for my Aunt Nona and her pain. There were no words.

Leland held me and comforted me until my tears subsided. He knew how deeply this revelation affected not just me but Rowan and his family. There was only one solution, and we both knew what it was.

"Leland, I can't tell Rowan and his family. And I must hear from you the right way to handle my family's secret is to keep the secret. You're my one confidant."

Leland sat quietly for several minutes. "I agree with you Valentine. What possible good would come from telling Rowan and his family? There's nothing to be ashamed of in all this, but it would be hurtful to Rowan and his family. You and Rowan are the only ones affected. There is no reason to further complicate lives."

"You know, Leland, I do care for Rowan deeply so I can't explain why I've felt something has been missing with us or rather something holding me back. Now the reason for my reluctance is apparent and could be what prevented me from fully committing to Rowan. I'm sad I have to once and for all break up with him, but at the same time, I'm relieved I know why." Leland put his arms around me.

"We never did get that burger or chili dog." My peculiar quip resembled the special someone we both loved and missed. Thank you, Aunt Nona, for teaching me to see the lighter side.

Leland and I spent most of the afternoon talking about family both his and mine. We were concerned and explored any possible further family implications and damage. We agreed I had to break off my relationship with Rowan. The decision was right for Rowan and the Rossi's and it was right for me, for Aunt Nona, and for my family. His reassurance I was making the right decision reinforced my belief and gave me the courage of conviction for what I had to do. We also exchanged our memories about Aunt Nona and her amazing strength and unwavering spirit.

"If ever there was a reflection of Aunt Nona, I'm looking at her. Girl, don't doubt me, you're cut from the same cloth." Leland's shared feelings calmed my questioning. The Rowan-Valentine romance had ended with no chance for us to spend our lives together. But I was grateful for having Rowan in my life.

Pfft. No problem, Aunt Nona, your secret is safe with me.

∞

Chapter 39
Cosmic Alignment

"Hello Caroline. It's Valentine. May I speak to Rowan?"

"Hello there. It's good to hear your voice, Valentine. Hold on, I'll get Rowan. He will be thrilled."

My heart beat like a bongo. The thunder of my pulse throbbed in my ears. What would I say and how could I face him? Did he think I was crazy or just beyond help? Did he hate me for making life difficult? But more horrific, did he think I was playing games?

"Hello, Valentine. How are you? I've been worried about you."

"Hi, Rowan. I'm okay, and it's nice to hear you're concerned. I wondered if you would come over to the house for a few minutes so we could talk. It would mean a lot to me."

He assured me he'd be here in about an hour. I looked in the mirror. I'd powder my nose and apply a little lip gloss. Amazing! My cheeks had a rosy glow and my eyes sparkled. Who knew after the last few days? There's something to Aunt Nona's advice about a healthy glow from within. No radiance from a jar needed today which was remarkable. I will not look pitiful because I *wasn't* pitiful.

The doorbell rang as I faced myself in the mirror. I had no golden wand, end of discussion.

"Hi, Rowan. It's good to see you." I embraced him with affection but restraint.

"You, too. It's been too long. I hope you will say what I want you to say. Have you spoken to Pastor Leland?"

"I just came from spending the afternoon with him. I can't tell you how much it means to me that you reached out to him. It's probably one of the most endearing things you've ever done. We have so many unresolved issues, Rowan, and you were trying to solve them. But it's no use. My mind has been made up since San Francisco. I knew then we were not meant to be together, and I'm even more convinced than ever. I care about you too much to give false hope. As much as I care, I want to be free and want you to be free as well. We've been trying to love each other for a long time and now it's time to let go. I hope you understand."

Rowan stared at me for a moment and then took my hand in his. "I only want you to be happy, Valentine, and I have to trust you when you say we are not better together but better apart. I don't understand why we couldn't make it, but I accept your decision. We've had a long road and some rough patches. It wouldn't be easy no matter how committed we are to solving our problems. In a way, it's a relief. You know I'll always care about you."

"Thank you, Rowan, for loving me and being patient with me. You taught me how to love and how to be loved. You made my dreams come true. You'll always have a special place in my heart."

He kissed me on the cheek and gave me a strong hug good-bye and was gone.

I had no regrets and I don't believe he did either. I had a dream of falling in love and my dream came true with Rowan. Along our thorny patch, we had fun and magic moments I'd treasure. And now we had our freedom. All was as it was intended.

I followed him outside and watched his car disappear in the night. I looked up. What a magnificent display! I took a deep breath of the dark night air and let the calm wash over me. The brightly lit blue velvet canopy bursting with millions of stars--stars in alignment--reassured. *Blessed with His peace.*

∞

CHAPTER 40
PROMISE OF TOMORROW

H e looked up from his work. I felt his eyes and knew he knew I was an outsider. He trudged across the gravel pathway so he wouldn't have to yell and to size me up. He needed assurance I had business here. "Good morning, young lady. Can I be of help? Our gardens can be confusing if you don't know your way around."

"Thank you. If I remember correctly, I'm headed in the right direction. It's called Tranquility Garden. I'm taking advantage of the quiet; such a welcome change from the rat race. It's a transformed world inside these gates. Makes me wonder what the hubbub is about."

"I know what you mean. It's hard on those folks in the traffic with the constant noise, stress, honking horns, and bad moods. It's getting dangerous to be on the road, makes me thankful I work here. Anyway, if I can be of help, just holler. I know this place pretty well as you can imagine. And, yes ma'am, you're absolutely correct. If you keep walking toward those large oaks, you'll be in the vicinity." He extended his arm pointing the direction.

"I will and thank you. This special day won't be complete without paying my respects."

"Take your time. We don't close the gates until sundown. I hope you find everything okay."

"Oh, I'm sure I will. By the way, my compliments. Your hard work is a tribute. What beautiful surroundings you have created."

"Thank you for the kind words. I guess because I enjoy what I do, satisfying. I appreciate the opportunity to share it and hope our sanctuary brings you comfort. I better get back to my work."

The faithful groundskeeper was much more. I saw he was reassured; he understood how his hard work and dedication translated into healing and consolation by creating the beauty of these surroundings. The gardens softened the sorrow of loved ones, strangers bonded by loss, and offered tangible evidence of another grueling eight hours of hard labor in the Texas heat. His work was of consequence.

A sea of white reached skyward against green, grassy knolls stretching toward the horizon. I sidestepped my way through the maze of marble stones etched with finality. Names and dates of countless souls surrounded me in cold serenity. Even the tranquility of this place was no match for my cluttered mind. I was trying to cram even more into a day already brimming over. I definitely was not as relaxed as I had envisioned and guilty again of adding more into my already full day. The obsession for instant peace suddenly halted. I gave in to my questioning and simultaneously wondered. How many *dark* secrets were buried in these graves? I answered my question with a question. How many headstones in the cemetery? My rational side knew all secrets were neither evil nor mysterious. People prefer anonymity about particular and peculiar things they do not want known for reasons known to them. *Benevolence* for one. Then I laughed out loud. My imagining was too obvious a signal of an off-kilter mind. Who obsesses with such irrelevant questions while seeking serenity? Leave it to me as provocateur to stir things up a bit to avert my attention.

A cemetery was not at the top of my list of favorite places, but I would rather be here at this moment than any other place. I planned this outing for months, dedicating both my time and mindset to this destination--the physical resting place of my two *adored* ones. I walked reverently toward the two graves directly in the middle of the local graveyard noticeably marked by two giant live oaks sheltering a small stone bench beneath their spread of shade. The well-manicured grounds welcomed all visitors seeking solitude and comfort. As I made a conscious effort to be still, I felt less like an intruder. In the midst of my consuming happiness of this day, I felt compelled to contemplate the reality of the absolute world--the Hereafter. In contrast to my customary preoccupation with the secular, the all-imposing predominance of Eternity overpowers here.

I placed the wilting blooms onto the green plots of my two *guardian angels*. One was a more recent fresh mound grave; the other almost twenty years before. They were side by side in death as in life. Both of the people I loved and the people who loved me without question rested here. The key was unconditional love although not without recognition of my imperfections. Throughout my life, I discovered how difficult (or impossible) a task to replace the quality of love of lost loved ones. My deep admiration of these women was impossible to quantify but even more critically I respected and was in awe of them. Our bond was not severed by death. Their presence and watchfulness continued through my complexities of everyday life--days filled with anxiety, quandary and questioning, exhilaration and sorrow. To this day, they remain with me. When blessed with love and life-changing care of this magnitude, the bond remains even though they're no longer in this world.

We may take for granted the select few who grace our lives as pillars. Exceptional people find their way into our lives and through the years remain steadfast in their love and genuine care; we don't understand how or why but we are grateful and inspired by their legacy. It took me almost a lifetime to grasp; my life was worthwhile. *No more, but no less than all the rest.* I experienced opportunity because of those caring few who offered hope to another struggling human. With deepest gratitude, I count them as my fellow warriors standing shoulder-to-shoulder as a major force in the struggle to burst free of self-imposed chains. Doomed without them and their interlocking link, they surrounded and supported me. My life reflects as a series of life-changing events and defining moments connected by those who kept me afloat so I might live up to *my responsibility of making the most of my life.*

Thank you my blessed ones for your vision. You taught me to look to the brilliance of the future lighting our way out of the darkness of the past. Waiting for the perfect arrangement yields little but passage of time and staggering disillusion. Aunt Nona empowered me to overcome relentless reminders attaching like a fungus that I was unacceptable. Leland by example guided me to burst free of memories weighing me down leaving me joyless. The dark ones seeking to destroy me slowly disintegrated taking their rightful place because of no right and no privilege to share any of my life, including my thoughts and memories and I feel profound pity for their tortured souls. I am thankful. *Broken child redemption.*

Today marks another beginning in my life as I venture to California and to the university as Dr. Valentine Monroe. I must leave the red brick storybook Tudor that has surrounded me in comfort but now will provide a home for another family as the parsonage for the church and their sanctuary. I treasure my memories of life on Morningstar, but the wonder of tomorrow and expanding vistas entice me to complete the circle of *my moment in time.*

∞

NOTE FROM THE AUTHOR

Word-of-mouth is crucial for any author to succeed. If you enjoyed *Beyond Morningstar Lane*, please leave a review online — anywhere you are able. Even if it's just a sentence or two. It would make all the difference and would be very much appreciated.

Thanks!
Miriam

ABOUT THE AUTHOR

Miriam C. Crouch lives in Irving, Texas with her husband Gilbert who is a retired City of Irving firefighter. She is a graduate of Texas Christian University and author of the novel *Daughter of the Town*. *Beyond Morningstar Lane* is a testament to the resilience of the human spirit and a tribute to our lifelines who inspire us to faithfully pursue our dreams.

Thank you so much for reading one of **Miriam C. Crouch's** novels. If you enjoyed the experience, please check out our recommended title for your next great read!

Daughter of the Town

"Heartwarming, poignant... a joy to read."

–WRITER'S DIGEST

www.ingramcontent.com/pod-product-compliance
Lightning Source LLC
Chambersburg PA
CBHW011131100726
47898CB00009B/2930